Birthday 1919.
from Marie.

RIM O' THE WORLD

"Put up your hands a little higher, Mr. Man!"

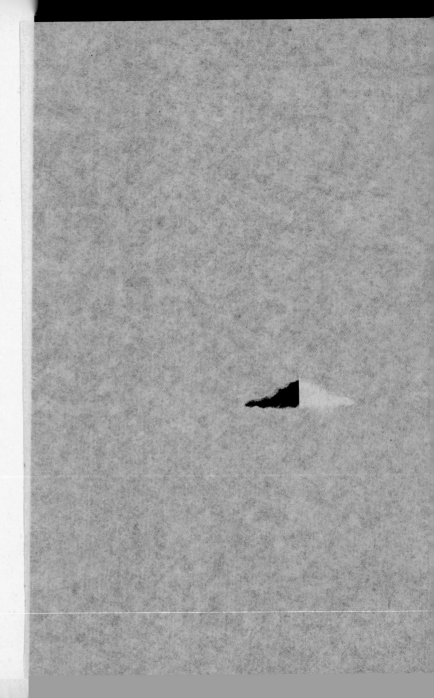

RIM O' THE WORLD

BY

B. M. BOWER

WITH FRONTISPIECE BY

ANTON OTTO FISCHER

BOSTON
LITTLE, BROWN, AND COMPANY
1919

Norwood Press
Set up and electrotyped by J. S. Cushing Co., Norwood, Mass., U.S.A.

CONTENTS

RIM O' THE WORLD

CHAPTER ONE

The Rim and What Lay Beneath It

NOT all of the West is tamed and trained to run smoothly on pneumatic tires and to talk more enthusiastically of the different " makes " of cars than of bits and saddles. There are still wide stretches unknown of tourists and movie men hunting locations for Western melodrama where men live in the full flavor of adventure and romance and never know it, because they have never known any other way to live.

In the Black Rim country there is such a place, — a wide, rough, sage-grown expanse where cattle and horses and sheep scarce know the look of barbed wire, and where brands are still the sole mark of ownership. Set down between high mountain ranges, remote, sufficient unto itself, rudely prosperous, the Black Rim country has yet to be tamed.

Black Rim country is called bad. The men from Black Rim are eyed askance when they burr their spur rowels down the plank sidewalks of whatever little town they may choose to visit. A town dweller will not quarrel with one of them. He will treat him politely, straightway seek some acquaintance whom he wishes to impress, and jerk a thumb toward the departing Black Rim man, and say importantly: " See that feller I was talking with just now? That's one of them boys from the Black Rim. Man, he'd kill yuh quick as look at yuh! He's bad. Yep. You want to walk 'way round them birds from the Rim country. They're a hard-boiled bunch up that way." And he would be as nearly correct in his estimate as such men usually are.

Tom Lorrigan's father used to carry a rifle across his thighs when he rode up the trail past Devil's Tooth Ridge to the benchland beyond, where his cattle fed on the sweet bunch grass. He never would sit close to a campfire at night save when his back was against a huge boulder and he could keep the glare of the fire from his eyes. Indians he killed as he killed rattlers, on the range theory that if they did not get him then they might some other time, and that every dead Indian counted one less to beware of. Tom Lorrigan's father was called a bad man even in Black Rim country, — which meant a good deal. Hard-bitted men of the Black Rim chose their words wisely when they spoke to Tom's father; chose wisely their words when they spoke of him, unless they had full faith in the listener's loyalty and discretion.

Tom Lorrigan's father lived to be sixty, — chiefly because he was "quick on the draw" and because he never missed anything that he shot at. But at sixty, when he was still hated by many, loved by a very few and feared by every one, he died, — crushed under his horse when it fell on the Devil's Tooth trail one sleety day in midwinter.

Young Tom Lorrigan learned to shoot when he learned to ride, and he was riding pitching horses before he could be certain which was p and which was q in his dad's old spelling book. Which does not by any means prove that young Tom was an ignoramus. Tom once had three brothers, but these were somehow unlucky and one by one they dropped out of the game of life. The oldest brother died with the smell of burnt black powder in his nostrils, and Tom's father stood over the body and called his dead son a fool for wearing his gun so it could stick in the holster. "If I ever ketch yuh doin' a trick like that, I'll thrash yuh till yuh can't stand," he admonished young Tom sternly. Young Tom always remembered how his dad had looked when brother Bill was shot.

The second brother was overtaken while riding a big sorrel horse that did not happen to carry the

Lorrigan brand. So he too died with the smell of powder smoke in his nostrils, taking three of his pursuers with him into the Dark Land. Him Tom's father cursed for being caught.

So young Tom learned early two lessons of the Black Rim book of wisdom: His gun must never stick in the holster; he must never get caught by the law.

He was twenty when Brother Jim was drowned while trying to swim his horse across the Snake in flood time on a dare. Young Tom raced along the bank, frantically trying to cast his forty-foot rope across sixty feet of rushing current that rolled Jim and his horse along to the boil of rapids below. Young Tom was a long, long while forgetting the terror in Jim's eyes, the helplessness of Jim's gloved hand which he threw up to catch at the rope that never came within twenty feet of him, and at the last, the hopeless good-by wave he sent Tom when he whirled into the moil that pulled him under and never let him go. Tom learned on the bank of the Snake another lesson: He must never be so weak as to let another man badger him into doing something against his own desires or judgment.

Jim's pitiful going left Tom in full possession of the Devil's Tooth ranch and the cattle and horses that fed on the open range of the Black Rim country, — and they were many. Young Tom was lonely, but his loneliness was smothered under

a consuming desire to add to his possessions and
to avoid the mistakes of his brothers and of his
father who had carelessly ridden where he should
have walked.

Men of the Rim country frequently predicted
that young Tom Lorrigan would die with his boots
on; preferably in mid-air. They said he was going
to be like his dad in more than looks, and that
times were changing and a man couldn't steal
cattle and kill off anybody that argued with him,
and get away with it as Tom's father had done.
They complained that the country was getting too
damn Sunday school, and young Tom had better
tame down a little before he got into trouble.

As Black Rim defines the word, Tom was quite
as bad as they called him. A handsome young
dare-devil he was, slanting his glance downward
when he looked into the eyes of a six-foot man, —
and every inch of him good healthy bone and
muscle. Women eyed him pleasantly, wistful for
his smile. Men spoke to him friendlywise and
consciously side-stepped his wrath. On the Black
Rim range his word was law, his law was made
for himself and the wealth he hankered for. That
wealth he named a million dollars, and he named
it often because he liked the sound of the word.
Without any ifs he declared it. There was a million to be had in Idaho, was there not? Very well,
he would have his million, and he would have it
in cattle and horses and land. He would not go

mucking in the gold mines for it; his million should graze on the bunch grass. He wanted, he said, to see a million dollars walking around. And since old Tom Lorrigan had left him a mere forty thousand — according to the appraisers of the Devil's Tooth estate — young Tom had a long way to go to see his dream a reality.

Men of the Black Rim hinted that young Tom rode with a long rope; meaning that his rope would reach the cattle of his neighbor cowmen if they came in his way. But they only hinted, for unless they could prove beyond the doubt of any twelve men in the county that his brand was burned on any cattle save his own, they had no wish to offend. For young Tom had learned well his three lessons from the fate of his three brothers; his gun never stuck in its holster; he was wily and not to be caught; he could neither be harried nor coaxed into setting aside his own judgment while it seemed to him good.

You would think that young Tom would speedily find himself a mate amongst the girls of the Black Rim country, — though they were as scarce as princesses of the royal blood and choice was of necessity restricted to a half dozen or so. None of the girls he knew pleased his fancy, untrained though that fancy might be. Instinct told him that they were too tame, too commonplace to hold his interest for long. A breathless dance or two, a kiss stolen in a shadowy corner, and blushes and giggles and inane remonstrances that bored him because he knew they would come. Tom had reached the sere age of twenty-two when he began to wonder if he must go beyond the Black Rim world for his wife, or resign himself to the fate of an old bachelor. None of the Black Rim girls, he told himself grimly, should ever have a share in that million.

Then that purple-lidded, putty-face jade we call Fate whimsically sent him a mate; curious, I suppose, to see what would happen when the two whose trails had lain so far apart should meet.

A girl from some far city she was; a small star that had twinkled behind the footlights and had fled — or had fallen — to the Black Rim country. Like many another, she had gone as far as her money would take her. That it took her to the end of the little branch railroad that stopped abruptly with its nose against a mountain twenty miles from the Devil's Tooth ranch was a coincidence, — or the whim of Fate. There she was, as strange to the outland as young Tom would have been to the city whence she had come; thinking perhaps to start life afresh in some little Western town; with no money to carry her back to the outskirts of civilization, and no town wherein she might win fresh successes. The train that had brought her panted upon a siding, deserted, its boiler cooling, its engineer, fireman, conductor and brakeman leaning over a bar in the shack that called itself a saloon. To-morrow it would rattle back to the junction, if all went well and the rails held fast to the ties, which was not certain.

The station's name was Jumpoff. The train's conductor, who had the misfortune to be considered a humorist, liked to say that Jumpoff was a knot at the end of the road to keep the track from unraveling. He had told the girl that, on the long, jolty ride from the junction. The girl replied that at any rate she liked the name.

What really held Jumpoff on the time-table in those days before it became a real town were the stockyards, where the Black Rim cattle came to start their journey to market. The trail over the mountains to the main line was rough, with a two-day drive without water. Yet the Black Rim country had many cattle, and a matter of a few tunnels and a trestle or two let the railroad in by a short cut which minimized the distance to the main line. The branch line paid a fair interest on the investment, — but not with its passenger service.

The girl found herself stranded in a settlement whose business was represented by one saloon, one section house, one stable, one twelve-by-twelve depot and a store that was no more than an addition to the saloon, with the bartender officiating in both places as customers required his services. Times when cattle were being shipped, the store was closed and the saloon had no rival.

"It sure ain't, Miss. Might you be looking for somebody in particular?"

"No-o — I'm just here. It would be a poor place to look for anybody, wouldn't it?"

"Sure would." Young Tom found his courage and smiled, and the girl looked at him again, as though she liked that white-toothed smile of Tom's.

"Well, I started out to find the jumping-off place, and this sounded like it on the railroad map. I guess it's It, all right; there's nothing to do but jump."

Young Tom pulled his black eyebrows together, studying her. By her speech she was human; therefore, in spite of her beauty that dazzled him, she was not to be feared.

"You mean you ain't got any particular place to go from here?"

The girl tilted her head and stared up the mountain's steep, pine-covered slope. She swung her head a little and looked at Tom. She smiled bravely still, but he thought her eyes looked sorry for something.

"Is there any particular place to go from here?" she asked him wistfully, keeping the smile on her lips as the world had taught her to do.

"Not unless you went back."

She shook her head. "No," she said, firmly, "I'll climb that mountain and jump off the top before I'll go back."

It was while the girl was hesitating half-way between the store-saloon and the section house, wondering which she would choose, that young Tom Lorrigan galloped up to the hitch rail, stopped his horse in two stiff-legged jumps, swung down and came toward her. Like a picture on a wall calendar she looked to young Tom, who had never seen her like in flesh and blood. He lifted his big, range hat, and she smiled at him, — though it must have been a stage smile, she had so little heart for smiling then.

Tom blinked as though he had looked at the sun. Such a smile he had never seen in his life; nor such hair, like real, gold-colored silk all in curls around her face; nor such eyes, which were blue as the sky at twilight when the stars first begin to show.

"Jumpoff is not much of a town," said the girl and laughed to hide how close she was to tears.

Young Tom caught his breath. He had thought that women had only two forms of laughter, the giggle of youth or the cackle of age. He had never dreamed that a woman could laugh like a mountain stream gurgling down over the rocks. Immediately he visioned young ferns dripping diamonds into a shadowed pool, though he did not attempt to formulate the vision in words. His answer was obvious and had nothing to do with gurgling brooks, or with ferns and shadowed pools.

Young Tom felt that she spoke in sober earnest in spite of her smile; which was strange. He had seen men smile in deadly earnest, — his dad had smiled when he reached for his gun to kill Buck Sanderson. But women cried.

"Don't you know anybody at all, around here?"

"Not a soul — except you, and I don't know whether your name is Tom or Bill."

"My name's Tom — Tom Lorrigan. Say! If you ain't got any place to go — why — I've got a ranch and about twenty-five hundred head of cattle and some horses. If you didn't mind marrying me, I could take you out there and give yuh a home. I'd be plumb good to you, if you're willing to take a chance."

The girl stood back and looked him over. Tall as Tom was she came almost to his chin. He saw her eyes darken like the sky at dusk, and it seemed to him quite possible that stars could shine in them.

"You'd be taking as great a chance as I would. I haven't any ranch or any cattle, or anything at all but myself and two trunks full of clothes and some things in my life I want to forget. And I have sixty cents in my purse. I can't cook anything except to toast marshmallows —"

"I've got a cook," put in young Tom quickly.

"And the clothes I've got would be a joke out here. And the things I came out here to forget I shall never tell you —"

"I ain't interested enough to ask, or to listen if you told me," said Tom.

"And myself can sing to you and dance to you, and I'm twenty years old by the family Bible —"

"I'm twenty-two — makes it about right," said Tom.

" And if you should count fifty and ask me again —"

" Ten, twenty, thirty, forty-fifty, will you marry me?" obeyed Tom with much alacrity.

"You might call me Belle. Belle Delavan. Well, I came to Jumpoff because — I meant to jump. Yes, I'll marry you — and the Lord have mercy on you, Tom Lorrigan, if I live to regret it."

"Amen. Same to you," grinned Tom. "It's an even break, anyway. They don't claim I'm sprouting wings. They say I've got split hoofs in my boots instead of feet, and wear my ears pointed at the top. But — but no girl has got any loop on me. I've been straight, as far as women goes. That's my record up to the present. If you can stand for a little drinkin' and gamblin' and shootin' —"

Belle waved aside his self-depreciation. Young Tom was a handsome devil, and his eyes were keen and clear and looked right into her own, which was sufficient evidence of good faith for any woman with warm blood in her body.

"Tom Lorrigan, I've eaten just three soda

crackers, six marshmallows and one orange since yesterday noon," said she irrelevantly. "I can't be emotional when I'm half starved. Is there any place where I can get a piece of bread or something?"

"My Lord! Think of me standing here and not thinkin' whether you'd had dinner or not! Sure, you can have something to eat."

He took her by the arm, too penitent to be diffident over the unaccustomed gallantry, and hustled her toward the section house. His mind registered the fact that the bartender, the fireman, the brakeman and the conductor would shortly apologize abjectly for standing outside the saloon gawping at a lady, or they would need the immediate ministrations of a doctor. He hoped the girl had not noticed them.

"They'll throw some grub together quick, over here," he explained to the girl. "Everybody eats at the section house. It ain't much of a place, but there ain't any other place. And while you're having dinner I'll have the operator wire down to Lava for a marriage license to be sent up on the next train. The saloon man is a justice of the peace, and he'll marry us right away, soon as you eat. And—"

"Without a license? I know it's always done that way on the stage, but — but this isn't going to be any stage marriage."

"Well, but the license will be all made out and

on the way, and he'll take my word for it and go ahead with the ceremony. If I tell him to, he will. It will be all right; I'll *make* it all right. And then I can get a team from a ranch back here a ways, and take you right out to Devil's Tooth. It's the best way. This ain't any place for a lady to stay. You'll be comfortable out at the Devil's Tooth — it's clean, anyway.'' He looked at her honest-eyed, and smiled again. ''Yuh needn't be afraid uh me. We're rough enough and tough enough, and we maybe shoot up each other now and again, but we ain't like city folks; we don't double-cross women. Not ever.''

She said nothing, and when they had walked four steps farther he added with a sincere wish to set her at ease: ''I could take you to some ranch and leave you till the license comes, if you think it wouldn't be all right to get married now. But the womenfolks would talk your arm off, and you wouldn't like it. And they'd talk about you when your back was turned. But if Scotty goes ahead and married us, I don't see why —''

''Oh, I'm not worrying about that. It's just cutting a corner instead of walking around. I was thinking,'' said Belle Delavan, while she dabbed at her lashes as though they were beaded with paint instead of tears and she must be careful not to smear them, ''I was just thinking how — how *good* you are. My God, I never knew they grew men like you, outside of plays and poetry.''

"Good!" echoed young Tom Lorrigan, feared of his kind for his badness. His tone was hushed with amazement, all aglow with pleasure. " *Good!* — my Lord!"

CHAPTER TWO

THE LORRIGAN TREE GROWS THRIFTILY

YOUNG Tom Lorrigan had found his mate. Had he known more about life in the big world beyond the Rim, he must have been amazed at his luck. Once a man dropped dead in a poker game when he had staked his last blue chip and drawn a royal flush. In the great game of hearts Tom had drawn a royal flush, but he did not drop dead. Instead, he went right on living, more determined than ever to own a million dollars' worth of cattle and horses before he died, considerably before he died, because he wanted to enjoy that million with Belle. And because of her he wanted that million to be honest money.

Everything he did now, he did for Belle more than for himself. As a matter of course she became his real reason for living. She was like the sun. He took her for granted, never questioning the blessed warmth of her presence, never stopping to wonder what life would be like if he lost her. She was beautiful, with a beauty that never palled and never paled. She laughed a great deal, and he never could keep laughter from his own lips while he listened. When she sang she put the meadow larks to shame, and afterwards when he rode the range alone Tom would whistle strange, new melodies that the Black Rim country never had heard before, — melodies which Belle had taught him unconsciously with her singing. He did not know that it would have astonished a city dweller to hear the bad man of Black Rim Country whistling Schubert's "Serenade" while he rode after cattle, or Wagner's "Prize Song," or "Creole Sue," perhaps, since Belle, with absolute impartiality, sang everything that she had ever heard sung. On billboards before eastern theatres Belle Delavan had been called "The Girl with a Thousand Songs." Audiences had been invited by the stage manager to name any selection they might choose, assured that Belle would sing it from memory. No wonder that her singing never grew stale to Tom Lorrigan!

But mostly she busied herself with little domesticities that somehow never included cooking, and with driving helter-skelter over the range with two horses hitched to a buckboard, following Tom when he rode after cattle. Do you think she should logically have learned to ride? She did try it once on the gentlest horse that Tom owned, which was not too gentle to run away with Belle. She rode that horse just two hundred yards before she jolted so far from the saddle that she could not find it again until some time after, when they had caught the horse and led him to the corral.

"Not any more for me, Tom Lorrigan!" she gasped, flapping her two pretty hands in eloquent disgust when Tom rode up to her. "I wouldn't get on a horse's back again to star for the Queen of England! I'll take that team of he-devils you've been breaking to drive, and I'll drive 'em or break every bone in their bodies. I'm willing to get behind any horse you've got; but to get on their backs — excuse me!" She limped painfully to the house with her yellow hair blowing around her shoulders and across her lips that would smile in spite of her mishap.

After that Belle drove the "he-devils" and others quite as devilish, and risked her bones with perfect equanimity. She drove horses that had to be thrown before the collar could be buckled on, and "forefooted" before they would submit to the harness. Indeed, Belle seemed to prefer that kind of horses. She wanted a team that could keep pace with Tom, — and she had it. Her buckboard lasted a year, with luck. She strewed the Devil's Tooth range with wheels and doubletrees and splinters and hairpins, and scattered sunshiny smiles and cuss-words and snatches of song wherever she went. And since she went wherever eight bronco feet could take her, Black Rim country came to know Belle Lorrigan as it knew Tom. Came to fear Belle Lorrigan's wrath, which bet-

tered the lightning for searing, lashing sword-
thrusts of venom; came to know her songs well
enough to hum snatches of them; came to laugh
when she laughed, — and to hope that the next
laugh would not be aimed at them; came to recognize her as a better shot than any one save Tom,
who taught her.

At the country dances on the various ranches,
Belle never missed quadrille, two-step, waltz or
schottische, and she danced by herself or sang
songs during the intervals, while the women of the
range sat stiffly along the walls on benches, stared
at Belle and whispered behind their weather-red-
dened hands, and tittered. She taught big-jointed,
bashful boys how to waltz, and she slapped a half-
drunken miner who squeezed her too tightly in a
square dance. Slapped Tom also when he came
hurrying up to kill the miner, and told him to keep
to his own quarrels and save his powder for something worth while. She didn't need help to step
on a worm, she added, and took a youth by the arm
and led him off to dance. The miner, I may say
to the curious, was next seen in Hailey, heading
south. He left a very good prospect up in the
hills and never went back to work out his assess-
ments.

As you have probably guessed, Belle Lorrigan
and the women of the Black Rim country did not
get on very well together. Black Rim women
thought that a woman who wore her hair in curls

down her back — yellow hair at that! — could not
be any too good if the truth were known. They
declared to one another that a woman who did not
talk about her past life, who never so much as
mentioned past illnesses, even, must have a great
deal to cover up. How did Tom Lorrigan get
acquainted with her, anyway? Through some
marriage agency, they were willing to bet. And
how did a decent woman happen to have all the
fancy clothes which Belle Lorrigan possessed?
And jewelry enough to stock a store with! Three
rings on one finger at one time and the same time
was going it pretty strong, in the opinion of the
Black Rim ladies. They also believed that she
used paint and powder, which damned her beyond
all hope of redemption.

Poor Belle Lorrigan (Black Rim country spoke
of her always as Belle Lorrigan without in the
least understanding why she remained an indi-
vidual personality to them instead of becoming
merely Mrs. Lorrigan — Mrs. Tom, even, since
many of the Black Rim women were designated by
the nicknames of their husbands)! She would
have been glad to be friendly, simply because
friendliness was in her blood and would out. She
would have been glad to receive them at the Devil's
Tooth ranch for one of those all-day visits which
were the custom of the country. But for a long
while they did not come. Sometimes she would
meet a family bundled to the eyes against the chill

winds of Idaho, bumping over the rough roads on
their way to visit some near neighbor who lived
only ten or fifteen miles away. She would flash
them a smile while she pulled up her bronco team
out of the trail to make a generous room for their
passing, and she would shout something pleasant
as they went by. And after they had gone on she
would shrug her fine, broad shoulders and call
them cats, going out to a scratching, with all the
kittens mewing along. She would flap a hand —
providing the bronco team left her a hand free to
flap — and shake her head, and say, "Not for
mine, thank you!" And would be hurt down deep
in her heart where it did not show, because they
never stopped at her door.

But when the boys began to come, then came the
neighbor women, making formal two-hour calls
upon the new mother, eager to see and to hear and
to go away and compare notes afterward. They
talked much of the names that Belle Lorrigan
called her children. The first one she named for
the hero in her first play; wanting, I suppose, a
souvenir of the time when she was fifteen and had
her first speaking part on the stage. She called
her first-born Algernon Adelbert. Algernon Adelbert Lorrigan, grandson of old Tom Lorrigan!
Think of that!

But Algernon Adelbert no sooner outgrew his
cradle than he was known to all and sundry as
Al Lorrigan, so that no harm was done him in

giving him such a name. He grew up lusty and arrogant, a good deal of a bully, six feet tall, a good rider — though not so good a rider as his dad — a good shot, willing to help gather that million together on the chance that he might have a share in the spending.

Al was a youth who hunted trouble for the thrill of meeting it more than half-way, but since Tom Lorrigan happened to be his father, Al rode off the Devil's Tooth ranch before he became the rampant young trouble-hunter. Belle had some anxious hours during the time Al was gone, but she never once betrayed her anxiety; which is doing pretty well for a mother.

The second was Marmaduke LeRoy, and the third and last she recklessly christened Lancelot Montgomery. Marmaduke never learned to spell his name correctly, and sometimes complained that Belle had gone and named him after a mess of preserves, — meaning marmalade, I suppose. But as he grew older he forgot his grievance. Belle was the only person who could remember offhand his full name, and she never called him by it except when she was very angry; when she usually attached so many adjectives that Marmaduke LeRoy was quite submerged. Commonly he was called Duke, which did well enough.

Tom used to study Duke through half-closed lids and the smoke of a cigarette, and wonder which side of the family had a yellow streak; not the Lorrigan side, so far as Tom could judge. Nor the Delavan side either, if Belle lived true to type. To be sure, Belle refused to ride a horse; but then Belle was a woman and women had whims. There was no yellow about Belle, except her hair which was pure golden.

Duke would invariably lie to dodge punishment. According to his own theory, Duke was always blameless, always the injured party, the boy who does right and never is given credit for his virtues. Even Belle, who would fight for her boys as a tigress fights for its young, looked askance at Duke while she tried, motherlike, to cover his faults from the keen eyes of Tom.

"I'd just like to know how you come by it," she once exclaimed exasperatedly, when Duke was ten and Lance eight. "I'd sure chop one limb off the family tree, if I knew which one gave you the gall to lie to me and Tom. Duke, for heaven's sake take a licking just once without trying to lay the blame on Al or Lance — and see how proud you'll feel afterwards!"

"Aw — lickins hur–rt!" Duke had protested, rubbing the arm Belle had gripped none too gently, and sidled away from her.

With her hands to her hips — gracefully posed there, as became an actress — Belle regarded him fixedly. "My Gawd!" she whispered, owning defeat before that invulnerable selfishness of Duke's.

Her tone stung even his young crocodile-hided

sensibility. "You're always blamin' me. You'n
Tom think I do everything mean on this ranch!
You think Lance is an angel! He's your pet and
you let him pick on me an' you never say a word.
Lance can do any darn thing he pleases, an' so
can Al. I'm goin' to run away, first thing you
know. You can have your sweet little angel pet
of a doggone ole cowardly-calf Lance!" Then he
whined, "Aw — you lemme go! I never done it,
I tell yuh! It was Lance!"

Belle gritted her teeth while she shook him.
"You yellow-hearted little whelp. *I saw you*
chasing that colt around the corral till he broke
the fence! If Tom was to know about it he'd lick
you good! Duke, why *can't* you be a man and take
the blame yourself, just once? I'd be — I'd be so
proud o' you if you only told the truth about
things. Don't you know — it's only a coward that
will lie to save his own skin?"

"Lance is a bigger coward than I am, an' you
never say a word to him. You think Lance is perfect."

"I guess you're hopeless all right," Belle retorted. "It's just a yellow streak in you somewhere. Living with the Lorrigans, I'm hoping
you'll outgrow it. The Lorrigans sure ain't
yellow!"

"I chased Blackie some, Belle," Lance volunteered, peering down over the stable eave at his
irate mother. "Duke started in and got him going

good, and when he come fogging over to this side I flopped my arms at him. Gee, but he did stop quick! I guess if you're going to lick Duke, you better give me about four good licks for that, Belle. And take 'em off Duke's licking. No use licking us both for the same thing."

Belle tilted her yellow head and looked up at her beloved youngest, grinning down at her cheerfully from the hay roof where he sprawled head downward, flat on his stomach.

"Well, thank the Lord one Lorrigan has got the nerve to own up to a thing. Come on down and get your four licks, then. I can be as square as the next one. But Duke's got it coming to him for lying to me. Tell me, Lance, did Duke chase Blackie through the fence?"

"Aw go on, Belle! What's matter with you, asking me what Duke done? He's the feller to ask about that. I chased Blackie about four licks' worth. Hurry up and let's get it over with. You know it ain't pleasant for either of us!"

"Smarty!" yelled Duke, quick to read in Belle's face what softening effect Lance had on her temper. "Tryin' to be smart — tryin' to be George Wash'nton! You little liar, you know you chased Blackie more'n what I done. Sneak out of it — yeah, that's you, every time. Own up just enough to make Belle think you're an angel. Doggone the whole doggone outfit!"

"*Now* what?" Tom's voice broke in upon

Duke's shrill tirade. From the back of his horse
Tom looked down quizzically upon them. "Duke,
what you been up to?"

"Aw, you always think it's me! Why don't you
ask Lance what he's been up to? Why don't you
lick Lance for being on the stable? If I was to get
up there and tromp around in the hay and make it
leak, I know what *I'd* git!"

Tom sent a glance up to where Lance was hastily
scrambling down a corner. "You'd better!" he
commented sternly. Then he looked at Belle, his
eyes twinkling under his scowl.

"If you can't handle these young devils, Belle,
turn 'em over to me. I'll mighty quick settle their
hash for 'em."

Belle gripped tighter the squirming Duke. "I'm
not a cripple yet, Tom Lorrigan. They've both
got a licking coming to 'em, and if you'll kindly
walk off stage R. C. I'll go on with the scene. You
weren't cued to come on here."

"It's your show, Belle," Tom assented, and
very obligingly rode to the other side of the stable
to unsaddle his horse, and grinned to himself when
the sound of wailing and pleading and promises of
the "I'll-never-do-it-again" variety came to his
ears. Belle's lickings were distinguished chiefly
by their uproar.

"Belle wallops 'em like brandin' calves," Tom
used to chuckle. "They beller a plenty while it's
going on, and kick up their heels when it's all over.

I wish't my dad had licked me like that when I was a kid. You can gamble, when I was thrashed, I knowed it!"

Duke grew up to be a very good cowpuncher, however. He knew every draw and dry wash, every creek bottom and every canyon on the Black Rim range; knew almost as well as the owner how many cattle carried every brand. In the Devil's Tooth round-ups Duke held his place alongside Al as a top hand, — disputing now and then the right of young Lance to compete with him, but never quite daring to bring his dispute to the point where action would take the place of words.

"Duke's sure enough a bad man — with his face," Tom once snarled to Belle. "Make it a talking match, and Duke could lick any old woman in the Black Rim country."

"There's been enough fighting Lorrigans, don't you think?" Belle smiled back at him. "Duke's dad can fight hard enough for the whole family. I didn't think you wanted your boys to be fighters."

"I don't. But I sure do want 'em to have the fightin' stuff in 'em, whether it ever comes out or not. Take Lance, there. Lance ain't a fighter, either; but by the Lord John, it's there! Once get Lance started, and I'd back him against any three men in the Black Rim. It's in him, if the play ever come up. And it's in Al. The Lorrigan is strong in Al. But that Duke —"

"Honey, I think maybe it's the Delavan in Duke. I remember an old maid aunt of mine that used to bolt the door and quarrel with my mother through the keyhole. I guess maybe Duke has got a little touch of Aunt Jane."

"Oh, sure! First I ever heard of Aunt Jane, Belle. Takes you to think up a reason."

"And the Lorrigan will come out, honey. He's got the look, now and then. It's in him, you'll see."

So that is how the Lorrigan boys grew up. They thought Belle the most beautiful, the most wonderful woman in the world, — though they never called her mother. Belle would not have it. She refused to become a motherly, middle-aged person, and her boys were growing altogether too big and too masterful to look upon a golden-curled, pink-cheeked, honey-throated Amazon as other Black Rim sons looked upon their faded, too-often shrewish maternal parent. She was just Belle. They knew no other like her, no one with whom they might compare her. We do not compare the sun and the moon with other suns and moons. Like Tom, they worshipped her in their hearts, and chummed with her even before they had outgrown her stormy chastisements. They mended her buckboards and her harness; they galloped alongside while she drove careening across the range, her hair flying in the wind, her mouth smiling and showing her white teeth. They danced with her,

— and having Belle for a teacher from the time they could toddle, you may guess how the Lorrigan boys could dance. They sang the songs she taught them; they tried to better her record at target practice and never did it; they quarreled with her when her temper was up and dodged her when it became too cyclonic.

They grew up without ever having ridden on the cars, save once or twice to Lava. Black Rim was the rim of the world to them, and their world held all that they yearned for. Belle sheltered them from too much knowledge of that other world, which held the past she hated and tried to forget. Much she taught them of city manners and the little courtesies of life. She would box the ears of the boy who neglected to rise and offer her a chair when she entered a room, and would smoke a cigarette with him afterward. Once she whipped her six-shooter out of its holster and shot a hole through the crown of Al's hat, as a tactful reminder that gentlemen always remove their hats when they come into a house. Al remembered, after that. At fourteen even the hardiest youth feels a slight shock when a bullet jars through his hat crown two inches above his hair.

CHAPTER THREE

Mary Hope Douglas Appears

DEVIL'S TOOTH ridge, which gave the Lorrigan ranch its name, was really a narrow hogback with a huge rock spire at one end. Crudely it resembled a lower jaw bone with one lone tooth remaining. Three hundred feet and more the ridge upthrust its barren crest, and the wagon road from the ranch crawled up over it in many switchbacks and sharp turns, using a mile and a half in the climbing. They called it the "dug road." Which meant that teams and scrapers and dynamite and much toil had been necessary in the making, distinguishing it from most Black Rim roads, which followed the line of least resistance until many passings had worn a definite trail; whereupon that trail became an established thoroughfare legalized by custom and not to be lightly changed for another.

Over in the next valley, beyond Devil's Tooth ridge, Alexander Douglas had made a ranch for himself and his family. Aleck Douglas was as Scotch as his name. He shaved his long upper lip, so that it looked longer and more uncompro-

mising than was necessary even to match the
Aleck Douglas disposition. His hair was wiry
and stood up from a forehead that might be called
beetling. His eyebrows were heavy and came so
near to meeting that Mary Hope used to wish that
she dared lay one small finger between father's
eyebrows, just to see if there would be room. His
eyes were as close together as his thin beak of a
nose would permit, and his ears were long and
narrow and set flat against his head. He was tall
and he was lank and he was honest to his last
bristling hair. He did not swear — though he
could wither one with vituperative epithets — and
he did not smoke and he did not drink — er — save
a wee nip of Scotch "whusky" to break up a cold,
which frequently threatened his hardy frame. He
was harshly religious, and had there been a church
in the Black Rim country you would have seen
Aleck Douglas drive early to its door every Sunday morn, and sit straight-backed in a front pew
and stare hard at the minister through the longest
of sermons, — providing, of course, that church
and minister were good Presbyterian.

He loved the dollars, how he did love his dollars!
He loved his cattle, because they represented dollars. He nursed them, dollars and animals alike,
and to lose one wrung the heart of him.

His wife was a meek little thing in his presence,
as the wives of such men as Aleck Douglas usually
are. She also was rigidly honest, dogmatically

religious and frugal and hard-working and intolerant of the sins of others.

Early she taught Mary Hope that beyond Devil's Tooth ridge lived those wicked Lorrigans, whose souls were bartered to the devil and whose evil ways were a stench in the nostrils of God. Mary Hope used to wonder if God turned up his nose when there was a stench in his nostrils, — for instance, when Belle Lorrigan hurtled past with her bronks and her buckboard and her yellow hair flying. Mary Hope wondered, too, what the Lorrigan boys had got from the devil in exchange for their souls. Some magic, perhaps, that would protect them from death and accident. Yet that seemed not true, for Al Lorrigan broke his leg, one spring round-up. The devil ought to have saved his horse from falling down with him, if the devil had Al Lorrigan's soul.

That had happened when Mary Hope was twelve and Al Lorrigan was eighteen. She heard her father tell her mother about it; and her father had set his whiskered lip against his long, shaven upper lip almost with a smack.

"They'll come to a bad end, all of them," he declared sententiously. "Violent deaths had all the Lorrigans before them — all save Tom, and the Lord but stays his hand for a time from that man. The wicked shall flourish as a green bay tree."

"Father, how can a tree be green and then bay

too?'' Mary Hope ventured to inquire. ''Is it just a Bible tree, or does it flourish somewhere really?''

Aleck Douglas hid his mouth behind his palm and coughed. '' 'Tis not bay like a horse, child. 'Tis not the color that I'm speaking of.''

''That painted Jezebel, Belle Lorrigan, drove past the house to-day within a stone's throw,'' Mrs. Douglas informed her husband. ''I wush, Aleck, that ye would fence me a yard to keep the huzzy from driving over my very doorstep. She had that youngest brat of hers in the seat with her — that Lance. And as they went past on the keen gallop — and the horses both in a lather of sweat — the boy impudently shook his fist at me where I was glancing from my window. And his mother lookit and laughed, the Jezebel!''

''Mother, Lance only waved his hand.''

''And why should Lance be waving his hand when he should pass the house? Did he think that a Douglas would come so low as to wave at a Lorrigan?''

Mary Hope ducked her sleek little pig-tailed head outside the door and shooed vehemently at a dingy black hen that happened to be passing. Mary Hope knew that a Douglas had stooped so low as to wave back at Lance Lorrigan, but it seemed unwise to tell her mother so.

When Mary Hope was permitted to have a gentle old cow-pony of her own, she rode as often

as she dared to Devil's Tooth ridge. By short
cuts down certain washes which the trail avoided
with many winding detours, she could lope to the
foot of the ridge in forty minutes by the old alarm
clock which she carried one day in her arms to
time the trip. She could climb by another short-
cut trail, to the Devil's Tooth in twenty minutes.
She could come down in fifteen, she discovered.
In a three-hour ride she could reach the Devil's
Tooth, spend a whole hour looking down upon the
ranch house of the wicked Lorrigans, and ride
home again. And by choosing the short cuts she
practically eliminated the chance of being observed.

If she could see Belle go tearing down the trail
with her bronks and her buckboard she would be
horrifiedly happy. The painted Jezebel fascinated
Mary Hope, who had read all about that wicked
woman in the Bible, and had shivered in secret at
her terrible fate. Belle Lorrigan might never be
eaten by dogs, since dogs are few in cattleland
and are kept strictly at home, but if Mary Hope's
mother was any true prophetess, the painted Jezebel's final doom would be quite as horrible.

At the infrequent parties which the Douglas
household countenanced, — such as Christmas
trees and Fourth of July picnics, Mary Hope
would sit and stare fixedly at Belle Lorrigan and
wonder if all painted Jezebels were beautiful and
happy and smiling. If so, why was unadorned

virtue to be commended? Mary tried not to wish
that her hair was yellow and hung in curls, and
that she had even white teeth and could sing and
dance so wonderfully that everything stopped and
every one looked and listened from the minute
she began until she stopped.

More than anything else in her starved young
life, Mary Hope wanted to see the inside of the
Lorrigan house. The painted Jezebel had a real
piano, and she could play it, people said. She
played ungodly songs, but Mary Hope had a ven-
turesome spirit. She wanted to see an instrument
of the devil, hear the painted Jezebel play on it
and sing her ungodly songs.

One day when she had ridden to the top of the
Devil's Tooth a great, daring plan came to her.
She wanted to ride down there — a half mile down
the bluff, a mile and a half by the road — but she
would never dare take that trail deliberately. Her
father might hear of it, or her mother. Nor could
she ask the Lorrigans not to tell of her visit. But
if her horse ran away with her and took her down
the ridge, she could ask them to please not tell her
father, because if he knew that her horse ran away
he would not let her ride again. It seemed to
Mary Hope that all the Lorrigans would sympa-
thize with her dilemma. They would probably ask
her into the house. She would see the piano, and
she could ask the painted Jezebel to play on it.
That would be only polite. It did seem a shame

that a girl thirteen years old, going on fourteen, should never have seen or heard a piano. Mary Hope looked at the sun and made breathless calculation. Having just arrived at the Devil's Tooth, she had an hour to spend. And if she took the steep, winding trail that the Lorrigans rode, the trail where old man Lorrigan's horse had fallen down with him, she could be at the house in a very few minutes.

" Ye look little enough like a runaway horse, ye wind-broken, spavined old crow-bait, you!" she criticized Rab as he stood half asleep in the sun. "I shall have to tell a lee about you, and for that God may wither the tongue of me. I shall say that a rattler buzzed beneath your nose — though perhaps I should say it was behind ye, Rab, else they will wonder that ye didna run away home. If ye could but lift an ear and roll the eye of you, wild-like, perhaps they will believe me. But I dinna ken — I wouldna believe it mesel!"

Rab waggled an ear when she mounted, switched his tail pettishly when she struck him with the quirt, reluctantly obeyed the rein, and set his feet on the first steep pitch of the Devil's Tooth trail. Old as he was, Rab had never gone down that trail and he chose his footing circumspectly. It was no place for a runaway, as Mary Hope speedily discovered when she had descended the first dip and entered the cleft which the Lorrigans called the Slide.

A slide it was, and down it Rab slid on his rump. An old watercourse, with sheer rock walls that formed the base of the Tooth itself. Had there been room Mary Hope would have turned back. But the cleft was so narrow that a pack horse must be adept at squeezing past protuberances and gauging the width of its pack if it would travel the trail. A sharp turn presently showed her the end of the cleft, and they emerged thankfully upon a sage-grown shelf along which the trail proceeded more gently.

Then came another cleft, with great boulders at the end, which a horse must negotiate carefully if he would not break a leg or two. It was here that old Tom Lorrigan had died under his horse before help came that way. But Rab had covered many rough trails, and he picked his way over the boulders safely, — though not as a runaway horse should have traveled.

After that there came a treacherous bit of shale, across which Mary Hope thought it best to lead her runaway steed which refused for a time to venture farther. Being a Douglas she was obstinate. Being obstinate, she would not turn back, especially since the trail would be even worse in the climbing than it was in the descent. Rab, she realized worriedly, could not slide up that narrow, rock-bottomed cleft down which he had coasted so readily.

"They must be devil horses that ride this way,

Rab," she sighed when she had remounted on the lower margin of the shale. "And the Lorrigans na doot have magic. But I dinna think that even they could run away down it."

She struck Rab sharply with the quirt and dug in her heels. If Rab was to run it must be immediately, for the level valley lay just below and the Lorrigan house was around the next point of the hill.

Rab would not run. He stopped abruptly and kicked with both feet. Mary Hope struck him again, a little harder, and Rab kicked again, more viciously. The trail was much better for kicking than for running, but Mary Hope would not accept the compromise, and at last Rab yielded to the extent of loping cautiously down the last steep declivity. When he reached level ground he laid back his ears and galloped as fast as his stiffened shoulders would let him. So Mary Hope very nearly achieved a dashing pace as she neared the corrals of the wicked Lorrigans.

"Well! Yuh traveling, or just goin' somewhere?" A young voice yelled at her as she went past the stable.

"My horse — is — he rinned away wi' me!" screamed Mary Hope, her pigtails snapping as Rab slowed up and stopped.

"He rinned away wi' you? When? You musta been purty young for riding when *that* horse rinned away!" Lance came toward her, grinning and slapping his hat against his fringed chaps before he set it upon his head; an uncommonly handsome head, by the way, with the Lorrigan's dark eyes and hair and his mother's provocative mouth. "Well, seeing your horse ain't going to rin no further, you might as well git down and stay awhile."

"I will not. I didna come to visit, if you please."

Mary Hope's cheeks were hot but confusion could not break her Scotch spirit.

"Want to borrow something?" Lance stood looking at her with much enjoyment. A girl in short skirts was fair game for any one's teasing, especially when she blushed as easily as did Mary Hope. "Want to borrow a horse that will rin away wi' you."

"Lance, you devil, get out and leave the girl alone. I'm ashamed of you! Haven't you got any manners at all? — after all the willows and the good powder I've wasted on you! Get back to that pasture fence before I take a club to you for such acting!"

Before Belle's wrath Lance retreated, and Mary Hope found the courage to wrinkle her nose at him when he glanced her way. "He rinned away to save himself a whupping," she commented, and made sure that he heard it, and hoped that he would realize that she spoke "Scotchy" just for his special benefit.

"All right for you, Belle Lorrigan!" Lance called back, retaliating for Mary Hope's grimace by a kiss thrown brazenly in the expectation of seeing her face grow redder; which it did immediately. "Careful of that horse — he might rinned away again!"

"That'll do for you, young man!" Whereupon Belle picked up a small stone and threw it with such accurate aim that Lance's hat went off. "Good thing for you that I haven't got a gun on me, or I'd dust your heels for you!" Then she turned to Mary Hope, who was listening with titillating horror to the painted Jezebel's unorthodox method of reproving her offspring. "Get right down, honey, and come in and rest. And don't mind Lance; he's an awful tease, especially when he likes a person. Tie your horse to the fence — or turn him in the corral, if he'll let you catch him again."

"I — I don't believe I could stop. I — I only came by because I — my horse —" Mary Hope stammered and blushed so red that her freckles were invisible. After all, it was very hard to tell a lie, she discovered.

"There's something I like about this horse," said Belle, running her plump white hand down the nose of Rab. "He's neighborly, anyway. He brought you here against your will, I can see that. And now he's here he sort of takes it for granted you'll be friendly and stop a while. Don't you think you ought to be as friendly as your horse, honey?"

"I — I am friendly. I — I always wished I could come and see you. But mother — mother doesna visit much among the neighbors; she — she's always busy."

"I don't visit much, myself," said Belle dryly. "But that ain't saying I can't be friendly. Come on in, and we'll have some lemonade."

Sheer astonishment brought Mary Hope down from her horse. All her life she had taken it for granted that lemonade was sacred to the Fourth of July picnics, just as oranges grew for Christmas trees only. She followed Belle dumbly into the house, and once inside she remained dumb with awe at what seemed to her to be the highest pinnacle of grandeur.

There was the piano with a fringed scarf draped upon its top, and pictures in frames standing upon the scarf in orderly rows. There were many sheets of music,— and never a hymn book. There were great chairs with deep upholstery which Mary observed with amazement was not red plush, nor even blue plush, yet which appealed to her instincts for beauty. There was no center table with fringed spread and family album and a Bible and a conch shell. Instead there was a long table before a window — a table littered with all sorts of things: a box of revolver cartridges, a rifle laid down in the middle of scattered newspapers, a bottle of oil, more music, a banjo, a fruit jar that did duty as a vase for wild flowers, a half-finished, braided quirt and four silver dollars lying where they had been carelessly flung down. To Mary Hope, reared in a household where dollars were precious things, that last item was the most amazing of all. The Lorrigans must be rich, — as rich as they were wicked. She thrilled anew at her own daring.

Belle brought lemonade, wonderful lemonade, with an egg beaten to yellow froth and added the last minute. Mary Hope sipped and marveled. After that, Belle played on the piano and sang songs which Mary Hope had never heard before and which she thought must be the songs the angels sang in Heaven, although there was nothing to suggest harps or hallelujahs. Love songs they were, mostly. The sun slipped around and shone through a window on Belle's head, so that her yellow hair glistened like fine threads of gold. Mary Hope watched it dreamily and wondered how a Jezebel could be so beautiful and so good.

"You'd better run along home now, honey," Belle said at last when she had finished her eighth song. "I'd love to have you stay all night — but I reckon there'd be trouble. Your dad ain't any too mild, I've heard. But I hope you won't wait until your horse runs away with you again. I want you to come real soon. And come early so you can stay longer. I'll teach you to play the piano, honey. You ought to learn, seeing you love it so.''

That night Mary Hope dreamed of playing strange, complex compositions on a piano which Lance Lorrigan had given her. The next morning and for many days after she still dreamed of playing entrancing strains upon a piano, and of Lance Lorrigan who had thrown her a kiss. Belle had said that Lance always teased a person he liked, and in that one remark lay the stuff of many dreams.

CHAPTER FOUR

A MATTER OF BRANDS

ON the grassy expanse known locally as Injun Creek, fifteen hundred head of cattle were milling restlessly in a close-held herd over which gray dust hovered and settled and rose again. Toward it other cattle came lowing, trotting now and then when the riders pressed close, essaying a retreat when the way seemed clear. From Devil's Tooth they came, and from Lava Bed way, and from the rough sandstone ridges of Mill Creek. Two by two the riders, mere moving dots at first against a monotone of the rangeland, took form as they neared the common center. Red cattle, black cattle, spotted and dingy white, with bandy-legged, flat-bodied calves keeping close to their mothers, kicking up their heels in sheer joy of their new life when the pace slowed a little, seeking a light lunch whenever the cows stopped to cast a wary glance back at their pursuer. A dozen brands were represented in that foregathering: The NL brand of Tom Lorrigan on most, with its various amendments which differentiated the property of other members of the family, since all of the Lorrigans owned cattle. There was the NL Block of Belle Lorrigan, the ANL which was Al's brand, the DNL of Duke and the LNL which belonged to Lance; monograms all of them, deftly constructed with the fewest possible lines. There was that invitation to the unlawful artistry of brand-working, the Eleven which Sleek Douglas thought quite sufficient to mark his cattle. It was merciful to the calves, he maintained, and as to thieves, the dishonest would be punished by law and the Douglas wrath. The Miller brand, a plain Block, showed now and then upon the rump of some animal. The AJ fled occasionally before a rider, and there were brands alien to the Black Rim; brands on cattle that had drifted down from the Snake through the Lava Creek pass, or over the sage-grown ridges farther north.

His rifle sheathed in a saddle holster under his thigh, his black eyes roving here and there and letting no small movement of men or animals escape their seeing glances, Tom Lorrigan rode to the round-up, lord of the range, steadfast upon the trail of his "million on the hoof" of which he dreamed. Beside him rode Al, and the two of them were talking while they rode.

" He ain't safe, I tell you," Al was saying in the tone of reiteration. " And you needn't ask me how I know. I know it, that's all. Maybe he's too damn' agreeable or something. Anyway,

I know I don't like the way his eyes set in his head.''

"A man that wasn't safe wouldn't dare come into the Black Rim and make the play he's makin','' Tom contended. "I've had my eye on him ever since he come. I've checked up what he says at different times — they tally like the truth. I can't find nothing wrong.''

"I've got him set down for a spotter,'' said Al.

"If he ain't on the level it'll show up sooner or later,'' Tom contended. "I've got my eye on him. I dunno what you pin your argument on, Al, I'll be darned if I do.''

"Well, watch out for Cheyenne. That's all. You're pretty keen, all right, but all a man's got to do to get on your blind side is to blow in here with his chin on his shoulder and his horse rode to a whisper and claim to you he's hidin' out. Cheyenne ain't right, I tell yuh. You take a tip from me and watch him.''

"Takes a kid to tell his dad where to head in at!'' growled Tom. "How do you reckon I ever got along before your time. Ever figure that out, Al?''

"Now, what's eatin' on old Scotty Douglas, do yuh reckon? That's him, all right. I could tell him on horseback ten mile off. He rides like a Mormon.''

Tom grunted. His boys, he had long ago discovered, were very apt to find some excuse for changing the subject whenever he mentioned the past which had not held their arrogant young selves. Tom resented the attitude of superior wisdom which they were prone to assume. They were pretty smart kids, but if they thought they were smarter than their dad they sure had a change of heart coming to them.

"Supposin' it is old Scotty. Do you reckon, Al, I've got you along for a guide, to point out what my eyes is getting too poor to see? As for Cheyenne," he reverted angrily to the argument, "as for Cheyenne, when you've growed to be a man, you'll find it's just as much the mark of a fool to go along suspecting everybody as it is to bank on everybody. You think now it's funny to put the Judas brand on every man you don't know. It ain't. It's a kid's trick. Boys git that way when they begin to sprout hair under their noses. I been pretty patient with yuh, Al. You're growing up fast, and you're feeling your oats. I make allowances, all kinds. But by the humpin' hyenas, don't you start in telling me where to head in at with my own outfit! If you do, I'll jest about wear out a willer switch on yuh!"

This to a youth almost old enough to vote was dire insult. Al pulled up his horse. "Run your own outfit and be darned to yuh!" he cried hotly, and spurred off in the direction of the ranch.

Tom laughed shortly and rolled a cigarette. "Thinks now it'll bust up the round-up if he

goes," he opined. "Lucky for my kids I ain't as
strict as my old dad was; they wouldn't have any
hide left, I reckon."

Up loped Aleck Douglas then, riding stiff-
legged, his bony elbows jerking awkwardly with
the motion of his horse, a rusty black vest dangling
open under his coat which flapped in the wind.
That the Douglas wrath rode with him Tom saw
from the corner of his eye and gave no sign.

"Hello," said Tom casually and drew a match
along the stamped fork of his saddle. "You're
quite a stranger." He lighted his cigarette, holding his reins lightly in one hand while he did so;
gave the reins a gentle flip to one side and sent
his horse after a cow and calf that showed symp-
toms of "breaking back."

"Mister Lorrigan, 'tis aboot a spotted yearlin'
that I've come to speak with ye. I've found the
hide of her in the brush beneath yon hill, and the
brand is cut from it. But I wad swear to the hide
wi'out the brand. 'Twas a yearlin' I ken weel,
Mister Lorrigan." He rode alongside, and his
close-set little eyes regarded keenly Tom's face.

"A spotted yearling with the brand cut out,
hey? That looks kinda bad. Have you got the
hide with you?"

"I have no got the hide wi' me, but I ken weel
whaur it lies, Mister Lorrigan, and I thinkit so do
you."

"Hm–m. You'd ought to of brought it along."

Tom's glance went out toward the herd and the cattle lumbering toward it far and near. "The range is plumb lousy with spotted yearlings, Scotty. What do you expect me to do about it?"

The Douglas face worked spasmodically before he spoke. "I expect ye, Mr. Lorrigan, to pay for yon beastie. I ken weel ye could name the mon that stickit the knife in her throat. An' she made fine eatin', I have na doot. But 'tis the law, Mister Lorrigan, that a mon should pay for the meat he consumes."

"Meaning, of course, that you think I'm feeding Douglas meat to my outfit. Don't you think you're kinda hasty? I kill a beef about every three or four days in round-up time. The boys work hard and they eat hard. And they eat NL beef, Scotty; don't overlook that fact. Hides ain't worth anything much, but salt's cheap, too. I ain't throwin' away a dollar when it's no trouble to save it. If you're any curious at all, you ride over to ranch and count all the green hides you can find. Belle, she'll show 'em to you. Take a look at the brands, and figure it out yourself. I don't know how many you'll find, but I'll gamble you a dozen cows against one that you'll wonder what went with all the beef that was in them hides. Humpin' hyenas! Ain't I got cattle enough of my own, without rustlin' off my neighbors?"

"Aye. Ye ha' cattle, Mister Lorrigan; I ken weel ye should no' be put to it for a wee bit meat

— but I ken weel yon spotty yearlin' was mine. I ken ye've been campin' thereabout — and it wad seem, Mister Lorrigan, that the salt was no sa plentifu' when the spotty yearlin' was kilt.''

The downright foolhardiness of the Douglas wrath held Tom's hand, — though of a truth that hand trembled and crept backward. Nor was Aleck Douglas nearsighted; he saw the movement and his bearded underlip met his shaven underlip in a straight line.

''Ye do weel to be reachin' for the gun, Mister Lorrigan. I dinna carry aye weapon save the truth.''

Tom flushed. ''Blame your oatmeal soul, if I reached for my gun, you wouldn't be telling me about it!'' he exploded. ''Carry the truth, do yuh? You've got to show me where you keep it, then. If you wasn't an old man — and a darn fool on top of that.''

'' 'Tis no brave to cover shame wi' bitter words, Tam Lorrigan. 'Tis the way of ye to bluster and bully until the neighbors all are affrighted to face ye and yere ill deeds.''

Toward them clattered two riders hotly pursuing a lean, long-legged steer with a wide spread of horns and a gift of speed that carried him forging past the disputants. Tom wheeled mechanically and gave chase, leaving the Douglas wrath to wax hotter or to cool if it would. It was a harsh accusation that Aleck Douglas had made, and that he did make it seemed to prove that he had what he considered very good evidence that he was right. Tom was well schooled in troubles of that kind. He did not take the matter so indifferently as Douglas believed.

Duke and Mel Wilson, riding hard, came upon Tom just as he had roped and thrown the steer in a shallow draw that hid them from the level where Aleck Douglas waited.

"Hey!" Tom beckoned them close. "Old Douglas says there's a hide in the willows this side of Squaw Butte, with the brand cut out; a spotted yearling, and he claims it's his and he can swear to it without the brand. I don't know a darn thing about it. Nobody does in this outfit; I'll stake all I've got on that. But he's on the fight — and a mule's a sheep alongside him when he's got his back up. He left the hide where he found it. Haze this steer and ride over there and see what there is to his talk. If you find a hide cachéd in the willows, put it outa sight. We don't want any rustling scraps started on this range; that's bad medicine always. If he can't produce any hide, he can't start anything but talk — and talk's cheap."

A few moments later they came tearing up out of the draw, the steer running strong, the three riders still hotly pursuing. Duke and Mel rushed it on to the herd, and Tom dropped out of the race and came along across to where Douglas wrath had not cooled but had smoldered and waited for the wind of opposition to fan it to flame again.

"Well, you still mournin' over your spotty yearlin'?" Tom called. "You must have more time than you know what to do with to-day. Us, we have to *work*."

"If it's to the round-up ye're going, then I'll ride wi' ye, Tom Lorrigan. I'm a fair mon and I wush na ill to my neighbors. But I canna twiddle the thumbs whilst others fare well on Douglas beef."

"You can ride where you please; it's open range. But if you ride to the herd I'll show you forty yearlings that I'll bet are dead ringers for the one that you claim was killed. I never seen that hide neither, unless maybe when the critter was using it.

"Now, I don't want any trouble with yuh, Scotty. But I tell yuh right now I can't stand for much more of this talk about beef rustling. Thief's a pretty hard word to use to a man's face — and get away with it."

" 'Tis a hard mon I'm usin' it tae," the Douglas retorted grimly.

"Braggin' about your nerve, are yuh, Scotty?"

"I have a name, Tam Lorrigan, and 'tisna Scotty." The Douglas face twisted with anger. "I will no bandy worrds with ye. 'Tis ill I should descend to the level o' them that deespitefully use me."

"Deespitefully!— why, humpin' hyenas! Ain't
I letting yuh *live?* And do yuh reckon any other
man could walk up to me and call me a thief and
live long enough to take it back? Just because
you're old, and such a blamed fool you go around
without a gun on yuh, I'm keepin' my hands off
you. I call yuh a coward. You wouldn't a dared
to come over here with a gun on yuh and talk the
way you've done. You've got me hog-tied. You
know it. And damn yuh, I'll fight yuh now with
the law — which is the only way a coward will
fight.

"You've done a heap of chawin' around about
the Lorrigans, Scotty. Don't think I ain't heard
it. Maybe it's your religion to backbite yore
neighbors and say what you wouldn't dare to say
to their face with a gun on you so we'd be equal.
I've passed it up. I've considered the source and
let it go. But when you come belly-achin' around
about me stealin' a spotty yearlin' — jest as if
there wasn't but one on the Black Rim range! —
why, damn it, *you'll prove it!* Do you get that?
You'll prove it before a jury, or I'll sue yuh for
libel and bust yuh. I don't go much on the law,
but by Henry, I'll use it on you!"

The Douglas eyes flickered uncertainly, but the
Douglas mouth was unyielding. "The law can no
be cheatit so easy, Tam Lorrigan. I hae no wush
to send ye tae jail — but ye ken weel that wad be
the penalty for killin' yon beastie in the willows.

I came to settle the matter fair between neighbors, and tae warn ye to cease your evil doings on the range. I wadna see yer woman come tae grief —"

"You can cut out that mercy talk, Scotty. And don't try to bring Belle into this. If it comes to a showdown, lemme advise you, you'd better side-step Belle. The grief would all be yourn, if you and Belle lock horns, and I'm telling yuh so."

They had reached the nearest margin of the herd. Cheyenne, a nameless estray from the Wyoming ranges, chanced to be holding herd where the two rode up. At him Tom looked, suspicion for the moment sharpening his glance.

"You can ask this man what he knows about any spotted hide over by Squaw Butte," he invited the Douglas stiffly. "He's practically a stranger to the outfit — been here about a month. Maybe his word'll be worth something to yuh — I dunno. You can ask him."

Douglas rode over to Cheyenne and said what he had to say. Tom meanwhile held the herd and meditated on the petty injustices of life — perhaps — and wished that a real he-man had come at him the way Douglas had come. It irked Tom much to be compelled to meet hard words with tolerant derision. Toleration was not much of a factor in his life. But since he must be tolerant, he swung his horse to meet the Douglas when the brief conversation with Cheyenne was over. The Douglas head was shaking slowly, owning disappointment.

"Well, yuh might as well make the rounds,
Scotty. Go on and ask all the boys. If I asked
'em myself you might think it was a frame-up.
And when you've made the rounds, take a look
through the herd. The chances are that you'll
find your spotty yearlin' walking around with her
hide on her. And when you're plumb through,
you make tracks away from my outfit. My patience is strainin' the buttons right now, looking at
your ugly mug. And lemme tell yuh — and you
mark it down in your little red book so yuh won't
forget it — after you've peddled your woes to the
hull outfit, you bring in that hide and some proof,
or you get down on them marrow bones and apologize! I'm plumb tired of the way you act."

Aleck Douglas scowled, opened his hard lips to
make a bitter answer and reconsidered. He went
off instead to interview the men, perhaps thinking
that adroit questioning might reveal a weak point
somewhere in their denial.

Tom rode over to Cheyenne. "Scotty's got his
war clothes on," he observed carelessly.

"Shore has," Cheyenne grinned. "But that's
all right. He didn't make nothin' off me. I never
give him any satisfaction at all."

Tom's brows pulled together. "Well, now, if
you know anything about any hide with the brand
cut out, you'd better come through, Cheyenne."

"I never said I knowed anything about it. I
guess mebby that's why I couldn't give him no

satisfaction." Cheyenne still grinned, but he did not meet Tom's eyes.

"You spoke kinda queer for a man who don't know nothing, Cheyenne. Did yuh think mebby it wasn't all NL beef you been eating?"

"Why, no. I never meant anything like that at all. I only said —"

"Straight talk don't need no explainin', Cheyenne. The Devil's Tooth outfit shore likes the taste of its own beef. If any man fails to agree with that, I want him to speak up right now."

Cheyenne pinched out the fire in his cigarette and flipped the stub away from him. He did not look at Tom when he said:

"NL beef shore suits me. I don't know about any other brand. I ain't et none to judge by."

"You bet your life you ain't," snapped Tom, as he turned away. "When you sample another brand you won't be drawin' wages with this outfit."

He rode away to the wagon, where a fire was already burning and the branding irons heating. Cheyenne, with his hat pulled down over his forehead so that he looked out from under the brim that shaded his face, watched Tom queerly, a corner of his lips lifted in a half smile that was not pleasant.

CHAPTER FIVE

They Ride and They Do Not Tell Where

ALECK DOUGLAS, having questioned the crew as Tom had suggested, and having inexorably ridden through the herd — in search of brands that had been "worked," or for other evidence of the unlawful acquisition of wealth, rather than in hope of finding his spotted yearling — rode away with the parting threat that he would "gang to the shuriff and hae a talk wi' him." Tom had advised him of one or two other destinations where he hoped the Douglas would arrive without any delay whatever, and the branding proceeded rather slowly with the crew three men short.

Duke and Mel Wilson rode in about three o'clock with a few cows and calves which they had gleaned from some brushy draw to cover their real errand. By the time they had snatched a hasty meal at the wagon a mile away, and had caught up fresh horses, the afternoon's work was nearly over. A little earlier than usual, Tom kicked the branding fire apart, ordered the herd thrown on water and grazed back to the bed-ground that had been used during round-up time ever since he could remember, and rode slowly toward camp, whither the lucky ones not on herd were speeding.

Cheyenne, Tom observed, seemed in a greater hurry than the others, and he beckoned to him a slim, swarthy-skinned youth who answered to the euphonious name of Sam Pretty Cow, who was three-quarters Indian and forgiven the taint for the ability to ride anything he ever tried to ride, rope anything he ever swung his loop at, and for his unfailing good humor which set him far above his kind.

"Cheyenne's in a hurry to-night, Sam."

"Yeah. Ride hell out of his horse. I dunno, me." Sam grinned amiably at his boss.

"I wish you would camp on his trail, Sam. He'll maybe ride somewhere to-night."

"Yeah. Uh-huh. You bet," acquiesced Sam, and leaned forward a little, meaning to gallop after Cheyenne.

"Hold on a minute! What did Scotty have to say, Sam?"

"Him? Talk a lot about spotty yearlin' he says is dead. Asking who kills them calf. Search me, I dunno."

"Hear any talk among the boys about beef rustling?"

"Uh-huh. First I hear is them sour-face asking me who kills them critter. Me, I dunno."

"If you hear anything about it, Sam, let me know. Scotty thinks we done it."

"Yeah. Uh-huh. Anybody does something mean, everybody says, 'Damn Lorrigans done it.' Too much talk in the Black Rim. Talking under their hats all the time but no liking to fight them Lorrigans. Uh-huh. They're scared, you bet."

"They'll have something to get scared at, if they ain't careful. I'm getting tired of it," said Tom gloomily.

"Yeah, you bet!" agreed Sam, his voice all sympathy. Then seeing that Tom had no immediate intention of saying more, he touched his horse with his long-shanked spurs and hurried on to "camp on the trail of Cheyenne."

Tom had nearly reached camp when Duke came pounding up behind him, coming from the herd. Duke set his horse up, in two jumps slowing from a gallop to a walk. Tom turned his head but he did not speak. Nor did Duke wait for questions.

"Dad, we didn't find any hide over by Squaw Butte," he announced abruptly. "Mel and I hunted every foot of the willows. I saw where a critter had been killed, all right. There was some scuffed-out tracks and blood on the ground. But there wasn't any hide. Scotty musta cachéd it somewheres."

"Scotty claims he left it where he found it, for evidence," Tom said gloomily.

"Darned if I'd take the blame for other folks' rustling," Duke declared. "I wisht he'd of come to me with his tale of woe. I'd a showed him where to head in, mighty darned sudden. I'd of asked where was his proof; there's other cow out-fits in the Black Rim besides the Devil's Tooth, I'd tell him. And if he didn't have mighty darned good evidence, I'd of —''

"Yes, I expect you would of tore the earth up all round him,'' Tom interrupted drily. ''You boys shore are fighty, all right — with your faces. What I'm interested in, is whereabouts you and Mel hunted. That hide wouldn't show up like the Devil's Tooth — understand. And Scotty was bawling around like a man that's been hurt in the pocket. He found a hide, and if it ain't his he shore thinks it is, and that's just about the same. And we camped over there three days ago. Where all did you and Mel look?''

"All over, wherever a hide could be cachéd. There ain't any over there. Scotty musta dreamt it — or else he buried it.''

"Scotty ain't the dreamy kind. Might be pos-sible that the ones that done the killing went back and had a burying — which they'd oughta have had at the time. I can't sabe a man rustling beef and leaving the hide laying around, unless —'' Tom pulled his eyebrows together in quick suspi-cion. ''It kinda looks to me like a frame-up,'' he resumed from his fresh viewpoint. ''Well, you and Mel keep it under your hats, Duke. Don't say nothing to any of the boys at all. But if any of the boys has anything to say, you listen. Scotty

made the rounds to-day — talked to the whole
bunch. They know all about his spotty yearlin',
gol darn him! I'd like to know if any of 'em has
got any inside dope. There's strangers in the outfit this spring. And, Duke, you kinda keep your
eye on Cheyenne. Al seems to think he ain't right
— but Al has got to the suspicious age, when every
man and his dog packs a crime on his conscience.
You kinda stall around and see if Cheyenne lets
slip anything.''

"What would happen to old Scotty Douglas if
he lost a bunch, for gosh sake? Drop dead, I
reckon," grumbled Duke. "He's sure making a
lot of fuss over one measly yearlin'.''

"Yeah — but I've saw bigger fusses made over
smaller matters, son," Tom drawled whimsically.
"I saw two men killed over a nickel in change,
once. It ain't the start; it's the finish that
counts.''

"Well, looking at it that way, uh course —''

"That's the only way to look at it, son. Did you
think, maybe, that I hazed you over to find that
hide and bury it, just to keep it from scentin' up
the scenery? It's what I could smell farther
ahead that I was after. If you'd looked ahead a
little further, maybe you'd of looked a little closer
in the willers.''

To this Duke had nothing to say; and presently
he loped on, leaving Tom to ride slowly and turn
the matter of the spotted yearling over and over

in his mind until he had reached some definite conclusion.

Tom had the name of being a dangerous man,
but he had not earned it by being hasty. His anger was to be feared because it smoldered long,
rather than because it exploded into quick violence.
He wanted to see the trail ahead of him — and just
now he thought he saw Trouble waiting on the
turn. No Lorrigan had ever ridden the other way
because Trouble waited ahead, but one Lorrigan
at least would advance with his eyes open and his
weapons ready to his hand.

"Bring your proof," he had said in effect to
Aleck Douglas, "or stand trial for libel. Since
you won't fight with guns, I'll fight you with the
law." Very good, if he could be sure that the
Douglas would fail to produce his proof.

Tom knew well enough the reputation he bore in
the Black Rim country. Before the coming of
Belle, and later, of the boys, Tom had done his
share toward earning that reputation. But Belle
and the boys had changed his life far more than
appeared on the surface. They had held his rope
from his neighbors' cattle, for one thing, though
his neighbors never had credited him with honesty.

It is true that Tom could remember certain incidents of the round-up that had added to his herd
and brought him a little nearer the million-dollar
mark. Without remorse he remembered, and
knew that any cowman in the country would do the

same, or worse if he dared.   For branding irons
do not always inquire very closely into the parent-
age of a calf that comes bouncing up stiff-legged
at the end of a cowpuncher's rope.   Nor need a
maverick worry very long because he belongs to
no one, so long as cowmen ride the range.   Cattle
would always stray into the Black Rim country
from ranges across the mountains, and of these the
Black Rim took its toll.   He supposed strange
irons were set now and then on the hide of an NL
animal across the mountains — but the branders
had better not let him catch them at it!   On the
other hand, he would see to it that they did not
catch him branding mavericks on his own range.
To Tom that seemed fair enough,— a give-and-take
game of the range-land.   According to Tom's code
he was as honest as his neighbors, and that was
honest enough for practical purposes.

It happened that he had not killed Aleck Douglas' spotted yearling.   And to be accused of the
theft hurt.

"Why, humpin' hyenas!   If I'd a beefed that
critter, old Scotty wouldn't ever have found no
hide to catch me on!   What kinda mark does he
think I am?   Rustle a beef and leave the hide
laying around? why, any darn fool would know
better than that!"

It was characteristic of the Lorrigan influence
that when Tom rode into camp every one of the
crew save his own sons quieted a little; not enough

to suggest timidity, but to a degree that told how well they knew that their master was present.

That master quietly took stock of his men while they ate their supper and loafed and smoked and talked. Cheyenne had unobtrusively retired to the bed tent. With his thumbs pushed down inside his belt Tom strolled past and slanted a glance inside. Cheyenne was squatted on his heels shaving with cold lather and a cracked looking-glass propped against a roll of bedding, and a razor which needed honing. In turning his head to look at Tom he nicked his chin and while he stopped the bleeding with a bit of old newspaper the size of a small finger-nail he congratulated himself in the mistaken belief that Tom had not seen him at all.

Cheyenne did not know Tom very well, else he would have taken it for granted that Tom not only had seen him, but had also made a guess at his reason for shaving in the middle of the week.

Tom walked on, making a mental tally of the girls within riding distance from camp. Jennie Miller was reported engaged to an AJ man, and besides, she lived too far away and was not pretty enough to be worth the effort of a twenty-five mile ride just to hear her play hymns distressingly on an organ with a chronic squeak in one pedal. There was Alice Boyle at the AJ, and there was Mary Hope Douglas, who was growing to be quite a young lady,— pretty good-looking, too, if she wouldn't peel her hair back so straight and tight. Mary Hope Douglas, Tom decided, was probably the girl. It struck Tom as significant that she should be the daughter of the man who mourned the loss of the yearling. He had not reached the rear of the tent before he decided that he himself would do a little riding that night. He caught and saddled Coaley, his own pet saddle horse that had never carried any man save Tom — never would, so long as Tom had anything to say about it — and set off toward the Devil's Tooth ranch. Cheyenne ducked his head under the tent flap when he heard the sound of hoof beats passing close, saw that it was his boss, noted the direction he was taking, and heaved a sigh of relief. While he labored with the knot in his handkerchief which must be tied exactly right before he would leave the tent, Cheyenne had been composing a reason for leaving camp. Now he would not need a reason, and he grinned while he plastered his hair down in a sleek, artistically perfect scallop over his right eyebrow. Tom was going to the home ranch,—to round up Al, very likely. He would be gone all night and he would not know how many of his men rode abroad that night.

So presently Cheyenne saddled the freshest horse in his string and loped off, making an insulting sign with one hand when the boys wished him luck with the girl and offered to go along and talk religion with "feyther" just to help him out.

Very soon after that Sam Pretty Cow drifted away, and no one noticed his absence. Sam Pretty Cow's wanderings never did attract much attention. He was Injun, and Injuns have ways strange to white men. For instance, he did not sleep in the tent, but spread his blankets under whatever shelter he could find within hailing distance from the others. He was always around when he was wanted, and that seemed to be all that was expected of him. Sleep settled on the Devil's Tooth round-up camp, and the night guard sang to the cattle while they rode round and round the herd, and never dreamed that this night was not as other nights had been.

CHAPTER SIX

BELLE MEETS AN EMERGENCY IN HER OWN WAY

A MEADOW LARK, his conscience comfortable after a generous breakfast of big and little worms carried to his mate hidden away under a thick clump of rabbit weed down by the creek, spread rigid wings and volplaned to the crooked post beside the corral gate, folded his feathers snug and tilted his head aslant. *"Cler, cler, cler, cler-ee, cler-ee!"* he sang, and perked a wary eye toward the low-roofed stable.

"Oh, I hear you, you sassy little sinner! I wouldn't think you'd have the nerve, after what you've done to my radishes. I'm sure going to mix with you, if you — Rosa! Lift a heel at me and you die! Stand over — don't you try squeezing me against the wall, or I'll take my quirt to you! Get over there, before I brain you! Hay-ah-h, you — "

From the sounds one would imagine that a bear, two lions and a mule had come to handgrips in the stable, and that a woman of the Amazons was battling with them all. The meadow lark knew

better.   This was his second season on the Devil's
Tooth ranch, and he knew that Belle Lorrigan was
merely harnessing her pinto team in the stable, and
that nothing out of the ordinary was taking place.
Being a wise bird as well as an inquisitive one, he
fluttered up to the ridge-pole of the roof and from
that sanctuary listened beady-eyed to the custom-
ary tumult.

Certain staccato epithets meant merely that Subrosa was objecting to the crupper. A sudden
stamping testified that Belle had approached Rosa
with the bridle. A high-keyed, musical voice
chanting man-size words of an intimidating nature
followed which proved that the harnessing was
progressing as well as could be expected. Then
came a lull, and the meadow lark tilted forward
expectantly, his head turned sidewise to see what
came next.

First came Belle Lorrigan, walking backward,
a shot-loaded quirt raised admonishingly to the
chin of Subrosa who walked stiff-legged and reluctant, his white-lashed, blue eyes rolling fearsomely,
his nostrils belling in loud snorts of protest. A
complexity of emotions stirred Subrosa. Afraid
to lunge forward, hating to walk circumspectly,
eager for the race yet dreading the discipline of
rein and whip, Subrosa yielded perforce to the inevitable. As his heels flicked over the low door-
sill he swung round and landed one final kick
against the log wall. threw up his head in anticipa-

tion of the quirt, stepped on a dragging trace chain and jumped as though it was a rattler.

"None of that, you cantankerous brute! One of these days I'm going to just naturally brain you, Sub. I'm getting good and tired of this circus business. You settle down, now, and act human, or —"

Subrosa kicked at the trace and flipped it up so that it struck him smartly on the rump. He jumped straight forward at Belle, who dodged and landed the quirt none too gently on his nose. Subrosa sat down violently, and Belle straightway kicked him in the paunch by way of hinting that she preferred him standing. Then they had it out, rampaging all over the round-pole corral until Belle, breathing a bit fast but sparkly-eyed and victorious, led Subrosa through the gate and up to the post where she snubbed him fast. She was turning to go after Rosa when a young voice called to her anxiously.

"Oh, Mrs. Lorrigan! Quick, I'm in a hurry. I mustn't stay, because they'll be here in a little while. But they're coming by the road and I came down the trail, and that gave me time. I can't take any more music lessons, Mrs. Lorrigan. Father is that angry wi' your husband — and oh, Mrs. Lorrigan! If you have any hide that isna your own, ye should hide it away at once! Because the shuriff —"

Belle laid her palms on her hips and stared

blankly up at Mary Hope, who sat nervously on old Rab at the gate.

"Heavens, child! My hide is my own — and at that it's pretty well hidden. What about the sheriff? What's he got to say about it?"

"It's the stealing, Mrs. Lorrigan. Father has the shuriff wi' him, and they are going to search the ranch for the hides —"

"Good Lord! *What* hides?"

"The hides of my father's cattle. And if you have any, put them away quick, where the shuriff canna find them, Mrs. Lorrigan! It's ill I should go against my father, but you have been so good to me with the music lessons, and —"

"Don't let the music lessons bother you, Hope. And I guess we're entitled to all the cowhides we've got on the place, if that's what you mean. What do you think we are — thieves, Hope Douglas?"

"I dinna say it. I only came to warn ye, so that you may have time tae put your hides way oot o' their sicht when they come. I dinna want that your husband should go to prison, Mrs. Lorrigan. But father is that angry —"

"Well, say! Let me tell you something, Hope. If there's any talk of stealing and prison for the Lorrigans, your dad had better keep outa my Tom's sight. And outa mine," she added grimly. "There'll be no searching for anything on this ranch when my Tom's not here to see what goes on.

You better go back and tell your dad I said it. If you don't and he brings the sheriff on here, don't blame me if somebody gets hurt.''

"Oh, but it's the law they're bringing on ye! Ye canna go contrary to the law!'' Mary Hope's voice quavered with fear.

"Oh, can't I!'' Belle gave her head a tilt. "You beat it, while the going's good. I hear voices up on the road. If you don't want your dad to come and catch you here —''

That settled it. Terror drove Mary Hope into the Devil's Tooth trail at Rab's best pace, which was a stiff-legged lope. Her last glance backward showed her Belle Lorrigan taking her six-shooter belt off the buckboard seat and buckling it around her waist so that the gun hung well forward. Mary Hope shuddered and struck Rab with the quirt.

Belle had led Rosa from the stable and was cautiously fastening the neck yoke in place when the sheriff and Aleck Douglas rode around the corner of the stable. Rosa shied and snorted and reared, and Belle used the rein-ends for a whiplash until Rosa decided that she would better submit to authority and keep her hide whole. She stood fairly quiet after that, with little nipping dance-steps in one spot, while Belle fastened buckles and snaps and trace chains. Subrosa, having had his tantrum, contented himself with sundry head-shakings and snorts. When the team was "hooked up" to

Belle's satisfaction, she tied them both firmly to the corral with short ropes, and finally turned her attention to her visitors.

"Howdy, Mr. Douglas? Fine day we're having," she greeted the dour Scotchman amiably.

The sheriff coughed behind his hand, looked sidelong at his companion, rode a step or two nearer to Belle, swung a leg over the cantle of his saddle. Perhaps he expected Aleck Douglas to introduce him, but he did not wait for the formality.

"Mrs. Lorrigan, I'm sheriff of the county," he began ingratiatingly, when his two feet were on the ground.

"You are?" Belle flashed a row of very white teeth. "You sure don't look it. I'd have taken you for a regular human being."

"Mr. Douglas, here, would like to take a look at some hides Mr. Lorrigan has got curing. He thinks possibly —"

" 'Tis useless to cover the truth wi' saft words, shuriff," Douglas interrupted glumly. " 'Tis stolen cattle we are tracing, and 'tis here we wad look for the hides of them. I hae guid reason —"

"You'll find my husband at the round-up. Before you do any searching, you had better go and have a talk with him. When he's gone strangers don't go prowling around this ranch."

"We'll have our talk with him after we've taken a look around," the sheriff amended, grinning a little. "It's just a matter of form — nothing you need to object to, one way or the other. I don't suppose we'll find anything —"

"No, I don't suppose you will. Not unless you find it on the road back. I hate to seem unfriendly, but I'll just have to ask you to crawl on your horse and go see Tom about it."

"Now, we don't want any unpleasantness at all, Mrs. Lorrigan. But this man has swore out a warrant —"

"Shucks! What he does never did interest me one way or the other, and does not now. I'm telling you there'll be no snooping around here while Tom's away."

"Oh, well, now!" The sheriff rather prided himself on his ability to "handle folks peaceable", as he expressed it. He injected a little more of the oil of persuasiveness into his voice. It was his standard recipe for avoiding trouble with a woman. "You don't think for a minute I'd take advantage of his absence, Mrs. Lorrigan? Nothing like that at all. We just want to see if a certain cowhide is here. If it isn't, then we won't need to bother Tom at all, maybe. Get down, Mr. Douglas, and we'll just have a look around. Mrs. Lorrigan ain't going to make no objections to that."

Belle smiled. "Oh, yes, she is. She's going to do quite a lot of objecting. You better stay right where you are, Scotty. You're a heap safer."

The sheriff began to lose patience. "Now, look

here, Mrs. Lorrigan! You're dealing with the law, you know. We can't have any nonsense.''

"We won't have," Belle assured him placidly. "That's what I've been trying to beat into your head. Why, good Lord! Can't you take the hint and see I'm trying not to have any trouble with yuh? I don't want to have to *run* you off the ranch — but as you say, there's not going to be any nonsense. I said, *go*. I'm waiting to see if you've got sense enough to do it.''

"Sa-ay! Just look here now! Do you know it's a State's prison offense to resist an officer?'' The sheriff's face was growing red.

Belle laughed. "Sure. But I'm not. You — you're irresistible! And I don't know you're an officer.''

This went over the sheriff's head and was wasted, though Aleck Douglas pulled down his mouth at the corners as though he was afraid he might smile if he were not careful.

The sheriff took up his bridle reins, preparing to lead his horse over to a post and tie him. He glanced at Belle and saw that she had a six-shooter in her hand and a glitter in her eyes. Quite naturally he hesitated. Then, at a perfectly plain signal from the gun, he turned his palms toward her at a level with his shoulders.

"You needn't tie up. Crawl into the saddle and drift.''

"I've got a search warrant —''

"You can keep it and show it to Tom. And get off this ranch just as quick as that horse can take you. I'll have you both arrested for trespassing. I'm not taking your word for anything, you see. *I* don't know anything about your warrant — hey, Riley!" This to the cook, who came, taking steps as long as his legs would let him, and swinging a damp dishcloth in one moist red hand.

"Riley, here's a man claims he's the sheriff and that he's got a warrant to search the ranch. I don't believe a word of it, and I've ordered him off the place. I wouldn't for the world resist an officer of the law — put your hands up a little higher, Mr. Man! — but when Tom ain't home no stranger is going to come snooping around here if I can stop him. Ain't that right, Riley?"

"That's right, Belle," Riley acquiesced, working his oversized Adam's apple convulsively. (Riley, by the way, would just as readily have approved of murder if Belle had asked for his approval.)

"Well, you're a witness that I'm from Missouri. I've told this man to go tell his troubles to Tom. If he's honest he'll do it. If he don't go in about ten seconds, I'm going to throw a bullet through his hat. *Then* if he hangs around, I shall shoot him in his left leg just about six inches above the knee. I can do it, can't I, Riley?"

"Well, now, you shore can, Belle!" Riley

nodded his head emphatically. "If you say six, I'd shore gamble a year's wages it won't be five, or seven. Six inches above his knee goes, if you say six."

"All right. I'm just defending the ranch when Tom's gone. You hear me, Mr. Man. Now, you git!"

The sheriff turned and opened his mouth to protest, and Belle shot the promised bullet through his hat-crown. The sheriff ducked and made a wild scramble for the stirrup.

"Open your mouth again and I'll be awfully tempted to shoot that crooked tooth out of it," Belle observed. "And in ten seconds, remember, you're going to get — "

The sheriff still had two of the ten seconds to spare when he left, Aleck Douglas following him glumly.

"It's him, all right. It's the sheriff, Belle," Riley informed her, while they watched the two clatter up the road to where the real grade began. "What's eatin' on 'em? Likely he did have a search warrant."

"He can use it, after I'm through. Old Scotty is trailing some rustled stock, they claim. They came here looking for hides. You keep an eye out, Riley, and see if they keep going. I guess they will — they'll go after Tom. I'm going to have a look at those cow-hides in the old shed."

"Better let me," Riley offered. "It ain't any job for a woman nohow. You watch the trail and I'll look."

Belle would not even consider the proposition. The Lorrigan reputation never had troubled her much,— but it sent her now to the shed where hides were kept stored until the hide buyer made his next annual visit through the country. She did not believe that she would find any brand save the various combinations of the NL monogram, but she meant to make sure before any stranger was given access to the place.

The job was neither easy nor pleasant, but she did it thoroughly. Riley, roosting meditatively on the top rail of the corral where he could watch the road down the bluff, craned his long neck inquiringly toward her when she returned.

"Nothing but NL stuff, just as I thought," said Belle, holding her hands as far away from her face as possible. "I knew Tom wouldn't have any stolen hides on the place — but it was best to make sure."

"No ma'am, he wouldn't. I'm shore surprised they'd come and try to find any. Looks bad to me, Belle. Looks to me like somebody is shore tryin' to start somethin'. There's plenty in the Black Rim would like to see Tom railroaded to the pen — plenty. Looks to me like they're aimin' to pin something on him. No, sir, I don't like it.

Uh course," he went on, letting himself loose-jointedly to the ground, "they couldn't get nothing on
Tom — not unless they framed something. But I
wouldn't put it a-past 'em to do it. No, ma'am, I
wouldn't."

"Your bread's burning, Riley. I can smell it.
Don't you never think they'll frame on Tom.
They may try it — but that's as far as they'll get.
They don't want to start anything with the Lorri-
gans!"

"Well, I left the oven door open. She ain't
burning to hurt. Yuh see, Scotty Douglas, he's religious and he don't never pack a gun. Them
kind's bad to tangle up with; awful bad. There
ain't nothing much a man can do with them religious birds. Them not being armed, you can't
shoot — it's murder. And that kinda ties a man's
hands, as yuh might say. They always take advantage of it, invariable. No, ma'am, it looks
bad."

"It'll look worse — for them that tries any
funny business with this outfit," Belle assured
him. "Go along and 'tend to your baking. You
know I hate burnt bread. I'm going to drive over
and see what they're up to."

She untied Rosa and Subrosa, and because she
was in a hurry she permitted Riley to hold them by
the bits while she climbed in, got the lines firmly in
one hand and her blacksnake in the other. Not
often did she deign to accept assistance, and Riley

was all aquiver with gratified vanity at this mark of her favor.

"Turn 'em loose — and get to that bread!" she cried, and circled the pintos into the road. "You, Sub! Cut that out, now — settle down! Rosa! Stead-dy, I ain't any Ben Hur pulling off a chariot race, remember!"

At a gallop they took the first sandy slope of the climb, and Belle let them go. They were tough — many's the time they had hit the level on top of the ridge without slowing to a walk on the way up. They had no great load to pull, and if it pleased them to lope instead of trot, Belle would never object.

As she sat jouncing on the seat of a buckboard with rattly spokes in all of the four wheels and a splintered dashboard where Subrosa landed his heels one day when he had backed before he kicked, one felt that she would have made a magnificent charioteer. Before she had gone half a mile her hair was down and whipping behind her like a golden pennant. Her big range hat would have gone sailing had it not been tied under her chin with buckskin strings. Usually she sang as she hurtled through space, but to-day the pintos missed her voice.

Five miles out on the range she overtook the sheriff and Aleck Douglas riding to the round-up. Aleck Douglas seldom rode faster than a jogging trot, and the sheriff was not particularly eager for

his encounter with Tom Lorrigan. For that matter, no sheriff had ever been eager to encounter a
Lorrigan. The Lorrigan family had always been
counted a hazard in the office of the sheriff, though
of a truth the present generation had remained
quiescent so far and the law had not heretofore
reached its arm toward them.

The two men looked back, saw Belle coming and
parted to let her pass. Belle yelled to her team
and went by with never a glance toward either,
and the two stared after her without a word until
she had jounced down into a shallow draw and
up the other side, the pintos never slowing their
lope.

"Well, I'm darned!" ejaculated the sheriff.
His name, by the way, was Perry. "I've heard
tell of Belle Lorrigan drivin' hell-whoopin' over
the country with a team of bronks, but I kinda
thought they was stretching the truth. I guess
not, though, if that's a sample."

"The woman hersel' is no so bad. 'Tis the men
folk that are black wi' sin. Drinkin', swearin',
gamblin' thieves they be, and 'tis well they should
be taught a lesson." The Douglas head wagged
self-righteously.

"Maybe it would be a good idea to go back and
search the ranch now, while she's gone." The
sheriff pulled up, considering. "I didn't want
any trouble with her; I never do quarrel with a
woman if I can get around it any way. She's a

holy terror. I guess I'll just ride back and take a look at them hides.''

Aleck Douglas eyed him sardonically, thinking perhaps of the black-edged bullet hole that showed plainly in the sheriff's hat-crown.

'' 'Tis a deal safer wi' the woman oot of the way,'' he agreed drily.

The sheriff nodded and turned back.

CHAPTER SEVEN

THE NAME

TOM LORRIGAN may have seen bigger fusses
made over smaller matters than the hide of a
spotty yearlin', but his boys never had.

No country is so isolated that gossip cannot find
it out. The story of the spotted yearling went
speeding through the country. Men made thin
excuses to ride miles out of their way that they
might air their opinions and hear some fresh bit
of news, some conjecture that grew to a rumor and
was finally repeated broadcast as truth. Children
cringed and wept while necks were scrubbed re-
lentlessly, for a fever of "visiting" attacked the
women of the range. Miles they would travel to
visit a neighbor. And there they talked and talked
and talked, while the guest in neighborly fashion
dried the dinner dishes for the hostess in hot, fly-
infested kitchens.

Aleck Douglas, infuriated by the contemptuous
attitude which Tom had taken toward him and his
spotty yearling, and by his failure to find any in-
criminating evidence on the Devil's Tooth ranch,

swore to a good many suspicions which he called facts, and had Tom arrested. The sheriff had taken two deputies along with him, because he fully expected that the Lorrigans would "go on the warpath" as Belle had done. He was vastly astonished and somewhat chagrined when Tom gave a snort, handed over his gun, and turned to one of his boys.

"Al," said Tom, "you go ahead with the round-up while I go in and fix this up. May take a few days — depends on the gait I can get 'em to travel. I'll have to rustle me a lawyer, too. But you know what to do; keep 'er moving till I get back."

Black Rim country talked and chortled and surmised, and wondered what made Tom so darned meek about it. They did not accuse him of any lack of nerve; being a Lorrigan, his nerve could scarcely be questioned. Opinion was about evenly divided. A few declared that Tom had something up his sleeve, and there would be a killing yet. Others insisted that Tom knew when he was backed into a corner. Old Scotty Douglas had him dead to rights, they said, and Tom knew better than to run on the rope. Men and women assumed the gift of prophecy, and all prophesied alike. Tom Lorrigan would go "over the road"; for how long they could only guess according to their secret hopes. Some predicted a fifteen-year term for Tom. Others thought that he might get off lightly — say with five or six years. They based their opinion on the fact that men have been sent to the penitentiary for fifteen years, there to repent of stealing a calf not yet past the age of prime veal. And it is not so long since men were hanged for stealing a horse; witness Tom's brother, who would surely have been lynched had he not been shot. Witness also divers other Lorrigans whose careers had been shortened by their misdeeds.

Much of the talk was peddled to Tom and the boys under the guise of friendship. Having lived all of his life in the Black Rim country, Tom knew how much the friendship was worth, knew that the Black Rim folk had drawn together like a wolf pack, and were waiting only until he was down before they rushed in to rend him and his family. Old grudges were brought out and aired secretly. It would go hard with the Lorrigan family if Tom were found guilty. Although he sensed the covert malice behind the smiles men gave him, he would not yield one inch from his mocking disparagement of the whole affair. He laid down a law or two to his boys, and bade them hold their tongues and go their way and give no heed to the clacking.

"The show ain't over till the curtain's down for good," he said, borrowing a phrase from Belle. "We got a long time yet to live in the Black Rim. We'll be right here when the smoke lifts. Hang and rattle now, and keep your mouths shut. This here's the law-sharp's job. I'm payin' him darn good money for it, too. When he's through, then we'll play. But mark this down in yore little red book, boys: The less yuh say right now, the stronger we can play the game when we're ready."

"If they do railroad yuh, dad, leave it to us. They'll be a sorry looking bunch when we're through," said Lance, and meant every word of it.

"They won't railroad me." Tom snorted and laughed his contempt of the whole affair. "I ain't ever used the law to fight with before — but shucks! When a scrap gets outside of gun range, one club's about the same as another to me."

Optimism is a good thing, but it does not altogether serve, as Tom discovered at the trial.

Evidence was produced which astonished him. For instance, an AJ man had seen him riding over by Squaw Butte, on the night after Douglas had accused him of stealing the spotted yearling. The AJ man seemed embarrassed at his sudden prominence in the case, and kept turning his big range hat round and round on one knee as he sat in the chair sacred to those who bore witness to the guilt or innocence of their fellow men in Black Rim country. He did not often look up, and when he did he swallowed convulsively, as though something stuck in his throat. But his story sounded matter-of-fact and honest.

He had ridden past Squaw Butte the night after Tom Lorrigan was accused by Douglas. Yes, he knew it was that night, because next day he heard about the fuss over at Devil's Tooth. He had been on his way from Jumpoff and had cut across country because he was late. There was a moon, and he had seen a man riding across an open space between the creek and the willows. The man had gone in among the willows. The AJ man had not thought much about it, though he did wonder a little, too. It was late for a man to be riding around on the range.

When he reached the place, he saw a man ride out of the brush farther along, into clear moonlight. It was Tom Lorrigan; yes, he was sure of that. He knew the horse that Tom was riding. It was a big, shiny black that always carried its head up; a high-stepping horse that a man could recognize anywhere. No, he didn't know of any other horse in the country just like it. He admitted that if he hadn't been sure of the horse he would not have been sure it was Tom. He did not think Tom saw him at all. He was riding along next the bank, in the shadow. He had gone on home, and the next day he heard that Scotty Douglas claimed the Lorrigans had rustled a yearling from him.

Later, Tom's lawyer asked him why he had not spoken to Tom. The AJ man replied that he didn't know — he wasn't very close; not close enough for talking unless he hollered.

That was all very well, and Black Rim perked its ears, thinking that the case looked bad for Tom. Very bad indeed.

But Tom's lawyer proved very adroitly that the AJ man had not been in Jumpoff at the time he claimed. He had been with his own outfit, and if he had ridden past Squaw Butte that night he must have gone out from the ranch and come back again. Which led very naturally to the question, Why?

On the other hand, why had Tom Lorrigan ridden to Squaw Butte that night? He himself explained that later on. He said that he had gone over to see if there was any hide in the willows as Douglas had claimed. He had not found any.

Thus two men admitted having been in the neighborhood of the stolen hide on that night. Tom's lawyer was quick to seize the coincidence, and make the most of it. Why, he asked mildly, might not the AJ outfit have stolen the yearling? What was the AJ man doing there? Why not suspect him of having placed the hide in the crevice where it had later been found? That night the hide had been removed from the willows where Douglas had first discovered it. Douglas had gone back the next day after it, and it had been missing. It was not until several days later that he had found it in the crevice. Why assume that Tom Lorrigan had removed it?

"If I'd set out to caché that hide," Tom here interposed, "I'd have buried it. Only a darn fool would leave evidence like that laying around in sight."

For this the court reprimanded him, but he had
seen several of the jury nod their heads, unconsciously agreeing with him.   And although his remark was never put on record, it stuck deep in the
minds of the jury and had its influence later on.
They remembered that the Lorrigans were no
fools, and they considered the attempt at conceal-
ing the hide a foolish one— not to say childish.

Tom's lawyer did not argue openly that a con-
spiracy had been hatched against Tom Lorrigan,
but he so presented the case in his closing argument
to the jury that each man believed he saw an angle
to the affair which the defense had overlooked.
It appeared to the jury to be a ''frame-up.''   For
instance, why had Cheyenne, a Lorrigan man, ridden over to the Douglas ranch and remained outside by the corral for a long time, talking with
Aleck Douglas, before he went inside to call on the
Douglas girl?   Sam Pretty Cow impassively testified to that.   He had been riding over to see a
halfbreed girl that worked for the Blacks, and he
had cut through the Douglas ranch to save time.
He saw Cheyenne's horse at the corral.

''Me, I dunno what she's doin' on that place.
Cheyenne, he's in camp when I'm go.   I'm stop by
the haystack.   I'm see Cheyenne talk to Scotty.
That don't look good, you bet.''

A full week the trial lasted, while the lawyers
wrangled over evidence and technicalities, and the
judge ruled out evidence and later ruled it in again.

A full week Tom slept in the county jail, — and for all their bad reputation, it was the first time a Lorrigan had lain down behind a bolted door to sleep, had opened his eyes to see the dawn light painting the wall with the shadow of bars.

There were nights when his optimism failed him, when Tom lay awake trying to adjust himself to the harrying thought that long, caged years might be his portion. Nights when he doubted the skill of his "law sharp" to free him from the dead-weight of the Lorrigan reputation and the malice of his neighbors. Of course, he would fight — to the last dollar; but there were nights when he doubted the power of his dollars to save him.

It was during those nights that the lawless blood of the Lorrigans ran swiftly through the veins of Tom, who had set himself to win a million honestly. It was then that he remembered his quiet, law-abiding years regretfully, as time wasted; a thankless struggle toward the regard of his fellow men. Of what avail to plod along the path of uprightness when no man would point to him and say, "There is an honest man."

"They've give me the name, and I ain't got the game," cried Tom bitterly, in the quiet of his cell. "Whether I go to the pen or whether I don't, they better stand from under. They'll sure know a Lorrigan's livin' in the Black Rim before I'm done."

CHAPTER EIGHT

The Game

AT the long table in the living room of the Devil's Tooth ranch Tom Lorrigan sat and sharpened an indelible pencil with the razor-edged small blade of his jackknife. On the open space which Tom had cleared with the sweep of his arm, a large-sized tablet of glazed and ruled paper, with George Washington pictured in red and blue and buff on the cover, received the wood parings from the pencil. It may have been significant that Tom was careful in his work and made the pencil very sharp.

Across the room, Belle swung around on the piano stool and looked at him. "Honey, if you're going to make out the order to Montgomery, Ward, I'd like to send on for some more music. I've been going over that new list —"

"I ain't," said Tom, removing his cigarette from the corner of his mouth and blowing the tiny, blue-painted shavings off George Washington's face. "You go ahead and make out the order yourself."

Belle eyed the pencil-sharpening and sent a keen glance at Tom's face. "Well, honey, from the way you're squaring up to that tablet, I thought you was going to send on for a new buckboard and mower."

Tom bent his head and blew again, gave George a sardonic grin and turned him face-down on the table, so that the ruled paper lay ready to his hand.

"Right now I'm going to figure up what that dang spotty yearlin' of old Scotty's cost me," he stated grimly. "And there's some other Black Rimmers I've got a bill against."

"Hope you don't try holding your breath till you collect," Belle retorted. "Honey, you'd best leave the Black Rimmers alone. I feel as if we'd had excitement enough for a while. I wouldn't start anything more right now, if I was you. Every last one of them is ready to jump on your neck — and the Lord only knows why, unless it's because you *didn't* steal that darned spotted yearling! Some folks sure do love to see the other fellow up to his eyebrows in trouble. They were sitting there in that courtroom just *wishing* you would be sent up. I saw it in their faces, Tom. And that old rock-hearted Scotchman looked as if he's just lost two bits when the jury said 'Not guilty.'"

"Mhm — hmm — that's what I'm figuring on now," said Tom, and bent to his problem. "My old dad woulda gone out and shot up a few, but times are changed and we're all getting so damn civilized we've got to stack the cards or quit the game. Belle, what do you reckon it's worth to a man to be hauled into court and called a cow thief?"

Belle's lips pressed together. "I don't know, Tom — but I know what it would have cost 'em if they had sent you over the road. I had a gun on me, and when that jury foreman stood up to give the verdict, it was looking him in the eye through a buttonhole in my coat. Him and Cheyenne and Old Scotty and two or three more would sure have got theirs, if he hadn't said, 'Not guilty.'"

"Lord bless yuh, I knew it all the time. Next time we go to court you'll leave the artillery at home, old girl. I like to got heart failure there for a minute, till I seen you ease down and lay your hand in your lap." He looked at her and laughed a little. "I've got a bill of damages against several of the folks around here, but I ain't fool enough to try and collect with a six-gun."

He settled himself to his task, writing at the top of the page the name of Aleck Douglas and after that "Dr." A full page he covered with items set against the names of various neighbors. When he had finished he folded the paper neatly and put it away with other important memoranda, picked up his big gray Stetson and went over to kiss Belle full on her red lips, and to smooth her

hair, with a reassuring pat on her plump shoulder
as a final caress.

"Don't you worry none about the Black Rimmers," he said, "and don't you worry about me.
I've got to ride high, wide and handsome now to
make up the time and money I lost on account of
the spotty yearlin', and maybe I won't be home so
much. But I ain't quarreling with my neighbors,
nor getting into any kind of ruckus whatever."

With the stilted, slightly stiff-legged gait born
of long hours in the saddle and of high-heeled riding boots, he walked unhurriedly to the corral
where the boys were just driving in a herd of
horses.

Few of them showed saddle marks, all of them
snorted and tossed untrimmed manes and tails as
they clattered against the stout poles, circling the
big corral in a cloud of dust and a thunder of hoof
beats. Pulling his hat down over his black brows
to secure it against the wind, Tom climbed the
corral fence and straddled the top rail that he
might scan the herd.

"Pretty good looking bunch, dad," said Al,
reining up beside Tom. "We had to ride some to
get 'em in — they're sure snuffy. What you going
to do with 'em? Break out a few?"

"Some. Did yuh take notice, Al, that Coaley
come within an ace of sending me over the road?
That there AJ man swore to the horse when he
wouldn't never have swore to me, but they all took

it as a cinch it was me he saw, because nobody else
ever rides Coaley. And by the Lord John, Al,
that's the last time any man's going to swear to
me in the dark by the horse I'm ridin'. The
Devil's Tooth outfit is going to have a lot more
saddle horses broke gentle than what they've got
now. And just between me and you, Al, any more
night-ridin' that's done in this outfit ain't going
to be done on cayuses that can be told a mile off
on a dark night!''

"You're durn tootin', dad." Al grinned while
he moistened the edge of his rolled cigarette. "I
thought at the time that Coaley was liable to
be a damn expensive horse for you to be ridin'."
His eyes traveled over the restless herd, singling
out this horse and that for brief study. "There's
some right speedy stuff in that bunch," he said.
"They've got the look of stayers, some of 'em.
Take that there bay over there by the post: He's
got a chest on him like a lion — and look at them
legs! There'd be a good horse for you, dad."

"One, maybe." Tom spat into the dust and,
impelled by Al's example, drew his own cigarette
papers from his shirt pocket. "I'm thinkin' of
breakin' all we've got time for this summer.
Darn this here makin' one horse your trademark!"

Up at the house, Riley appeared in the kitchen
doorway and gave a long halloo while he wiped his
big freckled hand on his flour-sack apron. "Hoo-
ee! Come an' git it!" He waited a moment, un-

til he saw riders dismounting and leading their horses into the little corral. Then he turned back to pour the coffee into the big, thick, white cups standing in single file around the long oil-cloth-covered table in the end of the kitchen nearest the side door where the boys would presently come trooping in to slide loose-jointedly into their places on the long, shiny benches.

Tom pinched out the blaze of his match and threw one long leg back over the corral fence. His glance went to the riders beyond the big corral.

"Where's Lance at?" he called to Al, who was riding around to the little corral.

"You can search me. He quit us when we got the horses into the corral, and rode off up the Slide trail. If I was to make a guess, I would say that he went to meet Mary Hope. They been doing that right frequent ever since she quit coming here. 'Tain't no skin off my nose — but Lance, he's buildin' himself a mess uh trouble with old Scotty, sure as you're a foot high."

"Darn fool kid — let the old folks git to scrappin' amongst themselves, and the young ones start the lovemakin'! I never knowed it to fail; but you can skin me for a coyote if I know what makes 'em do it." Grumbling to himself, Tom climbed down and followed Al. "You can tell Riley I'll be late to dinner," he said, when he had come up to where Al was pulling the saddle off his horse.

"I ain't much on buttin' into other folks' love affairs, but I reckon it maybe might be a good idea to throw a scare into them two. I'm plumb sick of Scotch — wouldn't take it in a highball right now if you was to shove one under my nose!"

Al laughed, looking over his shoulder at Tom while he loosened the latigo. "If you can throw a scare into Lance, you sure are a dinger," he bantered. "That youth is some heady."

"Looks to me like it runs in the family," Tom retorted. "You're some heady yourself, if you ever took notice. And I don't give a damn how heady any of you kids are; you can't run any rannies on your dad, and you want to put that down in your little red book so you won't forgit it!"

He led Coaley from the stable, mounted and rode away up the Slide trail, more than half ashamed of his errand. To interfere in a love affair went against the grain, but to let a Lorrigan make love to a Douglas on the heels of the trial was a pill so bitter that he refused to swallow it.

He urged Coaley up the trail, his eyes somber with resentment whenever he saw the fresh hoofprints of Lance's horse in the sandy places. Of the three boys, Lance was his favorite, and it hurt him to think that Lance had so little of the Lorrigan pride that he would ride a foot out of his way to speak to any one of the Douglas blood.

Up the Slide went Coaley, his head held proudly

erect upon his high arched neck, his feet choosing daintily the little rough places in the rock where long experience had taught him he would not slip. Big as Tom was, Coaley carried him easily and reached the top without so much as a flutter in the flanks to show that the climb had cost him an effort.

"It's a dang darn shame I got to straddle strange horses just because there ain't another in the country like you, Coaley," he muttered, leaning forward to smooth the silky hide under the crinkly mane. "It's going to set hard, now I'm tellin' yuh, to throw my saddle on some plain, ordinary cayuse. But it's a bet I can't afford to overlook; they made that plain enough."

Coaley pricked up his ears and looked, his big, bright eyes taking in the shadow of a horse beside a clump of wild currant bushes that grew in the very base of the Devil's Tooth. Tom grunted and rode over that way, Coaley walking slowly, his knees bending springily like a dancer feeling out his muscles.

Lance stood with his back toward them. His hat was pushed far back on his head, and he was looking at Mary Hope, who leaned against the rock and stared down into the valley below. Her hair, Tom observed, was not "slicked back" to-day. It had been curled a little, probably on rags twisted in after she had gone to bed and taken out before she arose in the morning, lest her mother discover her frivolity and lecture her long, — and, worse still, make her wet a comb and take all of the curl out. A loose strand blew across her tanned cheek, so that she reached up absently and tucked it behind her ear, where it would not stay for longer than a minute.

"I am sure I didna know you would be here," she said, without taking her eyes off the valley. "It is a view I like better than most, and I have a right to ride where I please. And I have no wish to ride out of my way to be friends with any one that tried to make my father out a liar and an unjust man. He may be hard, but he is honest. And that is more than some —"

"More than some can say — us Lorrigans, for instance!"

"I didna say that, but if the coat fits, you can put it on."

Mary Hope bit her lip and lashed a weed with her quirt. "All of this is none of my doing," she added, with a dullness in her voice that may have meant either regret or resentment. "You hate my father, and you are mad because I canna side with you and hate him too. I am sorry the trouble came up, but I canna see how you expect me to go on coming to see your mither when you know my father would never permit it."

"You say that like you were speaking a piece. How long did you lay awake last night, making it up? You can't make me swallow that, anyway. Your father never permitted you to come in the first place, and you know it. You made believe that old skate ran away with you down the trail, and that you couldn't stop him. You've been coming over to our place ever since, and you never asked old Scotty whether he would permit it or not. I'm not saying anything about myself, but it hurts Belle to have you throw her down right now. Under the circumstances it makes her feel as if you thought we were thieves and stole your dad's yearling.''

"I'm not saying anything like that."

"Maybe you're not, but you sure are acting it. If you don't think that, why don't you go on taking music lessons from Belle? What made you stop, all of a sudden?"

"That," said Mary Hope stiffly, "is my own affair, Lance Lorrigan."

"It's mine, let me tell you. It's mine, because it hits Belle; and what hits her hits me. If you think she isn't good enough for you to visit, why in thunder have you been coming all this while? She isn't any worse than she was two months ago, is she?"

"I'm not saying that she is."

"Well, you're acting it, and that's a darn sight worse."

"You ought to know that with all this trouble between your father and my father —"

"Well, can you tell me when they ever did have any truck together? Your father doesn't hate our outfit a darn bit worse than he ever did. He found a chance to knife us, that's all. It isn't that he never wanted to before.''

"I'll thank you, Lance Lorrigan, not to accuse my father of knifing anybody. He's my father and —"

"And that isn't anything to brag about, if you ask me. I'd rather have my father doing time for stealing, than have him a darned, hide-bound old hypocrite that will lie a man into the pen, and then go around and pull a long face and call himself a Christian!''

"My father doesna lie! And he is not a hypocrite either. If your father was half as —'' She stopped abruptly, her face going red when she saw Tom sitting on his horse beyond the shoulder of rock, regarding her with that inscrutable smile which never had failed to make her squirm mentally and wonder what he thought of her. She stood up, trembling a little.

Lance turned slowly and met Tom's eyes without flinching. "Hello," he said, on guard against the two of them, wondering what had brought his dad to this particular point at this particular time.

"Hello. How d'yuh do, Miss Douglas? Lance, dinner's getting cold waiting for you." Tom lifted his hat to Mary Hope, turned, and rode back whence he had come, never glancing over his shoulder but nevertheless keenly alert for the sound of voices.

He was not quite through the Slide when he heard the hoof beats of Lance's horse come clicking down over the rocks. Tom smiled to himself as he rode on, never looking back.

CHAPTER NINE

A Little Scotch

IN the Black Rim country March is a month of
raw winds and cold rains, with sleet and snow
and storm clouds tumbling high in the West and
spreading to the East, where they hang lowering
at the earth and then return to empty their burden
of moisture upon the shrinking live things below.

In the thinly settled places March is also the
time when children go shivering to school, harried
by weather that has lost a little of its deadliness.
In January and February their lives would not be
safe from sudden blizzards, but by the middle of
March they may venture forth upon the quest of
learning.

Black Rim country was at best but scantily supplied with schools, and on the Devil's Tooth range
seven young Americans — three of them adopted
from Sweden — were in danger of growing up in
deplorable ignorance of what learning lies hidden
in books. A twelve-mile stretch of country had
neither school-house, teacher nor school officers
empowered to establish a school. Until the Swedish family moved into a shack on the AJ ranch

there had not been children enough to make a teacher worth while. But the Swedish family thirsted for knowledge of the English language, and their lamenting awoke the father of four purely range bred products to a sense of duty toward his offspring.

Wherefore Mary Hope Douglas, home from two winters in Pocatello, where she had lived with a cousin twice removed and had gone to school and had learned much, was one day invited to teach a school in the Devil's Tooth neighborhood.

True, there was no schoolhouse, but there was a deserted old shack on the road to Jumpoff. A few benches and a stove and table would transform it into a seat of learning, and there were an old shed and corral where the pupils might keep their saddle horses during school hours. She would be paid five dollars a month per head, Jim Boyle of the AJ further explained. Seven "heads" at five dollars each would amount to thirty-five dollars a month, and Mary Hope felt her heart jump at the prospect of earning so much money of her own. Moreover, to teach school had long been her secret ambition, the solid foundation of many an air castle. She forthwith consented to become the very first school-teacher in the Devil's Tooth neighborhood, which hoped some day to become a real school district.

She would have to ride five miles every morning and evening, and her morning ride would carry her five miles nearer the Lorrigan ranch, two of them along their direct trail to Jumpoff. Mary Hope would never admit to herself that this small detail interested her, but she thought of it the moment Jim Boyle suggested the old Whipple shack as a schoolhouse.

Tom Lorrigan, riding home from Jumpoff after two days spent in Lava, pulled his horse down to a walk and then stopped him in the trail while he stared hard at the Whipple shack. Five horses walked uneasily around inside the corral, manes and tails whipping in the gale that blew cold from out the north. From the bent stovepipe of the shack a wisp of smoke was caught and bandied here and there above the pole-and-dirt roof. It seemed incredible to Tom that squatters could have come in and taken possession of the place in his short absence, but there was no other explanation that seemed at all reasonable.

Squatters were not welcome on the Devil's Tooth range. Tom rode up to the shack, dismounted and let Coaley's reins drop to the ground. He hesitated a minute before the door, in doubt as to the necessity for knocking. Then his knuckles struck the loose panel twice, and he heard the sound of footsteps. Tom pulled his hat down tighter on his forehead and waited.

When Mary Hope Douglas pulled open the door, astonishment held them both dumb. He had not seen the girl for more than a year, — he was not

certain at first that it was she. But there was no
mistaking those eyes of hers, Scotch blue and un-
compromisingly direct in their gaze. Tom pulled
loose and lifted the hat that he had just tightened,
and as she backed from the doorway he entered the
shack without quite knowing why he should do so.
Comprehensively he surveyed the mean little room,
bare of everything save three benches with crude
shelves before them, a kitchen table and a yellow-
painted chair with two-thirds of the paint worn off
under the incessant scrubbing of mother Douglas.
The three Swedes, their rusty overcoats buttoned
to their necks, goggled at him round-eyed over the
tops of their new spelling books, then ducked and
grinned at one another. The four Boyle children,
also bundled in wraps, exchanged sidelong glances
and pulled themselves up alert and expectant in
their seats.

"School, eh?" Tom observed, turning as Mary
Hope pushed the door shut against the wind that
rattled the small shack and came toward him shivering and pulling her sweater collar closer about
her neck. "When did this happen?"

"When I started teaching here, Mr. Lorrigan."
Then, mindful of her manners, she tempered the
pertness with a smile. "And that was yesterday.
Will you sit down?"

"No, thanks — I just stopped to see who was
livin' here, and — " He broke off to look up at
the dirt roof. A clod the size of his fist had been

loosened by the shaking of the wind, and plumped down in the middle of the teacher's desk. With the edge of his palm he swept clod and surrounding small particles of dirt into his hat crown, and carried them to the door.

"There's an empty calf shed over at the ranch that would make a better schoolhouse than this," he observed. "It's got a shingle roof."

Mary Hope was picking small lumps of dirt out of her hair, which she wore in a pompadour that disclosed a very nice forehead. "I just love a roof with shingles on it," she smiled.

"H'm." Tom looked up at the sagging poles with the caked mud showing in the cracks between where the poles had shrunken and warped under the weight. A fresh gust of wind rattled dust into his eyes, and the oldest Swede chortled an abrupt "Ka-hugh!" that set the other six tittering.

"Silence! *Shame* on you!" Mary Hope reproved them sternly, rapping on the kitchen table with a foot rule of some soft wood that blazoned along its length the name of a Pocatello hardware store. "Get to work this instant or I shall be compelled to keep you all in at recess."

"You better haze 'em all home at recess, and get where it's warm before you catch your death of cold," Tom advised, giving first aid to his eye with a corner of his white-dotted blue handkerchief. "This ain't fit for cattle, such a day as this."

"A north wind like this would blow through

anything," Mary Hope loyally defended the shack. "It was quite comfortable yesterday."

"I wouldn't send a dog here to school," said Tom. "Can't they dig up any better place than this for you to teach in?"

"The parents of these children are paying out of their own pockets to have them taught, as it is."

"They'll be paying out of their own pockets to have them planted, if they ain't careful," Tom predicted dryly. "How're you fixed for firewood? Got enough to keep warm on a hot day?"

Mary Hope smiled faintly. "Mr. Boyle hauled us a load of sage brush, and the boys chop wood mornings and noons — it's a punishment when they don't behave, or if they miss their lessons. But — the stove doesn't seem to draw very well, in this wind. It smokes more than it throws out heat." She added hastily, "It drew all right yesterday. It's this wind."

"What you going to do if this wind keeps up? It's liable to blow for a week or two, this time of year."

"Why — we'll manage to get along all right. They'd probably be out playing in it anyway, if they weren't in school."

"Oh. And what about you?" Tom looked at her, blinking rapidly with his left eye that was growing bloodshot and watery.

"I? Why, I've lived here all my life, and I ought to be used to a little bad weather."

"Hunh." Tom shivered in the draught. "So have I lived here all my life; but I'll be darned if I would want to sit in this shack all day, the way the wind whistles through it."

"You might do it, though — if it was your only way of earning money," Mary Hope suggested shrewdly.

"Well, I might," Tom admitted, "but I sure would stop up a few cracks."

"We've hardly got settled yet," said Mary Hope. "I intend to stuff the cracks with rags just as soon as possible. Is your eye still paining? That dirt is miserable stuff to stick in a person's eye. Shall I try and get it out? Yesterday I got some in mine, and I had an awful time."

She dismissed the children primly, with a self-conscious dignity and some chagrin at their boorish clatter, their absolute ignorance of discipline. "I shall ring the bell in ten minutes," she told them while they scuffled to the door. "I shall give you two minutes after the bell rings to get into your seats and be prepared for duty. Every minute after that must be made up after school."

"Ay skoll go home now, sen you skoll not keep me by school from tan minootes," the oldest of the Swedes stopped long enough to bellow at her from the doorway. "Ole og Helge skoll go med. Ve got long way from school, og ve don't be by dark ven ve come by home!"

He seized the square tobacco boxes, originally

made to hold a pound of "plug cut", and afterwards dedicated to whatever use a ranch man might choose to put them.. Where schools flourished, the tobacco boxes were used for lunch. The Swedes carried three tied in flour sacks and fastened to the saddles. The wind carried them at a run to the corral. The two smaller boys, Ole and Helge, rode, one behind the other, on one horse, a flea-bitten gray with an enlarged knee and a habit of traveling with its neck craned to the left. Christian, the leader of the revolt, considered himself well-mounted on a pot-bellied bay that could still be used to round up cattle, if the drive was not more than a couple of miles. Looking after them from the window that faced the corral, Tom could not wonder that they were anxious to start early.

"You better let the rest go, too," he advised the perturbed teacher, looking out at the four Boyle children huddled in the shelter of the shack, the skirts of the girl whipping in the wind like a pillow-slip on a clothesline in a gale. "There ain't any sense trying to teach school in a place like this, in such weather. Don't you know them kids have got all of twelve miles to ride, facing this wind most of the way? And you've got to ride five miles; and when the sun drops it's going to be raw enough to put icicles on your ribs under the skin. Tell 'em to go home. Pore little devils, I wouldn't ask a cow-critter to face this wind after sundown."

"You do not understand that I must have discipline in this school, Mr. Lorrigan.   To-morrow I shall have to punish those Swedes for leaving school without permission.   I shall make an example of Christian, for his impudence.   I do not think he will want to disobey me again, very soon!"   Mary Hope took her handkerchief from her pocket, refusing to consider for one moment the significance of its flapping in the wind while the windows and doors were closed.

"You're just plain stubborn," Tom said bluntly. "You've no business hanging out in a place like this!"

"I've the business of teaching school, Mr. Lorrigan.   I suppose that is as important to me as your business is to you.   And I can't permit my pupils to rebel against my authority.   You would not let your men dictate to you, would you?"

"They would have a right to call for their time if I asked them to do some damfool thing like sitting in this shack with the wind blowing through it at forty miles an hour."

"I am sorry, Mr. Lorrigan, that I must remind you that gentlemen do not indulge in profanity before a lady."

"Oh, hell!   What have I said that was outa the way?   I wasn't cussing; I was telling you what your father and mother ought to tell you, and what they would if they didn't think more of a few dollars than they do of their kid's health.   But I don't

reckon it's my put-in; only it's any man's business
to see that women and kids don't freeze to death.
And by the humpin' hyenas —''

With her lips in a straight line, her eyes very
hard and bright and with a consciousness of heap-
ing coals of fire on the head of an enemy of her
house, Mary Hope had twisted a corner of her
handkerchief into a point, moistened it by the
simple and primitive method of placing the point
between her lips, and was preparing to remove the
dirt from Tom's watering eye, the ball of which
was a deep pink from irritation. But Tom swung
abruptly away from her, went stilting on his high
heels to the door, pulled it open with a yank and
rounded the corner where the four Boyle children
stood leaning against the house, their chilled fingers clasped together so that two hands made one
fist, their teeth chattering while they discussed
the Swedes and tried to mimic Christian's very
Swedish accent.

"*Og* is *and*," said Minnie Boyle. "And *skoll*
is *shall*. Swede's easy. And *med* means *with* —''

"Aw, it's just the way they try to say it in English," Fred Boyle contradicted. "It ain't Swede
— but gee, when the Scotch and the Swede goes
in the air to-morrow, I bet there'll be fun. If
Mary Hope tries to lick Chris —''

"You kids straddle your cayuses and hit for
home," Tom interrupted them. "There ain't going to be any more school to-day. Them your

horses in the shed? Well, you hump along and saddle up and beat it. Go!''

He did not speak threateningly, at least he did not speak angrily. But the four Boyle children gave him one affrighted glance and started on a run for the corral, looking back over their shoulders now and then as if they expected a spatter of bullets to follow them.

At the corral gate Minnie Boyle stopped and turned as though she meant to retrace her steps to the house, but Tom waved her back. So Minnie went home weeping over the loss of a real dinner-bucket and a slate sponge which she was afraid the Swedes might steal from her if they came earlier to school than she.

When Tom turned to reënter the shack for a final word with Mary Hope, and to let her give first aid to his eye if she would, he found that small person standing just behind him with set lips and clenched fists and her hair blowing loose from its hairpins.

"Mr. Tom Lorrigan, you can just call those children back!" she cried, her lips bluing in the cold gale that beat upon her. "Do you think that with all your lawlessness you can come and break up my school? You have bullied my father —"

"I'd do worse than bully him, if I had him in handy reach right now," Tom drawled, and took her by the shoulder and pushed her inside. "Any man that will let a woman sit all day in a place like

this — and I don't care a damn if you *are* earning
money doing it! — oughta have his neck wrung.
I'm going to saddle your horse for yuh while you
bundle up. And then you're going home, if I have
to herd yuh like I would a white heifer. I always
have heard of Scotch stubbornness — but there's
something beats that all to thunder. Git yore
things on. Yore horse will be ready in about five
minutes."

He bettered his estimate, returning in just four
minutes to find the door locked against him.
"Don't you *dare* come in here!" Mary Hope called
out, her voice shrill with excitement. "I — I'll
brain you!"

"Oh, you will, will yuh?" Whereupon Tom
heaved himself against the door and lurched in
with the lock dangling.

Mary Hope had a stick of wood in her two hands,
but she had not that other essential to quick com-
bat, the courage to swing the club on the instant
of her enemy's appearance. She hesitated,
backed and threatened him futilely.

"All right — fine! Scotch stubbornness — and
not a damn thing to back it up! Where's your
coat? Here. Git into it." Without any prelude, any apology, he wrested the stick of wood
from her, pulled her coat off a nail near by, and
held it outspread, the armholes convenient to her
hands. With her chin shivering, Mary Hope
obeyed the brute strength of the man. She dug

her teeth into her lip and thrust her arms spitefully
into the coat sleeves.

"Here's yo're hat. Better tie it on, if yuh got
anything to tie it with. Here."

He twitched his big silk neckerchief from his
neck, pulled her toward him with a gentle sort of
brutality, and tied the neckerchief over her hat and
under her chin. He did it exactly as though he
was handling a calf that he did not wish to frighten
or hurt.

"Got any mittens? Gloves? Put 'em on."

Standing back in the corner behind the door,
facing Tom's bigness and his inexorable strength,
Mary Hope put on her Indian tanned, beaded buckskin gloves that were in the pockets of her coat.
Tom waited until she had tucked the coatsleeves
inside the gauntlets. He took her by the arm and
pulled her to the door, pushed her through it and
held her with one hand, gripping her arm while
he fastened the door by the simple method of pulling it shut so hard that it jammed in the casing.
He led her to where her horse stood backed to the
wind and tail whipping between his legs, and his
eyes blinking half shut against the swirls of dust
dug out of the dry sod of the grassland. Without
any spoken command, Tom took the reins and
flipped them up over Rab's neck, standing forward
and close to the horse's shoulder. Mary Hope
knew that she must mount or be lifted bodily into
the saddle. She mounted, tears of wrath spilling

from her eyes and making her cheeks cold where they trickled down.

The Boyle children, kicking and quirting their two horses — riding double, in the Black Rim country, was considered quite comfortable enough for children — were already on their way home. Mary Hope looked at their hurried retreat and turned furiously, meaning to overtake them and order them back. Tom Lorrigan, she reminded herself, might force her to leave the schoolhouse, but he would scarcely dare to carry his abuse farther.

She had gone perhaps ten rods when came a pounding of hoofs, and Coaley's head and proudly arched neck heaved alongside poor, draggle-maned old Rab.

"You're headed wrong. Have I got to haze yuh all the way home? Might as well. I want to tell yore dad a few things."

He twitched the reins, and Coaley obediently shouldered Rab out of the trail and turned him neatly toward the Douglas ranch. Even Rab was Scotch, it would seem. He laid his ears flat, swung his head unexpectedly, and bared his teeth at Coaley. But Coaley was of the Lorrigans. He did not bare his teeth and threaten; he reached out like a rattler and nipped Rab's neck so neatly that a spot the size of a quarter showed pink where the hair had been. Rab squealed, whirled and kicked, but Coaley was not there at that particular

moment. He came back with the battle light in his
eyes, and Rab clattered away in a stiff-legged run.
After him went Coaley, loping easily, with high,
rabbit jumps that told how he would love to show
the speed that was in him, if only Tom would
loosen the reins a half inch.

For a mile Tom kept close to Rab's heels.
Then, swinging up alongside, he turned to Mary
Hope, that baffling half smile on his lips and the
look in his eyes that had never failed to fill her
with trepidation.

"I ain't blaming yuh for being Scotch and stubborn," he said, "but you notice there's something
beats it four ways from the jack. Yo go on home,
now, and don't yuh go back to that board cullender
till the weather warms up. And tell yore folks
that Tom Lorrigan broke up yore school for yuh,
so they wouldn't have to break up a case of pneu-
monia."

Mary Hope was framing a sentence of defiance
when Coaley wheeled and went back the way they
had come, so swiftly that even with shouting she
could not have made herself heard in that whooping wind. She pulled Rab to a willing stand and
stared after Tom, hating him with her whole heart.
Hating him for his domination of her from the
moment he entered the schoolhouse where he had
no business at all to be; hating him because even
his bullying had been oddly gentle; hating him
most of all because he was so like Lance — and be-

cause he was not Lance, who was away out in California, going to college, and had never written her one line in all the time he had been gone.

Had it been Lance who rode up to the schoolhouse door, she would have known how to meet and master the situation. She would not have been afraid of Lance, she told herself savagely. She wouldn't have been afraid of Tom — but the whole Black Rim was afraid of Tom. Well, just wait until she happened some day to meet Lance! At least she would make him pay! For two years of silence and brooding over his hardihood for taking her to task for her unfriendliness, and for this new and unbearable outrage, she would make Lance Lorrigan pay, if the fates ever let them meet again.

CHAPTER TEN

The Lorrigan Way

THE Lorrigan family was dining comfortably in the light of a huge lamp with a rose-tinted shade decorated with an extremely sinuous wreath of morning glories trailing around the lower rim. A clatter of pots and pans told that Riley was washing his "cookin' dishes" in the lean-to kitchen that had been added to the house as an afterthought, the fall before. Belle had finished her dessert of hot mince pie, and leaned back now with a freshly lighted cigarette poised in her fingers.

"What have you got up your sleeve, Tom?" she asked abruptly, handing Duke her silver matchbox in response to a gestured request for it.

"My arm," Tom responded promptly, pushing back his wristband to give her the proof.

"Aw, cut out the comedy, Tom. You've been doing something that you're holding out on us. I know that look in your eye; I ought, having you and Lance to watch. You're near enough to double in a lead and not even the manager know which is who. You've been doing something, and

Lance knows what it is.   Now, I'll get it outa you
two if I have to shoot it out.''

Lance, just returned from Berkeley during Easter holidays, lifted one eyebrow at Tom, lowered
one lid very slowly, and gave his mother a level,
sidelong glance.

''Your husband, my dear madame, has been engaged in a melodramatic rôle created by himself.
He is painfully undecided whether the hisses of
the orchestra attest his success as a villian;
whether the whistling up in the gallery demands an
encore, or heralds an offering of cabbages and
ripe poultry fruit. I myself did not witness the
production, but I did chance to meet the star just
as he was leaving the stage. To me he confided
the fact that he does not know whether it was a
one-act farce he put on, or a five-act tragedy
played accidentally hind-side before, with the vil-
lian-still-pursuing-her act set first instead of
fourth. I am but slightly versed in the drama
as played in the Black Rim the past two years.
Perhaps if the star would repeat his lines —''

''For the Lord sake, Lance! As a dramatic
critic you're the punkest proposition I ever
slammed my door against. Talk the way you were
brought up to talk and tell me the truth. What
did Tom do, and how did he do it?''

Lance drew his black eyebrows together, studying carefully the ethics of the case. ''Belle, you
must remember that Dad is my father. Dad must

remember that you are my mother — technically speaking. By heck, if it wasn't for remembering how you used to chase me up on the barn every day or so with your quirt, I'd swear that you grew up with me and are at this present moment at least two years younger than I am. However, they *say* you are my mother. And — do you want to know, honestly, what dad has been doing?"

"I'm *going* to know," Belle informed him trenchantly.

"Then let me tell you. I'll break it gently. Tom, your husband, the self-confessed father of your offspring, to-day rode to an alleged school-house, threatened, ordered, and by other felonious devices hazed three Swedes and the four Boyle kids out of the place and toward their several homes and then when the schoolmarm very discreetly locked the door and mildly informed him that she would brain him with a twig off a sage-bush if he burst the lock, he straightway forgot that he was old enough to have a son quite old enough to frighten, abduct and otherwise lighten the monotonous life of said schoolmarm, and became a bold, bad man. He bursted that door off its hinges —"

"You're a liar. I busted the lock," Tom grunted, without removing the cigarette from his lips.

"He busted the lock of that door, madame; rushed in, wrested the sprig of sage —"

"It was a club the size of my arm."

"Wrested the club from that schoolmarm, brutally and ferociously forced her into her coat and hat, compelled her to mount her horse, and then deliberately drove her away from that —"

"Shut up, Lance. You remind me of one of those monstrosities they serve in the Lava House, that they call a combination salad. It's about two-thirds wilted lettuce and the rest beets and carrots. I don't ever eat them, but if I did they'd taste just like you sound."

"Oh, all right, then. With only two weeks' vacation I won't have time for a real spree of Black Rim dialect and sober up in time for the University. Let me mix it, Belle. I'll eat my own verbal combination salad, if anybody has to. I won't ask you."

"You'll eat 'em, all right," Tom stated briefly, lifting an eyebrow at him. "All I done, Belle, was to ride up to the Whipple shack to see who was camped there. It was that Douglas girl and the Boyle kids and them Swedes that live over beyond Boyle's. They was all setting there having school, — with their overcoats on, half froze, and the wind howling through like it was a corral fence. So when the Douglas girl got her Scotch up and said she wouldn't turn 'em loose to go home, I turned 'em loose myself and told 'em to beat it. And then I hazed her home. Seems like they think that shack is good enough for women and kids; but I wouldn't keep pigs in it, myself, without doing a lot of fixing on it first.''

"What dad seems to overlook is the attitude Boyle and old Scotty will take, when they hear how Tom Lorrigan broke up school for 'em. There'll be something drop, if you ask me — I hope it drops before I have to leave.''

Belle looked at him meditatively. "And where were you, Lance? With Mary Hope?''

For answer, Lance smiled, with his mouth twisted a little to one side, which made him resemble Tom more than ever. "A fellow sure does hate to have his own father cut in —''

"So that's what ails you! Well, you may just as well know first as last that Mary Hope hasn't spoken to one of us since the time they had Tom up in court for stealing that yearling. You know how they acted; and if you'd come home last summer instead of fooling around in California, you'd know they haven't changed a darn bit. It's a shame. I used to like Mary Hope. She always seemed kinda lonesome and half scared —''

"She's got over it, then,'' Tom interrupted, chuckling. "She's got spunk enough now for two of her size. Had that club lifted, ready to brain me when I went in, just because I'd spoiled her rules for her. If she had as much sense as she's got nerve —''

"Why don't they build her a schoolhouse, if

they want her to teach?'' Belle pushed back her chair.

"Ever know the AJ to spend a cent they didn't have to?" Duke asked. "Or old Scotty? The Swede ain't able. How're they paying her? This ain't any school district."

"So much a head," Tom answered. "Not much, I reckon. The girl's got nerve. I'll say that much for her. She was dodgin' clods of dirt from the roof, and shivering and teaching to beat hell when I got there."

"They're going to be awful sore at you, Tom, for this," Belle predicted. "They're going to say you did it because you hate the Douglases, and it was Mary Hope teaching. Jim Boyle will side with old Scotty, and there'll be the devil and all to pay. Did you tell those kids why you sent 'em home?"

"I told the girl. No, I never told the kids. The Swedes had sense enough to beat it when she let 'em out for recess. She got fighty over that, and wouldn't let the school out and wait for good weather, so I went out and told the Boyle kids to hit for home. Humpin' cats, *somebody* had to do something!

"So then the Scotch come out strong in the girl, and I made her go home too. If I see 'em in that shack to-morrow, and the weather like it is and like it's going to be, I'll send 'em home again. What in thunder do I care what old Scotty and

Jim Boyle says about it? If they want a woman to learn their kids to read, they'd oughta give her a better place than the Whipple shack to keep school in.''

"They won't," said Belle. "A roof and four walls is all you can expect of them. It's a shame. I expect Mary Hope is tickled to death to be earning the money, too. She was taking music all winter in Pocatello, I heard, and she and her mother saved up the money in nickels — Lord knows how, the way old Scotty watches them! — to pay for the lessons. It's a shame."

"What do they do for water? Old Man Whipple always hauled it in barrels when he tried to hold down the camp." Al, tilting back his chair, placidly picking his teeth, spoke for the first time.

"I didn't see no water barrel," Tom answered. "I reckon they make dry camp. They had a stove that smoked, and three benches with some kinda shelf for their books, and the girl was using a strip of tar-paper for a blackboard. But there was no water."

"Say, what sort of country is this Black Rim, anyway?" Lance studied the end of his cigarette, lifting his left eyebrow just as his father had done five minutes before. "I hope to heck I haven't come home to remodel the morals of the country, or to strut around and play college-young-man like a boob; but on the square, folks, it looks to me as though the Rim needs a lesson in citizenship. It doesn't mean anything in our lives, whether there is a schoolhouse in the country or not. Belle has looked out for us boys, in the matter of learning the rudiments and a good deal besides. Say, Belle, do you know they took my voice and fitted a glee club to it? I was the glee. And a real, live professor told me I had technique. I told him I must have caught it changing climates — but however, what you couldn't give us with the books, you handed us with the quirt — and here and now I want to say I appreciate it."

"All right, I appreciate your appreciation, and I wish to heaven you wouldn't ramble all over the range when you start to say a thing. That's one thing you learned in school that I'd like to take outa you with a quirt."

"I was merely pointing out how we, ourselves, personally, do not need a schoolhouse. But I was also saying that the Rim ought to have a lesson in real citizenship. They call the Lorrigans bad. All right; that's a fine running start. I'd say, let's give 'em a jolt. I'm game to donate a couple of steers toward a schoolhouse — a *regular* schoolhouse, with the Stars and Stripes on the front end, and a bench behind the door for the water bucket, and a blackboard up in front, and a woodshed behind — with a door into it so the schoolmarm needn't put on her overshoes and mittens every time she tells one of the Swedes to put a stick of wood in the stove. I'd like to do that, and not say a darn word until it's ready to move into. And then I'd like to stick my hands in my pockets and watch what the Rim would do about it.

"I've wondered quite a lot, in the last two years, whether it's the Black Rim or the Lorrigan outfit that's all wrong. I know all about grandad and all the various and sundry uncles and forbears that earned us the name of being bad; it makes darn interesting stuff to tell now and then to some of the fellows who were raised in a prune orchard and will sit and listen with watering mouths and eyes goggling. I've been a hero, months on end, just for the things that my grandad did in the seventies. Of course," he pulled his lips into their whimsical smile, "I've touched up the family biography here and there and made heroes of us all. But the fact remains there are degrees and differences in badness. I've a notion that the Black Rim, taken by and large, is a damn sight worse than the Devil's Tooth outfit. I'd like to try the experiment of making the AJ and old Scotty ashamed of themselves. I'd like to try a schoolhouse on 'em, and see if they're human enough to appreciate it."

Duke, turning his head slowly, glanced at Al, and from him to Tom. Without moving a muscle of their faces the two returned his look. Al slid his cigarette stub thoughtfully into his coffee cup and let his breath out carefully in a long sigh that

was scarcely audible. Tom took a corner of his
lower lip between his teeth, matching Lance, who
had the same trick.

"Honey, that's fine of you! There aren't many
that realize what a lot of satisfaction there is in
doing something big and generous and making the
other fellow ashamed of himself. And it would
be a God's mercy to Mary Hope, poor child.
Leave it to the AJ and whatever other outfit there
is to send pupils, and Mary Hope could teach in
the Whipple shack till it rattled down on top of
them. I know what the place is. I put up there
once in a hailstorm. It isn't fit for cattle, as Tom
says, unless they've fixed it a lot. I'll donate the
furniture; I'll make out the order right this evening for seats and blackboard and a globe and
everything, and make it a rush order!" Belle
pushed back her chair and came around to Lance,
slipped her arms around his neck and tousled his
wavy mop of hair with her chin. "If the rest
won't come through you and I'll do it, honey —"

"Who said we wouldn't?" Tom got up,
stretching his arms high above his head, — which
was very bad manners, but showed how supple he
still was, and how well muscled. "No one ever
called me a piker — and let me hear about it.
Sure, we'll build a schoolhouse for 'em, seeing
they're too cussed stingy to build one themselves.
There's the lumber I had hauled out for a new
chicken house; to-morrow I'll have it hauled up to

some good building spot, and we'll have it done before the AJ wakes up to the fact that anything's going on.''

''I'll chip in enough to make her big enough for dances,'' volunteered Duke. ''Darn this riding fifteen or twenty miles to a dance!''

''I'll paint 'er, if you let me pick out the color,'' said Al. ''Where are you going to set 'er?''

''What's the matter with doing the thing in style, and giving a house-warming dance, and turning it over to the neighborhood with a speech?'' bantered Lance, as they adjourned to the big living room, taking the idea with them and letting it grow swiftly in enthusiasm. ''That would celebrate my visit, and I'd get a chance to size up the Rim folks and *see* how they react to kindness. Lordy, folks, let's do it!''

''We might,'' Belle considered the suggestion, while she thumbed the latest mail-order catalogue, the size of a family bible and much more assiduously studied. ''They'd come, all right!'' she added, with a scornful laugh. ''Even old Scotty would come, if he thought it wouldn't cost him anything.''

''Well, by heck, we won't *let* it cost him anything!'' Lance stood leaning against the wall by the stove, his arms folded, the fingers of his left hand tapping his right forearm. He did not know that this was a Lorrigan habit, born of an old necessity of having the right hand convenient to a revolver butt, and matched by the habit of carrying a six-shooter hooked inside the trousers band on the left side.

Tom, studying Lance, thought how much he resembled his grandfather on the night Buck Sanderson was killed in a saloon in Salmon City. Old Tom had leaned against the wall at the end of the bar, with his arms folded and his fingers tapping his right forearm, just as Lance was doing now. He had lifted one eyebrow and pulled a corner of his lip between his teeth when Buck came blustering in. Just as Lance smiled at Duke's chaffing, Tom's father had smiled when Buck came swaggering up to him with bold eyes full of fight and his right thumb hooked in his chap belt. Old Tom had not moved; he had remained leaning negligently against the wall with his arms folded. But the strike of a snake was not so quick as the drop of his hand to his gun.

Tom was not much given to reminiscence; but to-night, seeing Lance with two years of man-growth and the poise of town life upon him, he slipped into a swift review of changing conditions and a vague speculation upon the value of environment in the shaping of character. Lance was all Lorrigan. He had turned Lorrigan in the two years of his absence, which had somehow painted out his resemblance to Belle. His hair had darkened to a brown that was almost black. His eyes had darkened, his mouth had the Lorrigan twist.

He had grown taller, leaner, surer in his movements, — due to his enthusiasm for athletics and the gym, though Tom had no means of knowing what had given him that catlike quickness, the grace of perfect muscular coördination. Tom thought it was the Lorrigan blood building Lance true to his forbears as he passed naturally from youth to maturity. He wondered if Lance, given the environment which had shaped his grandfather, would have been a "killer", hated by many, feared by all.

Even now, if it came to the point of fighting, would not Lance fight true to the blood, true to that Lorrigan trick of the folded arms and the tapping fingers? Would not Lance — ? Tom pulled his thoughts away from following that last conjecture to its logical end. There were matters in which it might be best not to include Lance, just as he had been careful not to include Belle. For Lance might still be a good deal like Belle, in spite of his Lorrigan looks and mannerisms. And there were certain Lorrigan traits which would not bear any mixture of Belle in the fiber.

"Well, now, that's all made out. I'll send to Salt Lake and get the stuff quicker. Wake up, Tom, and tell us how long it will take to put up the schoolhouse? Lance is going to give the dance — and there won't be so much as a soggy chocolate cake accepted from the Rimmers. What will you do, Lance? Put up a notice in Jumpoff?"

"Surely! A mysteriously worded affair, telling little and saying much. Music and refresh — no, by heck, that sounds too wet and not solid enough. Music and supper furnished free. Everybody welcome. Can't Riley drive the chuck-wagon over and have the supper served by a campfire? Golly, but I've been hungry for that old chuck-wagon! That would keep all the mess of coffee and sandwiches out of the nice, new schoolhouse."

"Who's going to hold their hat in front of the nice, new schoolhouse till it's done and ready? And how're you going to let 'em know where to come to, without giving away the secret?" Al, the practical, stretched his long legs to the stove and thrust his hands deep into his trousers pockets while he propounded these two conundrums. "Go on, Lance. This is yore party."

Lance unfolded his arms and disposed his big body on a bearskin covered lounge where he could take Belle's hand and pat it and playfully pinch a finger now and then.

"To look at your hand, Belle, a fellow would swear that a blonde manicure girl comes here twice a week," he said idly. "Where is the schoolhouse going to be built? Why not put it just at the foot of the ridge, at Cottonwood Spring? That's out of sight of the road, and if the notice said 'Cottonwood Spring', folks would know where to head for. It's close to the line of your land, isn't it, dad? A yard — corral-size — fenced around the place would keep the cattle off the doorstep, and they could water there just the same. If we're going to do it, why not do it right?"

"I guess we could get down there with a load," Tom assented easily. "I'd ruther have it on my land anyways."

"Don't think, Tom Lorrigan, that we'd ever take it back from Mary Hope. No matter how Scotty acts up. But if they ever gave her the double-cross and got some one else to teach — why it might be nice to know it's our schoolhouse, on our land." Belle pulled her hand away from Lance and went over to the piano. "It's all done but the shingling," she said cheerfully. "Come on, Lance, see if you can sing 'Asleep in the Deep.' And then show me what you mean by saying you can yodel now better than when I licked you the time you and Duke chased the colt through the corral fence!"

"All done but the shingling — and I ain't got 'em bought yet!" grumbled Tom, but was utterly disregarded in the sonorous chords of Belle's prelude to the song.

CHAPTER ELEVEN

A T fifteen minutes to four on a certain Tuesday afternoon, the first really pleasant day after the day of tearing, whooping wind that had blown Tom into the rôle of school bully, Lance loped out upon the trail that led past the Whipple shack a mile and a quarter farther on. Ostensibly his destination was the town of Jumpoff, although it was not the time of day when one usually started from the Devil's Tooth ranch to the post-office, with three unimportant letters as an excuse for the trip.

As he rode Lance sang lustily a love song, but he was not thinking especially of Mary Hope. In two years more than one California girl had briefly held his fancy, and memory of Mary Hope had slightly dimmed. In his pocket were two letters, addressed to two California towns. One letter had Miss Helene Somebody inscribed upon it, and on the other was Miss Mildred Somebody Else. The love song, therefore, had no special significance, save that Lance was young and perfectly normal and liked the idea of love, without being hampered by any definite form of it concentrated upon one girl.

For all that he had timed his trip so as to arrive at the Whipple shack just about the time when Mary Hope would be starting home.   He was curious to see just how much or how little she had changed; to know whether she still had that funny little Scotch accent that manifested itself in certain phrasings, certain vowel sounds at variance with good English pronunciation.   He wanted to know just how much Pocatello had done to spoil her.   Beneath all was the primal instinct of the young male dimly seeking the female whom his destiny had ordained to be his mate.

As a young fellow shut in behind the Rim, with the outside world a vast area over which his imagination wandered vaguely, Mary Hope had appealed to him.   She was the one girl in the Black Rim country whom he would ride out of his way to meet, whose face, whose voice, lingered with him pleasantly for days after he had seen her and talked with her.   He reflected, between snatches of song, that he might have thought himself in love with Mary Hope, might even have married her, had Belle not suddenly decided that he should go beyond the Rim and learn the things she could not teach him.   Belle must have wanted him, her youngest, to be different from the rest.   He wondered with a sudden whimsical smile, whether she was satisfied with the result of his two years of exile. Tom, he suspected, was not,— nor were Duke and Al. The three seemed to hold themselves apart from him, to look upon him as a guest rather than as one of the family returned after an absence. They did not include him in their talk of range matters and the business of the ranch. He had once observed in them a secret embarrassment when he appeared unexpectedly, had detected a swift change of tone and manner and subject.

Surely they could not think he had changed sufficiently to make him an outsider, he meditated. Aside from his teasing of Belle, he had dropped deliberately into the range vernacular, refraining only from certain crudities of speech which grated on his ears. He had put on his old clothes, he had tried to take his old place in the ranch work. He had driven a four-horse team up the Ridge trail with lumber for the schoolhouse, and had negotiated the rock descent to Cottonwood Spring with a skill that pleased him mightily because it proved to him — and to Tom and the boys — that his range efficiency had not lessened during his absence. He had done everything the boys had done, except ride out with them on certain long trips over the range. He had not gone simply because they had made it quite plain that they did not want him.

Nor did the hired cowboys want him with them, — ten of them in the bunk house with a cook of their own, and this only the middle of March! In two years the personnel of the bunk house had changed almost completely. They were men whom he did not know, men who struck him as "hard-boiled", though he could not have explained just wherein they differed from the others. Sam Pretty Cow and Shorty he could hobnob with as of yore, — Sam in particular giving him much pleasure with his unbroken reserve, his unreadable Indian eyes and his wide-lipped grin. The others were like Duke, Tom and Al, — slightly aloof, a bit guarded in their manner.

"And I suppose Mary Hope will be absolutely spoiled, with small-town dignity laid a foot deep over her Scotch primness. Still, a girl that has the nerve to lift a club and threaten to brain Tom Lorrigan —"

He had forgotten the love song he was singing, and before he reached farther in his musings he met the Swedes, who stared at him round-eyed and did not answer his careless hello. A little farther, the Boyle children rode up out of a dry wash, grinned bashfully at him and hurried on.

A saddlehorse was tied to a post near the Whipple shack. With long legs swinging slightly with the stride of his horse, reins held high and loose in one hand, his big hat tilted over his forehead, Lance rode up and dismounted as if his errand, though important, was not especially urgent. The door stood open. He walked up, tapped twice with his knuckles on the unpainted casing, and entered, pulling off his hat and turning it round and round in his gloved fingers while he ducked his head, pressed his lips together with a humorous quirk, shuffled his spurred feet on the dirty floor and bowed again as awkwardly as he could. In this manner he hoped to draw some little spark of individuality from Mary Hope, who sat behind her yellow-painted table and stared at him over her folded arms. But Mary Hope, he observed, had been crying, and compunction seized him suddenly.

"Well, what is it?" she asked him curtly, rubbing a palm down over one cheek, with the motion obliterating a small rivulet of tears.

"If you please, ma'am, I was sent to mend a lock on a door."

"What lock? On what door?" Mary Hope passed a palm down her other cheek, thus obliterating another rivulet that had ceased to flow tears and was merely wet and itchy.

"If you please, ma'am, you can search me." Lance looked at her innocently. "I didn't bring any lock with me, and I didn't bring any door with me. But I've got some screws and three nails and — lots of good intentions."

"Good intentions are very rare in this country," said Mary Hope, and made meaningless marks on the bare tabletop with a blunt pencil.

Lance heard a twang of Scotch in the "very rare" which pleased him. But he kept his position by the doorway, and he continued bashfully turning his big hat round and round against his chest, — though the action went oddly with the Lorrigan look and the athletic poise of him. "Yes, ma'am. Quite rare," he agreed.

"In fact, I don't believe there is such a thing in the whole Black Rim country," stated Mary Hope, plainly nonplussed at his presence and behavior.

"Could I show you mine?" Lance advanced a step. He was not sure, at that moment, whether he wanted to go with the play. Mary Hope was better looking than when he had seen her last. She had lost a good deal of the rusticity he remembered her to have possessed, but she was either too antagonistic to carry on the farce, or she was waiting for him to show his hand, to betray some self-consciousness. But the fact that she looked at him straight in the eyes and neither frowned nor giggled, set her apart from the ordinary range-bred girl.

"You talk like a country peddler. I'm willing to accept a sample, and see if they are durable. Though I can't for the life of me see why you'd be coming here with good intentions."

"I'd be mending a lock on a door. Is this the door, ma'am? And is this the lock?"

Since the door behind him was the only door within five miles of them, and since the lock dangled from a splintered casing, Mary Hope almost smiled. "It is a door," she informed him. "And it is a lock that has been broken by a Lorrigan."

She was baiting him, tempting him to quarrel with her over the old grudge. Because she expected a reply, Lance made no answer whatever. He happened to have a dozen or so of nails in his coat pocket, left-overs from his assiduous carpentry on the house being builded for her comfort. The screws he possessed were too large, and he had no hammer. But no man worries over a missing hammer where rocks are plentiful, and Lance was presently pounding the lock into place, his back to Mary Hope, his thoughts swinging from his prospective party to the possible religious scruples of the Douglas family.

Mary Hope used to dance — a very little — he remembered, though she had not attended many dances. He recalled suddenly that a Christmas tree or a Fourth of July picnic had usually been the occasions when Mary Hope, with her skirts just hitting her shoe tops in front and sagging in an ungainly fashion behind, had teetered solemnly through a "square" dance with him. Mother Douglas herself had always sat very straight and prim on a bench, her hands folded in her lap and her eyes blinking disapprovingly at the ungodly ones who let out an exultant little yip now and then when they started exuberantly through the mazes of the "gran'-right-n-left."

Would Mary Hope attend the party? Should he tell her about it and ask her to come? Naturally, he could not peacefully escort her partyward,

— the feud was still too rancorous for that. Or
was it? At the Devil's Tooth they spoke of old
Scotty as an enemy, but they had cited no particular act of hostility as evidence of his enmity.
At the Devil's Tooth they spoke of the whole Black
Rim country as enemy's country. Lance began to
wonder if it were possible that the Lorrigans had
adopted unconsciously the rôle of black sheep,
without the full knowledge or concurrence of the
Black Rimmers.

He did what he could to make a workable lock
of one that had been ready to fall to pieces before
his father heaved against it; hammered in the loosened screws in the hinges, tossed the rock out into
the scuffed sod before the shack, and picked up
his hat. He had not once looked toward Mary
Hope, but he turned now as if he were going to
say good-by and take himself off; as if mending
the lock had really been his errand, and no further interest held him there.

He surprised a strange, wistful look in Mary
Hope's eyes, a trembling of her lips. She seemed
to be waiting, fearing that he meant to go without
any further overtures toward friendship.

The Whipple shack was not large. Ten feet
spanned the distance between them. Impulsively
Lance covered that distance in three steps. At
the table he stopped, leaned toward her with his
palms braced upon the table, and stared full into
Mary Hope's disturbed eyes.

"Girl," he said, drawing the word softly along a vibrant note in his voice that sent a tremor through her, "Girl, you're more lonesome than Scotch, and you're more Scotch than the heather that grows in your front yard to make your mother cry for the Highlands she sees when her eyes blur with homesickness. You were crying when I came — crying because you're lonely. It's a big, wild country — the Black Rim. It's a country for men to ride hell-whooping through the sage and camas grass, with guns slung at their hips, but it's no country for a little person like you to try and carry on a feud because her father made one. You're — too little!"

He did not touch her, his face did not come near her face. But in his eyes, in his voice, in the tender, one-sided little smile, there was something, — Mary Hope caught her breath, feeling as if she had been kissed.

"You little, lonesome girl! There's going to be a party at Cottonwood Spring, a week from Friday night. It's a secret — a secret for you. And you won't tell a soul that you were the first to know — and you'll come, you girl, because it's your party. And not a soul will know it's your party. If your father's Scotch is too hard for dancing — you'll come just the same. You'll come, because the secret is for you. And —" He thought that he read something in her eyes and hastened to forestall her intention "— and you won't go near Cottonwood Spring before the time of the party, because that wouldn't be playing fair.

"Don't be lonely, girl. The world is full of pleasant things, just waiting to pop out at you from behind every bush. If you're good and kind and honest with life, the Fates are going to give you the best they've got. Don't be lonely! Just wait for the pleasant things in to-morrow and to-morrow — in all the to-morrows. And one of them, girl, is going to show you the sweetest thing in life. That's love, you girl with the tears back of your Scotch blue eyes. But wait for it — and take the little pleasant things that minutes have hidden away in the to-morrows. And one of the pleasant times will be hidden at Cottonwood Spring, a week from Friday night. Wonder what it will be, girl. And if any one tries to tell it, put your hands over your ears, so that you won't hear it. Wait — and keep wondering, and come to Cottonwood Spring next Friday night. Adios, girl."

He looked into her eyes, smiling a little. Then, turning suddenly, he left her without a backward glance. Left her with nothing to spoil the haunting cadence of his voice, nothing to lift the spell of tender prophecy his words had laid upon her soul. When he was quite gone, when she heard the clatter of his horse's hoofs upon the arid soil that surrounded the Whipple shack, Mary Hope still stared out through the open doorway, seeing nothing of the March barrenness, seeing only the tender, inscrutable, tantalizing face of Lance Lorrigan,— tantalizing because she could not plumb the depths of his eyes, could not say how much of the tenderness was meant for her, how much was born of the deep music of his voice, the whimsical, one-sided smile.

And Lance, when he had ridden a furlong from the place, had dipped into a shallow draw and climbed the other side, turned half around in the saddle and looked back.

"Now, why did I go off and leave her like that? Like an actor walking off the stage to make room for the other fellow to come on and say his lines. There's no other fellow — thank heck! And here are two miles we might be riding together — and me preaching to her about taking the little, pleasant things that come unexpectedly!" He swung his horse around in the trail, meaning to ride back; retraced his steps as far as the hollow, and turned again, shaking his head.

"Anybody could stop at the schoolhouse just as school's out, and ride a couple of miles down the road with the schoolma'am — if she let him do it! Anybody could do that. But that isn't the reason, why I'm riding on ahead. What the hell *is* the reason?"

He stopped again on the high level where he could look back and see the Whipple shack squatted forlornly in the gray stretch of sage with wide, brown patches of dead grass between the bushes.

"Lonesome," he named the wild expanse of un-peopled range land. "She's terribly lonely — and sweet. Too lonely and sweet for me to play with, to ride a few miles with — and leave her lonelier than I found her. I couldn't. There's enough sadness now in those Scotch blue eyes. Damned if I'll add more!"

He saw Mary Hope come from the shack, pause a minute on the doorstep, then walk out to where her horse was tied to the post. He lifted the reins, pricked his horse gently with the spurs and galloped away to Jumpoff, singing no more.

CHAPTER TWELVE

She Will, and She Won't

COTTONWOOD SPRING was a dished-out oasis just under the easy slope of Devil's Tooth Ridge. From no part of the Jumpoff trail could it be seen, and the surrounding slope did not offer much inducement to cattle in March, when water was plentiful; wherefore riders would scarcely wander into the saucer-like hollow that contained the cottonwoods and the spring. A picnic had once been held there, but the festivities had been marred by a severe thunder-storm that came just as a wordy quarrel between two drunken cowpunchers was fast nearing the gun-pulling stage. Lightning had struck the side hill just beyond the grove, and the shock of it had knocked down and stunned the two disputants, and three saddle horses standing in the muddy overflow from the spring. For this reason, perhaps, and because it was on Lorrigan land, the place had never thereafter been frequented save by the stock that watered there.

But from the head of the little basin a wide view was had of the broken land beyond Devil's

Tooth. The spring was clear and cold and never affected by drouth. By following the easy slope around the point of the main trail from Jumpoff to the Lorrigan ranch, no road-building was necessary, and in summer the cottonwoods looked very cool and inviting — though at certain times they harbored buffalo gnats and many red ants that would bite, which rendered the shade less grateful than it looked. But to the Lorrigans it seemed an ideal site for a schoolhouse.

Ten days after they had planned the deed, the schoolhouse stood ready for the dance. In the lean-to shed, twelve shiny yellow desks that smelled strongly of varnish were stacked in their heavy paper swaddlings, waiting to be set in place when the dance was done. Belle herself had hemmed scrim curtains for the windows, which Riley had washed copiously. The blackboard, with the names of various Devil's Tooth men and a "motto" or two scrawled upon it was in place; the globe was on the teacher's desk, and the water bucket on its shelf in the corner, with a shiny new tin dipper hanging on a nail above it.

If you were to believe the frequent declarations, every puncher on the ranch had done his durnedest to put 'er up, and put 'er up right. Sam Pretty Cow had nailed a three-foot American flag to the front gable, and had landed on a nail when he jumped from the eaves. On the night of the dance he was hobbling around the chuck-wagon with half a pound of salt pork bound to his foot, helping Riley, who had driven over to the spring early, burdened with the importance of his share in the entertainment.

A dance in the Black Rim country has all the effect of a dog fight in a small village with empty streets. No sooner does it start than one wonders where all the people came from.

At eight o'clock toiling horses drawing full loads of humanity began to appear over the rim of the hollow, to pick their way carefully down toward the lighted windows, urged by their drivers. Men on horseback made the descent more swiftly, with a clatter of small rocks kicked loose as they came. They encountered a four-wire fence, circled it to where a lantern, hung on a post, revealed a gate that lay flat on the ground to leave a welcoming space for teams and saddle horses to pass through.

Beside the schoolhouse, with two lanterns shedding a yellow glow on his thin, sandy hair, Riley, at the chuck-wagon, arranged doughnuts, sandwiches, pies and cakes to his liking, wiped his red hands frequently on his clean floursack apron, and held carefully unprofane conversation with the women who came fluttering over to him, their arms burdened.

"No, mom, sorry! I know I'm turnin' down something that's better than anything I got here, but this here party's on the Lorrigans. No, mom, I got orders not to take in s'much as a sour pickle from nobody. You jest put it back in the rig, whatever you got there, and consider't you got some Sat'day bakin' did up ahead.

"Yes, mom, it's Lance's party. He's home for a visit, an' he kinda wanted to have a dance an' meet the folks, seein' he's been away quite a spell and kain't stay long.

"Yes, mom, he's goin' back to college first the week.

"Hey! I wisht you'd tie up yore cayuses other side the shack. Folks'll be comin' around here for their supper, and they don't wanta git their faces kicked off whilst they're huntin' grub to fill 'em.

"No, mom, we ain't takin' any cakes or nothin' off nobody. Lance, he wanted to give this dance an' give it *right*. Ain't goin' to cost nobody a thing but sore corns, t'night!"

Lance had hired an Italian violinist and his boy who played a harp much taller than himself and people coming from Jumpoff had brought them out. The Millers had come, with all their outfit. The AJ outfit was there to a man. The Swedes were present, sitting together in the corner by the water bucket, and the Conleys, who lived over by Camas Creek beyond the AJ, had come. The Conleys had sheep, and were not firmly settled in the Black Rim, sheepmen being looked at askance. There were families from nearer Jumpoff, — one really did wonder where they all came from, when the country seemed so wide and unpeopled.

Lance was surprised to see how many were there who were total strangers. Until the dancing began the men stood outside and smoked, leaving the women and children to arrange themselves on benches along the wall inside. Lance knew the custom well enough, and he did not go in. But he tried to see who came with every load that was deposited within the circle of light on the narrow platform that embellished the front.

At nine o'clock, when the musicians were trying their instruments tentatively and even the most reluctant male was being drawn irresistibly to the humming interior, Lance frankly admitted to himself that he was not happy, and that his condition was the direct result of not having seen Mary Hope enter the door.

He sought out Tom, who was over at the chuckwagon, taking an early cup of coffee. Tom blew away the steam that rose on the chill night air and eyed Lance. "Well, when do we make the speech? Or don't we?" he demanded, taking a gulp and finding the coffee still too hot for comfort. "Don't ask me to; I done my share when I built 'er. You can tell the bunch what she's for."

"Oh, what the heck do we want with a speech?" Lance remonstrated. "They know it's a schoolhouse, unless they're blind. And I thought maybe some one — you, probably, since you're the one who hazed her out of the other place — would just tell Mary Hope to bring her books over here and

teach. And I thought, to cinch it, you could tell
Jim Boyle that you felt you ought to do something
toward a school, and since you couldn't furnish
any kids, you thought you'd furnish the house.
That ought to be easy. It's up to you, I should
say. But I wouldn't make any speech.''

Tom grunted, finished his coffee and proceeded
to remove all traces of it from his lips with his best
white handkerchief. ''Where's Jim Boyle at?''
he asked, moving into the wide bar of dusk that
lay between the lights of the chuck-wagon and the
glow from the two windows facing that way.

''I believe I'd speak about it first to Mary
Hope,'' Lance suggested, coming behind him.
''But she hasn't come yet —''

As if she heard and deliberately moved to con-
tradict him, Mary Hope danced past the window,
the hand of a strange young man with a crisp white
handkerchief pressed firmly between her shoulder
blades. Mary Hope was dancing almost as solemnly as in the days of short skirts and sleek hair,
her eyes apparently fixed upon the shoulder of her
partner who gazed straight out over her head, his
whole mind centered upon taking the brunt of col-
lisions upon the point of his upraised elbow.

''I'll ketch her when she's through dancing,''
promised Tom. But Lance had another thought.

''Let me tell Mary Hope, dad. I'm going to
dance with her, and it will be easy.''

In the darkness Tom grinned and went on to

find Jim Boyle standing in a group of older men
on the platform that served as a porch.   Jim Boyle
was smoking a cheap cigar brought out from
Jumpoff by the section boss.   He listened reflec-
tively, looked at the glowing tip of the evil-smelling
cigar, threw the thing from him and reached for
his cigarette papers with an oath.

"Now, that's damn white of yuh, Tom," he said.
"I leave it to the boys if it ain't damn white.   Not
having no school district I'm puttin' up the money
outa my own pocket to pay the teacher.   And
havin' four kids to feed and buy clothes for, I
couldn't afford to build no schoolhouse, I tell yuh
those.   And uh course, I didn't like to go round
askin' fer help; but it's damn white of yuh to step
in an' do yore share towards making the Rim look
like it was civilized.   Sederson, he'll feel the same
way about it.   And I'm gitting a foreman that's
got a kid, school age; we sure'n hell do need a
schoolhouse.   Rim's settlin' up fast.   I always
said, Tom, that you was white.   I leave it to the
boys here."

Inside, Lance was not finding it so easy to make
the announcement.   Last Tuesday, Mary Hope
had not understood just why he had ridden on
ahead of her for two miles — she could see the
small dust cloud kicked up by his horse on the
Jumpoff trail, so there could be no mistake —
when he knew perfectly well that she must ride
that way, when he could not have failed to see her

horse saddled and waiting at the door. It seemed to Mary Hope an obscure form of mockery to tell her not to be lonely — to tell her in a caressing tone that left with her all the effect of kisses — and then to ride away without one backward glance, one word of excuse. Until she had mounted and had seen him on the trail ahead, she had not realized how he had mocked her.

For days — until Friday, to be explicit — she had been quite determined not to go near Cottonwood Spring. Then she had suddenly changed her mind, dismissed school half an hour early, put old Rab in a lather on the way home, dressed herself and announced to her mother that she must ride into Jumpoff for school supplies, and that she would stay all night with the Kennedys. It had taken two years and the dignity of schoolteacher to give Mary Hope the courage to announce things to her mother. As it was, she permitted her mother to explain as best she might to Hugh Douglas. Her courage did not reach to that long, uncompromising upper lip of her father's.

She had folded her prettiest dress carefully into a flat bundle, had thrown it out of her window and left the house in her riding clothes. There was a saddle horse, Jamie, a Roman-nosed bay of uncertain temper and a high, rocking gait, which she sometimes used for long trips. She saddled him now and hurried away, thankful to be gone with

her package and her guilty conscience before her
father arrived. She was very good friends with
the Kennedys, at the section house. If there was
a dance within forty miles, the Kennedys might
be counted upon to attend; and that is how Mary
Hope arrived at the schoolhouse with a load from
Jumpoff. She had seen Lance standing near the
door, and Lance had paid no attention to her, but
had left an AJ man to claim the first two-step.
Wherefore Lance walked straight into trouble
when he went to Mary Hope and asked for the next
dance with her.

"So sorry — it's promised already," said Mary
Hope, in her primmest tone.

"There's a dance after the next one," he hinted,
looking down from his more-than-six feet at her
where she sat wedged between Mrs. Boyle and
Jennie Miller.

"So sorry — but I think that one is promised
also," said Mary Hope.

Lance drew a corner of his lip between his teeth,
let it go and lifted his eyebrows whimsically at
Jennie Miller, whom he had once heard playing
on her organ, and whom he had detested ever since
with an unreasoning animosity born solely of her
musical inability and her long neck that had on its
side a brown mole with three coarse hairs in it.

"If Miss Douglas has two dances engaged in
advance, it's quite hopeless to hope for a dance
with Miss Miller," he said, maliciously drawing

the sentence through certain vibrant tones which experience had taught him had a certain pleasing effect upon persons. "Or is it hopeless? Are you engaged for every dance to-night, Miss Miller? And if you are, please may I stand beside you while you eat a sandwich at midnight?"

Jennie Miller giggled. "I ain't as popular as all that," she retorted, glancing at Mary Hope, sitting very straight and pretty beside her. "And if I was, I don't go and promise everybody that asks. I might want to change my mind afterwards if some other fellow comes along I liked better — and I've saw too many fights start over a girl forgetting who she's promised to dance with."

"You don't want to see a fight start now, do you?" Lance smiled down at her without in the least degree betraying to Mary Hope that he would like to pull Jennie Miller by force from that seat and occupy it himself.

"I never can see why men fight over things. I hate fights," Miss Miller stammered, agitated by a wild feeling that perhaps she was going to be made love to.

"Then don't forget that you are going to dance with me." The music just then started again, and he offered her his arm with a certain import that made Mary Hope clench her hands.

Mary Hope was punished for her lie. She had not promised that dance, and so she sat on the plank bench and saw Lance and Jennie Miller sway past her four times before a gawky youth who worked for her father caught sight of her and came over from the water-bucket corner to ask her for the dance. That was not the worst. On the fourth round of Lance and Jennie, and just as the gawky one was bowing stiffly before her, Lance looked at her over Jennie Miller's shoulder, and smiled that tantalizing, Lorrigan smile that always left her uneasily doubtful of its meaning.

CHAPTER THIRTEEN

A Way He Had with Him

IT was at the chuck-wagon at midnight, while Riley and Sam Pretty Cow were serving tin cups of black coffee to a shuffling, too-hilarious crowd, that Lance next approached Mary Hope. She was standing on the outskirts of a group composed mostly of women, quite alone so far as cavaliers were concerned, for the gawky youth had gone after coffee. She was looking toward the sagebrush camp-fire around which a crowd of men had gathered with much horseplay at which they were laughing loudly, and she was wondering how best she could make Lance Lorrigan aware of her absolute indifference to him, when his voice drawled disconcertingly close to her ear:

"You're not lonely now, you girl — and you did find a secret at Cottonwood Spring. A pleasant little secret, wasn't it?"

Mary Hope's hands became fists at her side, held close against her best frock. "I think the fellows over by the fire have discovered your pleasant secret," she said, and did not turn her face toward him.

With his arms folded and his eyebrows pulled together and his lip between his teeth, Lance stared down at her face, studying it in the flicker of the distant firelight and the two lanterns. If her combativeness roused in him any resentment, he did not permit it to show in his voice.

"Some of the fellows from Jumpoff brought a bottle or two. That's no secret, except that I don't know where they have it cachéd. The schoolhouse is your —"

"I heard it was included in the Lorrigan refreshments."

"The schoolhouse is ready for your pleasure Monday morning," Lance spoke with that perfect impersonal courtesy that is so exasperating to a person who listens for something to resent. "I knew of it, of course — dad wanted it kept for a surprise. And he wanted me to tell you. It's the Lorrigan expression of their appreciation of the need of a school."

The gawky youth came stumbling up, his outstretched hands carefully holding two tin cups filled with coffee close to the boiling point. Being a youth of good intentions, he tried very hard not to spill a drop. Being gawky, he stubbed his toe as he was rounding the group of women, and Mrs. Miller shrieked and swung back her hand, cuffing the gawky one straight into the thickest of the crowd. Other women screamed.

Lance reached a long arm and plucked the youth

out by the slack of his coat, shook him and propelled him into the darkness, where he collided
violently with Sam Pretty Cow. Some one had
been over-generous with Sam Pretty Cow. A
drunken Indian is never quite safe. Sam Pretty
Cow struck out blindly, yelling Piegan curses
hoarsely as he fought. The crowd of men around
the camp-fire came running. For a short space
there was confusion, shouting, the shrill voices of
scalded women denouncing the accident as a deliberate outrage.

Mrs. Miller whirled on Lance. "You pushed
him on me! If that ain't a Lorrigan trick!—"

"Yeah — what yuh mean? Throwin' bilin' hot
coffee on — "

"Who says it's a Lorrigan trick?"

"Might 'a' known what to expect — "

"Get back here, away from the crowd. There
may be shooting," Lance muttered to Mary Hope,
and pulled her to the rear of the wagon and around
upon the farther side. She could not resist. His
strength was beyond any hope of combating it
with her small strength. Mrs. Miller, whose
scalded shoulder led her to wild utterances without
thought of their effect upon others, shouted at him
as he hustled Mary Hope away:

"Yeah — *run!* You're the one that done it —
now run! That's like a Lorrigan — do your dirty
work and then crawl out and let somebody else
take the blame! That kid never —"

"Aw, come back and fight, you big sneak!" A drunken voice bellowed hoarsely, and a gunshot punctuated the command.

"Go on — get on the other side of the schoolhouse. Run! The fools will all start to shooting now!"

Mary Hope stopped stubbornly. "I will not!" she defied him; and Lance without more argument lifted her from the ground, stooped and tossed her under the wagon, much as he would have heaved a bag of oats out of the rain.

"Don't you move until I tell you to," he commanded her harshly, and ran back, diving into the thick of the crowd as though he were charging into a football scrimmage.

"Who was it called me back to fight? Put up your guns, — or keep them if you like. It's all one to me!"

In the dim light he saw the gleam of a weapon raised before him, reached out and wrenched it away from the owner, and threw it far over his shoulder into the weeds. "Who said a Lorrigan run? I want that man!"

"I said it," bellowed a whisky-flushed man whose face was strange to him. "I said it, and I say it agin. I say — a Lorrigan!"

He lifted his gun above the pressure of excited men and women. Lance sprung upward and forward, landed on some one's foot, lunged again and got a grip on the hand that held the gun. With his left hand he wrenched the gun away. With his right he pulled the man free of the crowd and out where there was room. The crowd — men, now, for the women had fled shrieking — surged that way.

"Stand back there! I'll settle with this fellow alone." He held the other fast, his arms as merciless as the grip of a grizzly, and called aloud:

"This is a Lorrigan dance, and the Lorrigans are going to have order. Those of you who brought chips on your shoulders, and whisky to soak the chips in, can drink your whisky and do your fighting among yourselves, off the Lorrigan ranch. We all came here to have fun. There's music and room to dance, and plenty of chuck and plenty of coffee, and the dance is going right on without any fuss whatever.

"This poor boob here who thinks he wants to fight me just because I'm a Lorrigan, I never saw before. It wouldn't be a fair fight, because he's too drunk to do anything but make a fool of himself. There's nothing to fight about, anyway. A fellow was carrying two cups of boiling hot coffee, and he stubbed his toe, and some one got scalded a little. That's nothing to break up a dance over. The rest of you heard the noise and jumped at the conclusion there was trouble afoot. There isn't. I think you all want to go on with the dance and have a good time, except perhaps a few who are drunk. They are at liberty to go off somewhere and beat each other up to their hearts' content. Come on, now, folks — get your partners for a square dance — and *everybody dance!*"

His voice had held them listening. His words were not the words of a coward, yet they were a plea for peace, they seemed reasonable even to the half-drunken ones who had been the readiest to fight. The old-time range slogan, *"Everybody dance!"* sent three or four hurrying to find the girls they wanted. The trouble, it would appear, had ended as suddenly as it had begun and for a moment the tension relaxed.

The drunken one was still cursing, struggling unavailingly to tear himself away from Lance so that he could land a blow. Lance, looking out across the crowd, caught Belle's glance and nodded toward the schoolhouse. Belle hurried away to find the musicians and set them playing, and a few couples strayed after her. But there were men who stayed, pushing, elbowing to see what would happen when Lance Lorrigan loosened his hold on the Jumpoff man.

Lance did not loosen his hold, however. He saw Tom, Al, three or four Devil's Tooth men edging up, and sent them a warning shake of his head.

"Who knows this fellow? Where does he belong? I think his friends had better take care of him until he sobers up."

"We'll take care of him," said another stranger, easing up to Lance. "He won't hurt yuh; he was only foolin', anyway. Bill Kennedy, he always gits kinda happy when he's had one or two.''

There was laughter in the crowd. Two or three voices were heard muttering together, and other laughs followed. Some one produced a bottle and offered the pugnacious one a drink. Lance let him go with a contemptuous laugh and went to where the Devil's Tooth men now stood bunched close together, their backs to the chuck-wagon.

''We'll have to clean up this crowd, before it's over,'' Al was saying to his father. ''Might as well start right in and git 'er over with.''

''And have it said the Lorrigans can't give a dance without having it end in rough-house!'' Lance interrupted. ''Cut out the idea of fighting that bunch. Keep them out of the house and away from the women, and let them have their booze down in the grove. That's where I've seen a lot of them heading. Come on, boys; it takes just as much nerve not to fight as it does to kill off a dozen men. Isn't that right, dad?''

''More,'' said Tom laconically. ''No, boys, we don't want no trouble here. Come on in and dance. That's yore job — to keep 'er moving peaceable. I'll fire any man I ketch drinking Jumpoff booze. We've got better at the ranch. Come on!''

He led the way and his men followed him, — not as though they were particularly anxious to avoid trouble, but more like men who are trained to

obey implicitly a leader who has some definite purpose and refuses to be turned from it. Lance,
walking a few steps in the rear, wondered at the
discipline his father seemed to maintain without
any apparent effort.

"And they say the Lorrigans are a tough outfit!" he laughed, when he had overtaken Tom.
"Dad, you've got the bunch trained like soldiers.
I was more afraid our boys would rough things up
than I was worried over the stews."

"Shucks! When we rough things up, it's when
we want it rough. Al, he was kinda excited. But
at that, we may have to hogtie a few of them smart
Alecks from town, before we can dance peaceable."

Mary Hope, Lance discovered, was already in
the schoolhouse. Also, several of the intoxicated
were there, and the quadrille was being danced
with so much zest that the whole building shook.
That in itself was not unusual — Black Rim dances
usually did become rather boisterous after supper
— but just outside the door a bottle was being cir-
culated freely, and two or three men had started
toward the cottonwood grove for more. Duke,
coming up to Lance where he stood in the doorway,
pulled him to one side, where they could not be
overheard.

"There's going to be trouble here, sure's you're
knee-high to a duck. Dad won't let our bunch
light into 'em, but they'll be fighting amongst
themselves inside an hour. You better slip it to

the women that the dance breaks up early. Give
'em a few more waltzes and two-steps, Lance, and
then make it Home-Sweet-Home, if you don't
want to muss up your nice city clothes," he added,
with a laugh that was not altogether friendly.

"Mussing up nice city clothes is my favorite
pastime," Lance retorted, and went inside again
to see who was doing all the whooping. The chief
whooper, he discovered, was Bill Kennedy, the
man whom he had very nearly thrashed. Mary
Hope was looking her Scotch primmest. Lance
measured the primness, saw that there was a vacant space beside her, and made his precarious way
toward it, circling the dancers who swung close to
the benches and trod upon the toes of the wall
flowers in their enthusiasm. He reached the vacant space and sat down just in time to receive Bill
Kennedy in his lap. But Bill was too happy just
then to observe whose lap he landed in, and
bounced up with a bellowing laugh to resume his
gyrations.

"Don't dance any more, girl," Lance said, leaning so that he could make himself heard without
shouting in the uproar. "It's getting pretty wild
— and it will be wilder. They must have hauled it
out in barrels!"

Mary Hope looked at him, but she did not smile,
did not answer.

"I'm sorry the secret is no nicer," Lance went
on. "Now the floor will have to be scrubbed

before a lady girl can come out and teach school here. I thought it would be great to have a house-warming dance, — but they're making it too blamed warm!''

Some one slipped and fell, and immediately there was a struggling heap where others had fallen over the first. There were shrieks of laughter and an oath or two, an epithet and then a loud-flung threat.

Lance started up, saw that Tom and Al were heading that way, and took Mary Hope by the arm.

''It's time little girls like you went home,'' he said smiling, and somehow got her to the door without having her trampled upon. ''Where are your wraps?''

''There,'' said Mary Hope dazedly, and pointed to the corner behind them, where cloaks, hoods, hats and two sleeping children were piled indiscriminately.

Through the doorway men were crowding, two or three being pushed out only to be pushed in again by others eager to join the mêlée. In the rear of the room, near the musicians, two men were fighting. Lance, giving one glance to the fight and another to the struggling mass in the doorway, pushed up the window nearest them, lifted Mary Hope and put her out on the side hill. He felt of a coat or two, chose the heaviest, found something soft and furry like a cap, and followed her. Behind the door no one seemed to look.

A solid mass of backs was turned toward him when he wriggled through on his stomach.

"Where's your horse?" he asked Mary Hope, while he slipped the coat on her and buttoned it.

"It does seem to me that a Lorrigan is *always* making me put on a coat!" cried Mary Hope petulantly. "And now, this isn't mine at all!"

"A non-essential detail. It's a coat, and that's all that matters. Where is your horse?"

"I haven't any horse here — oh, they're killing each other in there! The Kennedys brought me — and he's that drunk, now —"

"Good heck! Bill Kennedy! Well, come on. You couldn't go back with them, that's sure. I'll take you home, girl." He was leading her by the arm to the fence behind the house. "Wait, I'll lift a wire; can you crawl under?"

"Now, I've torn it! I heard it rip. And it isn't my coat at all," said Mary Hope. "Oh, they're murdering one another! I should think you'd be ashamed, having a dance like —"

"Coats can be bought — and murdered men don't swear like that. I'll have to borrow Belle's pintos, but we don't care, do we? Come on. Here they are. Don't get in until I get them untied and turned around. And when I say get in, you'd better make it in one jump. Are you game?"

"No Lorrigan will ever cry shame on a Douglas for a coward! You must be crazy, taking this awful team."

"I am. I'm crazy to get you away from here before they start shooting, back there." He spoke to the team gruffly and with a tone of authority that held them quiet, wondering at his audacity perhaps. He untied them, got the lines, stepped in and turned them around, the pintos backing and cramping the buckboard, lunging a little but too surprised to misbehave in their usual form.

"Get in — and hang on. There's no road much — but we'll make it, all right."

Like the pintos, Mary Hope was too astonished to rebel. She got in.

The team went plunging up the hill, snorting now and then, swerving sharply away from rock or bush that threatened them with vague horrors in the clear starlight. Behind them surged the clamor of many voices shouting, the confused scuffling of feet, a revolver shot or two, and threading the whole the shrill, upbraiding voice of a woman.

"That's Mrs. Miller," Mary Hope volunteered jerkily. "She's the one that was scalded."

"It wasn't her tongue that was hurt," Lance observed, and barely saved the buckboard from upsetting on a rock as Rosa and Subrosa shied violently and simultaneously at a rabbit scuttling from a bush before them.

He swung the pintos to the right, jounced down into some sort of trail, and let them go loping along at their usual pace.

"Belle has her own ideas about horse-training," Lance chuckled, steadying Subrosa with a twitch of the rein. "They'll hit this gait all the way to your ranch."

Mary Hope gave a gasp and caught him by the arm, shaking it a little as if she were afraid that otherwise he would not listen to her. "Oh, but I canna go home! I've a horse and my riding clothes in Jumpoff, and I must go for them and come home properly on horse-back to-morrow! It's because of the lie I told my mother, so that I could come to the dance with the Kennedys. Set me down here anywhere, Lance Lorrigan, and let me walk until the Kennedys overtake me! They'll be coming soon, now — as soon as Bill Kennedy gets licket sober. You can stop the horses — surely you can stop them and let me out. But please, *please* do not take me home to-night, in this party dress — and a coat that isna mine at all!"

"I'm not taking you home, girl. I'm taking you to Jumpoff. And it won't matter to you whether Bill Kennedy is licked sober or not. And to-morrow I'll find out who owns the coat. I'll say I found it on the road somewhere. Who's to prove I didn't? Or if you disapprove of lying about it, I'll bring it back and leave it beside the road."

"It's a lot of trouble I'm making for you," said Mary Hope quite meekly, and let go his arm. "I should not have told the lie and gone to the dance.

And I canna wear my own coat home, because it's there in the pile behind the door, and some one else will take it. So after all it will be known that I lied, and you may as well take me home now and let me face it.''

To this Lance made no reply. But when the pintos came rattling down the hill to where the Douglas trail led away to the right, he did not slow them, did not take the turn.

Mary Hope looked anxiously toward home, away beyond the broken skyline. A star hung big and bright on the point of a certain hill that marked the Douglas ranch. While she watched it, the star slid out of sight as if it were going down to warn Hugh Douglas that his daughter had told a lie and had gone to a forbidden place to dance with forbidden people, and was even now driving through the night with one of the Lorrigans, — perchance the wickedest of all the wicked Lorrigans, because he had been away beyond the Rim and had learned the wickedness of the cities.

She looked wistfully at the face of this wickedest of the Lorrigans, his profile seen dimly in the starlight. He did not look wicked. Under his hat brim she could see his brows, heavy and straight and lifted whimsically at the inner points, as though he were thinking of something amusing. His nose was fine and straight, too, — not at all like a beak, though her father had always maintained that the Lorrigans were but human vultures.

His mouth, — there was something in the look of
his mouth that made her catch her breath; something tender, something that vaguely disturbed
her, made her feel that it could be terribly stern
if it were not so tender. He seemed to be smiling
— not with his mouth, exactly, but away inside of
his mind — and the smile showed just a little bit,
at the corner of his lips. His chin was the Lorrigan chin absolutely; a nice chin to look at, with
a little, long dimple down the middle. A chin
that one would not want to oppose, would not want
to see when the man who owned it was very angry.

Mary Hope had gone just so far in her analysis
when Lance turned his head abruptly, unexpectedly, and looked full into her eyes.

"Don't be afraid, girl. Don't worry about the
lie — about anything. It was a sweet little lie —
it makes you just human and young and — sweet.
Let them scold you, and smile, 'way down deep in
your heart, and be glad you're human enough to
tell a lie now and then. Because if you hadn't,
we wouldn't be driving all these miles together to
save you a little of the scolding. Be happy. Be
just a little bit happy to-night, won't you, girl —
you lonely little girl — with the blue, blue eyes!"

There it was again, that vibrant, caressing note
in his voice. It was there in his eyes while he
looked at her, on his lips while he spoke to her.
But the next moment he looked ahead at the trail,
spoke to Rosa who had flung her head around to

bite pettishly at Subrosa, who snapped back at her.

Mary Hope turned her face to the starlit range-land. Again she breathed quickly, fought back tears, fought the feeling that she had been kissed. All through the silent ride that followed she fought the feeling, knew that it was foolish, that Lance knew nothing whatever about that look, that tone which so affected her. He did not speak again. He sat beside her, and she felt that he was think-ing about her, felt that his heart was making love to her — hated herself fiercely for the feeling, fought it and felt it just the same.

"It's just a way he has with him!" she told her-self bitterly, when he swung the team up in front of the section house and helped her down. "He'd have the same way with him if he spoke to a — a rabbit! He doesna mean it — he doesna know and he doesna care!"

"Thank you, Mr. Lorrigan. It was very kind of you to bring me." Her voice was prim and very Scotch, and gave no hint of all she had been thinking.

"I'm always kind — to myself," laughed Lance, and lifted his hat and drove away.

CHAPTER FOURTEEN

IN WHICH LANCE FINISHES ONE JOB

IN the Traffic saloon, whither Lance had gone to find a fire and an easy chair and something cheering to drink while he waited for the pinto team to rest and eat, he found a sleepy bartender sprawled before the stove, a black-and-white dog stretched flat on its side and growling while it dreamed, and an all-pervading odor of alcoholic beverages that appealed to him.

"A highball would make me happy, right now," he announced cheerfully, standing over the bartender, rubbing his fingers numbed from the keen air and from holding in the pintos, to which a slackened pull on the bits meant a tacit consent to a headlong run.

"Been to the dance?" The bartender yawned widely and went to mix the highball. "I been kinda waitin' up — but shucks! No tellin' when the crowd'll git in — not if they drink all they took with 'em."

"They were working hard to do just that when I left." Lance stood back to the stove. Having left in a hurry, without his overcoat, he was chilled to the bone, though the night had been mild for that time of the year. He hoped that the girl had not been uncomfortable — and yawned while the thought held him. He drank his highball, warmed himself comfortably and then, with some one's fur overcoat for a blanket, he disposed his big body on a near-by pool table, never dreaming that Mary Hope Douglas was remembering his tone, his words, his silence even; analyzing, weighing, wondering how much he had meant, or how little, — wondering whether she really hated him, whether she might justly call her ponderings by any name save curiosity. Such is the way of women the world over.

What Lance thought does not greatly matter. Such is the way of men that their thoughts sooner or later crystallize into action. The bartender would tell you that he went straight to sleep, with the fur coat pulled up over his ears and his legs uncovered, his modishly-shod feet extending beyond the end of the table. The bartender dozed in his chair, thinking it not worth while to close up, because the dance crowd might come straying in at any time with much noise and a great thirst, to say nothing of the possibility of thirsty men coming on the midnight freight that was always four or five hours late, and was now much overdue.

The freight arrived. Three men entered the saloon, drank whisky, talked for a few minutes and departed. The bartender took a long, heat-warped poker and attacked the red clinkers in the body of the stove, threw in a bucket of fresh coal, used the poker with good effect on the choked draft beneath, and went back to his chair and his dozing.

During the clamor of the fire-building Lance turned over, drawing up his feet and straightway extending them again; making a sleepy, futile clutch at the fur coat, that had slipped off his shoulders when he turned. The bartender reached out and flung the coat up on Lance's shoulders, and bit off a chew of tobacco and stowed it away in his cheek. Presently he dozed again.

Dawn seeped in through the windows. Lance, lying flat on his stomach with his face on his folded arms, slept soundly. The unpainted buildings across the street became visible in the gloomy, life-less gray of a sunless morning. With the breeze that swept a flurry of gray dust and a torn news-paper down the street, came the rattle of a wagon, the sound of voices mingled in raucous, incoherent wrangling.

"They're comin'," yawned the bartender, glanc-ing at the sleeper on the pool table. "Better wake up; they're comin' pickled and fighty, judgin' by the sound."

Lance sighed, turned his face away from the light and slept on, untroubled by the nearing tu-mult.

Galloping horses came first, *ka-lup, ka-lup, ka-lup,* a sharp staccato on the frosted earth. The rattle of the wagon ceased, resumed, stopped outside the saloon. Other galloping horsemen came up and stopped. The door was flung open violently, letting in men with unfinished sentences hot on their tongues.

"Next time a Lorrigan dance comes off —"

"What I'd a done, woulda —"

"Fix them damn Lorrigans!"

Detached phrases, no one man troubling to find a listener, the words came jumbled to the ears of Lance, who fancied himself in the bunk-house at home, with the boys just in from a ride somewhere. He was wriggling into a freshly uncomfortable posture on the table when the fur coat was pulled off him, letting the daylight suddenly into his eyes as his brain emerged from the fog of sleep.

"And here's the — guy that run away from me!" Bill Kennedy jerked off his hat and brought it down with a slap on Lance's face. "Run off to town, by jiminy, and hid! Run —"

Half asleep as he was — rather, just shocked awake — Lance heaved himself off the table and landed one square blow on Bill Kennedy's purple jaw. Bill staggered, caught himself and came back, arms up and fists guarding his face. Lance disentangled his feet from the fur coat, kicked it out of his way and struck again just as Kennedy was slugging at him.

At the bar the long line of men whirled, glasses in hand, to watch the fight. But it did not last long. Kennedy was drunk, and Lance was not. So presently Kennedy was crawling on his knees amongst some overturned chairs, and Lance was facing the crowd, every inch of him itching to fight.

"Who was it said he was going to fix them damn Lorrigans?" he demanded, coming at them warily. "I'm not packing a gun, but I'd like to lick a few of you fellows that tried to rough-house the dance I gave. Didn't cost you a cent; music, supper, everything furnished for you folks to have a good time — and the way you had it was to wreck the place like the rotten-souled hoodlums you are. Now, who is it wants to fix the damn Lorrigans?"

"Me, for one; what yuh go'n take my girl away from me for?" a flushed youth cried, and flung the dregs of his whisky glass at Lance. There was not more than a half teaspoon in the glass, but the intent was plain enough.

Lance walked up and knocked that young man staggering half across the room, slapped with the flat of his hand another who leered at him, whirled to meet some one who struck him a glancing blow on the ear, and flung him after the first.

"You're all of you drunk — it's a one-sided fight all the way through," he cried, parrying a blow from Kennedy, who had gotten to his feet and came at him again mouthing obscenity. "But I'll lick you, if you insist."

His coat had hampered him until it obligingly slit up the back. He wriggled out of the two halves, tore off his cuffs, and went after the crowd with his bare fists. Some one lifted a chair threateningly, and Lance seized it and sent it crashing through a window. Some one else threw a beer mug, but he ducked in time and broke a knuckle on the front teeth of the thrower. He saw a gap in the teeth, saw the man edge out of the fray spitting blood while he made for the door, and felt that the blow was worth a broken knuckle.

It was not a pretty fight. Such fights never are pretty. Lance himself was not a pretty sight, when he had finished. There had been shooting — but even in Jumpoff one hesitated to shoot down an unarmed man, so that the bar fixtures suffered most. Lance came out of it with a fragment of shirt hanging down his chest like a baby's bib, a cut lip that bled all over his chin, a cheek skinned and swelling rapidly, the bad knuckle and the full flavor of victory.

The saloon looked as though cattle had been driven through it. Bill Kennedy lay sprawled over a card table, whimpering inarticulately because he had lost his gun at the dance. The flushed youth who had rashly claimed Mary Hope as his girl was outside with a washbasin trying to stop his nose from bleeding. Others were ministering to their hurts as best they might, muttering the thoughts that they dared not express aloud.

Lance looked up from examination of his knuckle, caressed his cut lip with the tip of his tongue, pulled the fragment of shirt down as far as possible, gently rubbed his swelling cheek, and turned to the bartender.

"I never licked a man yet and sent him home thirsty," he said. "Set it out for the boys — and give me another highball. Then if you'll lend me a coat and a pair of gloves, I'll go home."

Peace was ratified in whisky drunk solemnly. Lance paid, and turned to go. One of the vanquished wabbled up to him and held out his hand to shake.

"You damn Lorrigans, you got us comin' and goin'," he complained, "but shake, anyway. I'm Irish meself, and I know a rale fight when I see it. What we didn't git at the dance before we left, by heavins you give us when we got into town — so I'm one that's game to say it was a fine dance and not a dull momint anywhere!"

"That's something," Lance grinned wryly and wriggled into the fur overcoat which the bartender generously lent him. He rejected the gloves when he found that his hands were puffed and painful, and went out to find breakfast.

Over a thick white cup of dubious coffee and a plate of sticky hot-cakes he meditated glumly on the general unappreciativeness of the world in general, and of the Black Rim in particular. What had happened at the schoolhouse he could

only surmise, but from certain fragmentary re-
marks he had overheard he guessed that the schoolhouse probably had suffered as much as the saloon.
Black Rim, it would seem, was determined that the
Lorrigans should go on living up to their reputa-
tions, however peacefully inclined the Lorrigans
might be.

Two disquieting thoughts he took with him to
the stable when he went after the pinto team:
Mary Hope would say that it was not a pleasant
surprise which he had given her at Cottonwood
Spring. And Belle, — he was not at all sure
whether he was too big for Belle's quirt to find the
tender places on his legs, but he was very sure
that the Irishman spoke the truth. There would
still be no dull moments for Lance when he con-
fronted the owner of that pinto team.

CHAPTER FIFTEEN

He Tackles Another

MUCH to the disgust of Rosa and Subrosa, their new driver turned them from the main trail just as they were beginning to climb joyously the first grade of Devil's Tooth Ridge. Rosa and Subrosa were subdued, plainly resentful of their subjection, and fretting to be in their own stalls. Belle they could and did bully to a certain extent. They loved to fight things out with Belle, they never missed an opportunity for "acting up"— yet this morning they had been afraid to do more than nag at each other with bared teeth; afraid to lope when this big man said, "Hey — settle down, there!" with a grating kind of calm that carried with it a new and unknown menace.

Some one had exuberantly fired the Whipple shack, and the pintos wanted to whirl short around in their tracks when they saw the smoking embers. They had wanted to bolt straight out across the rocky upland and splinter the doubletree, and per-haps smash a wheel or two, and then stand and

kick gleefully at the wreck. If headshakings and
flattened ears meant anything, Rosa and Subrosa
were two disgruntled pintos that morning. They
had not dared do more than cut a small half-circle
out of the trail when they passed the blackened
spot that had been the Whipple shack.

Now they turned down the rocky, half-formed
trail to Cottonwood Spring, reluctantly but with
no more than a half-hearted kick from Subrosa
to register their disgust. And to that Lance gave
no heed whatever. He did not so much as twitch
a rein or yell a threat. He drove surely — with
one hand mostly because of the broken knuckle,
which was painful in the extreme — ignoring the
pintos for the most part.

He was meditating rather gloomily upon the in-
nate cussedness of human nature as it was de-
veloped in Black Rim Country. He was thinking
of Mary Hope — a little; of her eyes, that were so
obstinately blue, so antagonistically blue, and then,
quite unexpectedly, so wistfully blue; of her voice,
that dropped quite as unexpectedly into pure Scottish melody; of her primness, that sometimes was
not prim at all, but quaintly humorous, or wistfully shy.

He was thinking more often of the dance that
had started out so well and had ended — Lord
knew how, except that it ended in a fight. He remembered striking, in that saloon, faces that had
been pummeled before ever he sent a jab their way.

There had been eyes already closed behind purple, puffy curtains of bruised flesh. He had fought animosity that was none of his creating.

Thinking of the fight, he thought of the wrecked saloon when the fight was over. Thinking of the wrecked saloon led him to think of the probable condition of the nice new schoolhouse. Thinking of that brought him back to Mary Hope, — to her face as it looked when she rode up to the place on Monday morning. Ride up to it she must, if she meant to go on teaching, for there was no more Whipple shack.

"Rotten bunch of rough-necks," he summed up the men of Black Rim and of Jumpoff. "And they'll blame the Devil's Tooth outfit — they'll say the Lorrigans did it. Oh, well — heck!"

So he drove down into the hollow, tied the pintos to the post where they stood the night before, crawled through the wire fence where Mary Hope had left a small three-cornered fragment of the coat that "wasna" hers at all, and went over to the schoolhouse, standing forlorn in the trampled yard with broken sandwiches and bits of orange peel and empty whisky flasks accentuating the unsightliness and disorder.

The door swung half open. The floor was scored, grimy with dirt tracked in on heedless feet and ground into the wax that had been liberally scattered over it to make the boards smooth for dancing. A window was broken, — by some one's elbow or by a pistol shot, Lance guessed. The planks placed along the wall on boxes to form seats were pulled askew, the stovepipe had been knocked down and lay disjointed and battered in a corner. It was not, in Lance's opinion, a pleasant little surprise for the girl with the Scotch blue eyes.

He pulled the door shut, picked up the empty whisky flasks and threw them, one after the other, as far as he could send them into a rocky gulch where Mary Hope would not be likely to go. Then he recrossed the enclosure, crawled through the fence, untied the pintos and drove home.

The bunk house emanated a pronounced odor of whisky and bad air, and much snoring, just as Lance expected. The horses dozed in the corral or tossed listlessly their trampled hay; the house was quiet, deserted looking, with the doors all closed and the blinds down in the windows of the room that had been the birthplace of Belle's three boys.

Lance knew that every one would be asleep to-day. The Devil's Tooth ranch had always slept through the day after a dance, with certain yawning intermissions at mealtimes.

He unhitched the pintos, turned them loose in the corral, caught his own horse, which one of the boys must have led home, and tied it to a post. From the chuck-wagon, standing just where Riley had driven it to a vacant spot beside the woodpile, Lance purloined a can of pork and beans, a loaf of bread, and some butter. These things he put in a bag.

For a minute he stood scowling at the silent house, undecided, wondering just how soundly Belle was sleeping. He was not afraid of Belle; no real Lorrigan was ever afraid of anything, as fear is usually defined. But he wanted to postpone for a time her reckoning with him. He wanted to face her when he had a free mind, when she had slept well, when her temper was not so edgy. He wanted other things, however, and he proceeded to get those things with the least effort and delay.

He wanted soft cloths. On the clothesline dangled three undershirts, three pair of drawers and several mismated socks. The shirts and drawers were of the kind known as fleece-lined — which means that they are fuzzy on the inside. They were Riley's complete wardrobe so far as underwear went, but Lance did not trouble himself with unimportant details. He took them all, because he had a swift mental picture of the schoolhouse floor which would need much scrubbing before it would be clean.

He was ready to mount and ride away when he remembered something else that he would need. "Lye!" he muttered, and retraced his steps to the house. Now he must go into the kitchen shed for what he wanted, and Riley slept in a little room next the shed. But Riley was snoring with

a perfect rhythm that bespoke a body sunk deep
in slumber, so Lance searched until he found what
he wanted, and added a full box of a much-adver-
tised washing powder for good measure. He was
fairly well burdened when he finally started up the
trail again, but he believed that he had everything
that he would need, even a lump of putty, and a
pane of glass which he had carefully removed from
a window of the chicken house, and which he hoped
would fit.

You may think that he rode gladly upon his errand; that the thought of Mary Hope turned the
work before him into a labor of love. It did not.
Lance Lorrigan was the glummest young man in
the whole Black Rim, and there was much glumness amongst the Rim folk that day, let me tell you.
He ached from fighting, from dancing, from sleeping on the pool table, from hanging for hours to
those darned pintos. His left hand was swollen,
and pains from the knuckle streaked like hot
wires to his elbow and beyond. His lips were sore
— so sore he could not even swear with any comfort — and even the pulling together of his black
eyebrows hurt his puffed cheek. And he never
had scrubbed a floor in his life, and knew that he
was going to hate the work even worse than he
hated the men who had made the scrubbing necessary.

While he went up the Slide trail he wished that
he had never thought of giving a dance. He

wished he had gone down to Los Angeles for his Easter holiday, as one of his pals had implored him to do. He wished Mary Hope would quit teaching school; what did she want to stay in the Black Rim for, anyway? Why didn't she get out where she could amount to something?

If there were any caressing cadences in the voice of Lance Lorrigan, any provocative tilt to his eyebrows, any tenderness in his smile, anything enigmatical in his personality, none of these things were apparent when he set the first bucket of water on the stove to heat. He had added to his charms a broad streak of soot across his forehead and a scratch on his neck, acquired while putting up the stovepipe. He had set his lip to bleeding because he forgot that it was cut, and drew it sharply between his teeth when the stovepipe fell apart just when he was sure it was up to stay. He had invented two new cuss-words. What he had not done was weaken in his determination to make that small schoolhouse a pleasant surprise for Mary Hope.

He did the work thoroughly, though a woman might have pointed out wet corners and certain muddy splashes on the wall. He lost all count of the buckets of water that he carried from the spring, and it occurred to him that Mary Hope would need a new broom, for the one Belle had provided was worn down to a one-sided wisp that reminded him of the beard of a billy goat. He used two cans of condensed lye and all of the washing powder, and sneezed himself too weak too swear over the fine cloud of acrid dust that filled his nostrils when he sprinkled the powder on the floor. But the floor was clean when he finished, and so was the platform outside.

Of Riley's underwear there was left the leg of one pair of drawers, which Lance reserved for dusting the desks and the globe that had by some miracle escaped. While the floor was drying he took out the broken windowpane, discovered that the one from the chicken house was too short, and cut his thumb while he chipped off a piece of glass from the other to fill the space. He did not make a very good job of it. To hold the glass in place, he used shingle nails, which he had to hunt for on the ground where they had dropped from the roof during shingling, and when they had been driven into the frame — with the handle of the screwdriver — they showed very plainly from the inside. Then the putty did not seem to want to stick anywhere, but kept crumbling off in little lumps. So Lance threw the putty at a gopher that was standing up nibbling one of Riley's sandwiches, and went after the desks.

These took some time to unwrap and carry into place. There were only twelve, but Lance would have sworn before a jury that he carried at least fifty single desks into the schoolhouse that afternoon, and screwed them to the floor, and unscrewed

them because the darned things did not line up
straight when viewed from the teacher's desk,
and he had a vivid impression that blue, blue eyes
can be very critical over such things as a crooked
line of desks!

Perhaps it was because his head ached splittingly and his injured hand throbbed until it was
practically useless; at any rate the cleaning of the
schoolhouse, especially the placing of the desks,
became fixed afterward in his memory as the biggest, the most disagreeable incident in his whole
vacation.

At four-thirty however the task was accom-
plished. At the spring, Lance scrubbed the water
bucket clean, washed the dipper, placed them behind the door. He got wearily into the borrowed
fur coat, took a last comprehensive survey of the
room from the doorway, went back to erase certain sentences scrawled on the blackboard by some
would-be humorist, took another look at the work
of his aching hands, and went away with the coffee-
pot in his hand and the screwdriver showing its
battered wooden handle from the top of his pocket.
He was too tired to feel any glow of accomplish-
ment, any great joy in the thought of Mary Hope's
pleasure. He was not even sure that she would
feel any pleasure.

His chief emotion was a gloomy satisfaction in
knowing that the place was once more presentable,
that it was ready for Mary Hope to hang up her

hat and ring her little bell and start right in teaching. That what the Lorrigans had set out to do,
the Lorrigans had done.

At the ranch he found Riley at the bunk house
wrangling with the boys over his lost wardrobe.
In Riley's opinion it was a darned poor idea of a
darned poor joke, and it took a darned poor man
to perpetrate it. Lance's arrival scarcely interrupted the jangle of voices. The boys had bruises
of their own to nurse, and they had scant sympathy for Riley, and they told him so.

Lance went into the house. He supposed he would
have to replace Riley's clothes, which he did, very
matter-of-factly and without any comment whatever, restitution being in this case a mere matter
of sorting out three suits of his own underwear,
which were much better than Riley's, and placing
them on the cook's bed.

"That you, Lance? Where in the world have
you been all this while? I came mighty near going
gunning after the man that stole my team, let me
tell you — and I would have, if Tom hadn't found
your horse tied up to the fence and guessed you'd
gone to take Mary Hope home. But I must say,
honey, you never followed any short cut!"

This was much easier than Lance had expected,
so he made shift to laugh, though it hurt his lip
cruelly. "Had to take her to Jumpoff, Belle.
Then I had to clean up that crowd of toughs
that —"

"You cleaned up Tom's leavin's, then!" Belle made grim comment through Lance's closed door. "I didn't think there was enough left of 'em to lick, by the time our boys got through. Haven't you been to bed yet, for heaven's sake?"

"I'm going to bed," mumbled Lance, "when I've had a bath and a meal. And to-morrow, Belle, I think I'll hit the trail for 'Frisco. Hope you don't mind if I leave a few days early. I've got to stop off anyway to see a fellow in Reno I promised — any hot water handy?"

There was a perceptible pause before Belle answered, and then it was not about the bath water. She would not have been Belle Lorrigan if she had permitted a quiver in her voice, yet it made Lance thoughtful.

"Honey, I don't blame you for going. I expect we are awful rough — and you'd notice it, coming from civilized folks. But — you know, don't you, that the Lorrigans never spoiled your party for you? It — it just happened that the Jumpoff crowd brought whisky out from town. We *tried* to make it pleasant — and it won't happen again —"

"Bless your heart!" Clad with superb simplicity in a bathrobe, Lance appeared unexpectedly and gathered her into his arms. "If you think I'm getting so darn civilized I can't stay at home, take a look at me! By heck, Belle, I'll bet there isn't a man in the whole Black Rim that got as much fun out of that scrap as I did! But I've got to go.'' He patted her reassuringly on the head, laid his good cheek against hers for a minute and turned abruptly away into his own room. He closed the door and stood absent-mindedly feeling his swollen hand. "I've got to go," he repeated under his breath. "I might get foolish if I stayed. Darned if I'll make a fool of myself over any girl!"

CHAPTER SIXTEEN

ABOUT A PIANO

IN the lazy hour just after a satisfying dinner, Lance stood leaning over an end of the piano, watching Belle while she played — he listened and smoked a cigarette and looked as though he hadn't a thing on his mind.

"I remember you used to sing that a lot for the little Douglas girl," he observed idly. "She used to sit and look at you — my word, but her eyes were the bluest, the lonesomest eyes I ever saw! She seemed to think you were next to angels when you sang. I saw it in her face, but I was too much of a kid then to know what it was." He lighted a fresh cigarette, placed it between Belle's lips so that she need not stop playing while she smoked, and laughed as if he were remembering something funny.

"She always looked so horrified when she saw you smoking," he said. "And so adoring when you sang, and so lonesome when she had to ride away. She was a queer kid — and she's just as unexpected now — just as Scotch. Didn't you find her that way, dad?"

"She was Scotch enough," Tom mumbled from

his chair by the fire. "Humpin' hyenas! She was like handlin' a wildcat!"

"The poor kid never did have a chance to be human," said Belle, and ceased playing for a moment. "Good heavens, how she did enjoy the two hours I gave her at the piano! She's got the makings of a musician, if she could keep at it."

"We-ell—" Having artfully led Belle to this point, Lance quite as artfully edged away from it. "You gave her all the chance you could. And she ought to be able to go on, if she wants to. I suppose old Scotty's human enough to get her something to play on."

"Him? *Human!*" Tom shifted in his chair. "If pianos could breed and increase into a herd, and he could ship a carload every fall, Scotty might spend a few dollars on one."

"It's a darned shame," Belle exclaimed, dropping her fingers to the keys again. "Mary Hope just *starves* for everything that makes life worth living. And that old devil—"

"Say—don't make me feel like a great, overgrown money-hog," Lance protested. "A girl starving for music, because she hasn't a piano to play on. And a piano costs, say, three or four hundred dollars. Of course, we've got the money to buy one—I suppose I could dig up the price myself. I was thinking I'd stake our schoolhouse to a library. That's something it really needs. But a piano—I wish you hadn't said anything about starving. I know I'd hate to go hungry for music, but —''

"Well, humpin' hyenas! I'll buy the girl a piano. I guess it won't break the outfit to pay out a few more dollars, now we've started. We're outlaws, anyway — might as well add one more crime to the list. Only, it don't go to the Douglas shack — it goes into the schoolhouse. Lance, you go ahead and pick out some books and ship 'em on to the ranch, and I'll see they get over there. Long as we've started fixin' up a school, we may as well finish the job up right. By Henry, I'll show the Black Rim that there ain't anything small about the Lorrigans, anyway!''

"Dad, I think you're showin' yourself a real sport,'' Lance laughed. "We-ell, if you're game to buy a piano, I'm game to buy books. We staked Black Rim to a school, so we'll do the job right. And by the way, Belle, if you're going to get me to Jumpoff in time for that evening train, don't you think it's about time you started?''

That is how it happened that Mary Hope walked into the schoolhouse one Monday and found a very shiny new piano standing across one corner of the room where the light was best. On the top was a pile of music. In another corner of the room stood a bookcase and fifty volumes; she counted them in her prim, frugal way that she had learned from her mother. They were books evidently approved by some Board of Education for school libraries, and did not interest her very much.   Not when a piano stood in the other corner.

She was early, so she opened it and ran her fingers over the keys. She knew well enough who had brought it there, and her mouth was pressed into a straight line, her eyes were troubled.

The Lorrigans — always the Lorrigans! Why did they do these things when no one expected goodness or generosity from them? Why had they built the schoolhouse — and then given a dance where every one got drunk and the whole thing ended in a fight?   Every one said it was the Lorrigans who had brought the whisky.   Some one told her they had a five-gallon keg of it in the shed behind the schoolhouse, and she thought it must be true, the way all the men had acted.   And why had they burned the Whipple shack and all the school books, so that she could not have school until more books were bought? — an expense which the Swedes, at least, could ill afford.

Why had Lance taken her to Jumpoff, away from the fighting, and then gone straight to the saloon and gotten so drunk that he fought every one in town before he left in the morning? Why had he never come near her again?   And now that he was back in California, why did he ignore her completely, and never send so much as a picture postal to show that he gave her a thought now and then?

Mary Hope would not play the piano that day. She was more stern than usual with her pupils, and would not so much as answer them when they asked her where the piano and all the books had come from. Which was a foolish thing to do, since the four Boyle children were keen enough to guess, and sure to carry the news home, and to embellish the truth in true range-gossip style.

Mary Hope fully decided that she would have the piano hauled back to the Lorrigans. Later, she was distressed because she could think of no one who would take the time or the trouble to perform the duty, and a piano she had to admit is not a thing you can tie behind the cantle of your saddle, or carry under your arm. The books were a different matter. They were for the school. But the piano — well, the piano was for Mary Hope Douglas, and Mary Hope Douglas did not mean to be patronized in this manner by Lance Lorrigan or any of his kin.

But she was a music-hungry little soul, and that night after she was sure that the children had ridden up over the basin's brim and were out of hearing, Mary Hope sat down and began to play. When she began to play she began to cry, though she was hardly conscious of her tears. She seemed to hear Lance Lorrigan again, saying, "Don't be lonely, you girl. Take the little pleasant things that come —" She wondered, in a whispery, heart-achey way, if he had meant the piano when he said that. If he had meant — just a piano, and a lot of books for school!

The next thing that she realized was that the
light was growing dim, and that her throat was
aching, and that she was playing over and over a
lovesong that had the refrain:

" Come back to me, sweetheart, and love me as before —
  Come back to me, sweetheart, and leave me nevermore! "

Which was perfectly imbecile, a song she had always hated because of its sickly sentimentality.
She had no sweetheart, and having none, she certainly did not want him back. But she admitted
that there was a certain melodious swing to the
tune, and that her fingers had probably strayed
into the rhythm of it while she was thinking of
something totally different.

The next day she played a little at noontime for
the children, and when school was over she played
for two hours. And the next day after that
slipped away — she really had meant to ride over to
the AJ, or send a note by the children, asking Jim
Boyle if he could please remove the piano and saying that she felt it was too expensive a gift for
the school to accept from the Lorrigans.

On the third day she really did send a prim little
note to Jim Boyle, and she received a laconic reply,
wholly characteristic of the Black Rim's attitude
toward the Devil's Tooth outfit.

" Take all you can git and git all you can without going
to jale. That's what the Lorrigans are doing, Yrs truly,
                                        " J. A. Boyle."

It was useless to ask her father. She had known that all along. When Alexander Douglas slipped the collars up on the necks of his horses, he must see where money would be gained from the labor. And there was no money for the Douglas pocket in hauling a piano down the Devil's Tooth Ridge.

But the whole Black Rim was talking about it. Mary Hope felt sure that they were saying ill-natured things behind her back. Never did she meet man or woman but the piano was mentioned. Sometimes she was asked, with meaning smiles, how she had come to stand in so well with the Devil's Tooth. She knew that they were all gossiping of how Lance Lorrigan had taken her home from the dance, with Belle Lorrigan's bronco team. She had been obliged to return a torn coat to Mrs. Miller, and to receive her own and a long lecture on the wisdom of choosing one's company with some care. She had been obliged to beg Mrs. Miller not to mention the matter to her parents, and the word had gone round, and had reached Mother Douglas — and you can imagine how pleasant that made home for Mary Hope.

Because she was lonely, and no one seemed willing to take it away, she kept the piano. She played it, and while she played she wept because the Rim folk simply would not understand how little she wanted the Lorrigans to do things for her. And then, one day, she hit upon a plan of redeeming herself, for regaining the self-respect

she felt was slipping from her with every day that
the piano stood in the schoolhouse.

She would give a series of dances — they would
be orderly, well-behaved dances, with no refreshments stronger than coffee and lemonade! — and
she would sell tickets, and invite every one she
knew, and beg them to come and help to pay for the
school piano.

Even her mother approved that plan, though she
did not approve dances. "But the folk are that
sinfu' they canna bide wi' any pleasure save the
hoppin' aboot wi' their arms around the waist
of a woman," she sighed. "A church social wad
be far more tae my liking, Hope — if we had only
a church!"

"Well, since there isn't any church, and people
won't go to anything but a dance, I shall have to
get the money with dances," Mary Hope replied
with some asperity. The subject was beginning
to wear her nerves. "Pay for it I shall, if it takes
all my teacher's salary for five years! I wish the
Lorrigans had minded their own business. I've
heard nothing but piano ever since it came there.
I hate the Lorrigans! Sometimes I almost hate
the piano."

"Ye shud hae thought on all that before ye ac-
cepit a ride home wi' young Lance, wi' a coat ye
didna own on your back, and disobedience in your
heart. 'Tis the worst of them a' ye chose to escort ye, Hope, and if he thought he could safely

presume to gi' ye a present like yon piano, ye hae but yersel' tae blame for it.''

"He didn't give it!" cried Mary Hope, her eyes ablaze with resentment. "He wasna here when it came. I havena heard from him and I dinna want to hear from him. It was Belle Lorrigan gave the piano, as I've said a million times. And I shall pay for it —"

"Not from your ain pocket will ye pay. Ye can give the dance — and if ye make it the Fourth of July, with a picnic in the grove, and a dance in the schoolhouse afterwards, 'tis possible Jeanie may come up from Pocatello wi' friends — and twa dollars wad no be too much to ask for a day and a night of entertainment.''

"Well, mother! When you do —" Mary Hope bit her tongue upon the remainder of the sentence. She had very nearly told her mother that when she did choose to be human she had a great head for business.

It was a fine, practical idea, and Mary Hope went energetically about its development. She consulted Mrs. Kennedy. Mrs. Kennedy also had friends in Pocatello, and she obligingly gave the names of them all. She strongly advised written invitations, with a ticket enclosed and the price marked plainly. She said it was a crying shame the way the Lorrigans had conducted their dance, and that Mary Hope ought to be very careful and not include any of that rough bunch in this dance.

"Look how that young devil, Lance Lorrigan, abused my Bill, right before everybody!" she cited, shifting her youngest child, who was teething, to her hip that she might gesticulate more freely. "And look how they all piled into our crowd and beat 'em up! Great way to do — give a dance and then beat up the folks that come to it! And look at what Lance done right here in town — as if it wasn't enough, what they done out there! Bill's got a crick in his back yet, where Lance knocked him over the edge of a card table. You pay 'em for the piano, Hope; I'll help yuh scare up a crowd. But don't you have none of the Lorrigans, or there'll be trouble sure!"

Mary Hope flushed. "I could hardly ask the Lorrigans to come and help pay for their own present," she pointed out in her prim tone. "I had never intended to ask the Lorrigans."

"Well, maybe not. But if you did ask them, I know lots of folks that wouldn't go a step — and my Bill's one," said Mrs. Kennedy.

So much depends upon one's point of view. Black Rim gossip, which persisted in linking Mary Hope's name with Lance Lorrigan, grinned among themselves while they mentioned the piano, the schoolhouse, and the library as evidence of Lance's being "stuck on her." The Boyle children had frequently tattled to Mary Hope what they heard at home. Lance had done it all because he was in love with her.

Denial did not mend matters, even if Mary Hope's pride had not rebelled against protesting that the gossip was not true. Lance Lorrigan was not in love with her. Over and over she told herself so, fiercely and with much attention to evidence which she considered convincing. Only twice she had seen him in the two weeks of his visit. Once he had come to mend the lock his father had broken, and he had taken her home from the dance because of the fighting. Never had he made love to her. . . . Here she would draw a long breath and wonder a little, and afterwards shake her head and say to herself that he thought no more of her than of Jennie Miller. He — he just had a way with him.

Mary Hope's point of view was, I think, justifiable. Leaving out the intolerable implication that Lance had showered benefits upon her, she felt that the Lorrigans had been over-generous. The schoolhouse and the books might be accepted as a public-spirited effort to do their part. But the piano, since it had not been returned, must be paid for. And it seemed to Mary Hope that the Lorrigans themselves would deeply resent being invited to a dance openly given for the purpose of raising money to repay them. It would never do; she could not ask them to come.

Moreover, if the Lorrigans came there would be trouble, whether there was whisky or not. At the house-warming dance the Lorrigans had practi-

cally cleaned out the crowd and sent them home
long before daylight. There had been no serious
shooting — the Lorrigans had fought with their
fists and had somehow held the crowd back from
the danger-line of gun-play. But Mary Hope
feared there would be a killing the next time that
the Jumpoff crowd and the Lorrigans came together.

She tried to be just, but she had heard only one
side of the affair, — which was not the Lorrigan
side. Whispers had long been going round among
the Black Rim folk; sinister whispers that had to
do with cattle and horses that had disappeared
mysteriously from the Rim range. Mary Hope
could not help hearing the whispers, could not help
wondering if underneath them there was a basis of
truth. Her father still believed, in spite of Tom's
exoneration, that his spotty yearling had gone
down the gullets of Devil's Tooth men. She did
not know, but it seemed to her that where every one
hinted at the same thing, there must be some truth
in their hints.

All of which proves, I think, that Mary Hope's
point of view was the only one that she could logically hold, living as she did in the camp of the enemy; having, as she had, a delicate sense of propri-
ety, and wanting above all things to do nothing
crude and common. As she saw it, she simply
could *not* ask any of the Lorrigans to her picnic
and dance on the Fourth of July.

CHAPTER SEVENTEEN

THE LORRIGAN VIEWPOINT

I HAVE said that much depends upon one's point of view. Mary Hope's viewpoint was not shared by the Devil's Tooth. They had one of their own, and to them it seemed perfectly logical, absolutely justifiable.

They heard all about the Fourth of July picnic and dance, to be held at Cottonwood Spring and in the schoolhouse of their own building. Immediately they remembered that Cottonwood Spring was on Lorrigan land, that Lorrigan money had paid for the material that went into the schoolhouse, that Lorrigan labor had built it, Lorrigan generosity had given it over to the public as represented by Mary Hope Douglas and the children who came to her to be taught. In their minds loomed the fact that Lorrigan money had bought books for the school, and that Tom Lorrigan himself had paid close to four hundred dollars for the piano.

They heard that invitations were being sent broadcast, that a crowd was coming from Pocatello, from Lava, from Jumpoff —invited to come and spend a day and night in merry-making. Yet no invitation came to the Devil's Tooth ranch, not a word was said to them by Mary Hope, not a hint that they were expected, or would be welcome.

Belle met Mary Hope in the trail one day, just a week before the Fourth. Mary Hope was riding home from school; Belle was driving out from Jumpoff. It is the custom of the outland places for acquaintances to stop for a bit of friendly conversation when they meet, since meetings are so far between. But, though Belle slowed the pintos to a walk, Mary Hope only nodded, said, "How do you do," and rode on.

"She looked guilty," Belle reported wrathfully to Tom and the boys at the supper table. "Guilty as sin. She seemed to be afraid I was going to ask her if I couldn't come to her dance. The little fool! Does she think for a minute I'd *go?* She hasn't so much as thanked you for that piano, Tom. She hasn't said one word."

"Well, I didn't put my name and *ad*-dress on it," Tom palliated the ingratitude, while he buttered a hot biscuit generously. "And there wasn't any name on the books to show who bought 'em. Maybe she thinks —"

"I don't care what she thinks! It's the way she acts that counts. Everybody in Jumpoff has got invitations to her picnic and dance. They say it's to pay us for the piano — and they think she's do-

ing some wonderful stunt. And we're left out in
the cold!"

"We never was in where it was right warm,
since I can remember," said Al. "Except when
we made it warm ourselves."

"Sam Pretty Cow was saying yesterday — "
and Duke repeated a bit of gossip that had a gibe at
the Lorrigans for its point. "He got it over to
Hitchcocks. It come from the Douglases. I guess
Mary Hope don't want nothing of us — except
what she can get out of us. We been a good thing,
all right — easy marks."

Duke had done the least for her and therefore
felt qualified to say the most. His last sentence
did its work. Tom pulled his eyebrows together,
drew his lip between his teeth and leaned back in
his chair, thinking deeply, his eyes glittering between his half-closed lids.

"Easy marks, ay?" he snorted. "The Lorrigans have been called plenty of things, fur back
as I can remember, but by the humpin' hyenas,
they never was called easy marks before!"

That was Tom's last comment on the subject.
Belle, not liking the look on his face, because she
knew quite well what it portended, passed him two
kinds of preserves and changed the subject. Al
and Duke presently left for the bunk house. Mary
Hope's party and her evident intention to slight
the Lorrigans was not mentioned again for days.

But Tom's wrath was smoldering. He was not

hasty. He waited. He himself met Mary Hope in the trail one day, lifted his hat to her without a word and rode on. Mary Hope let him go with a chilly nod and a murmured greeting which was no more than an empty form. Certainly she did not read Tom's mind, did not dream that he was thinking of the piano, — and from an angle that had never once presented itself to her.

So, now that you see how both were justified in their opinions, as formed from different points of view, let me tell you what happened.

Mary Hope had her picnic, with never a thunderstorm to mar the day. Which is unusual, since a picnic nearly always gets itself rained upon. She had sent out more than a hundred invitations — tickets two dollars, please — and there were more who invited themselves and had to be supplied with tickets cut hastily out of pasteboard boxes that had held sandwiches.

Mary Hope was jubilant. Mother Douglas, as official hostess, moved here and there among the women who fussed over the baskets and placated with broken pieces of cake their persistent offspring. Mother Douglas actually smiled, though her face plainly showed that it was quite unaccustomed to the expression, and tilted the smile downward at the corners. Mother Douglas was a good woman, but she had had little in her life to bring smiles, and her habitual expression was one of mournful endurance.

It was sultry, and toward evening the mosquitoes swarmed out of the lush grass around the
spring and set the horses stamping and moving
about uneasily. But it was a very successful picnic, with all the chatter, all the gourmandizing, all
the gossip, all the childish romping in starched
white frocks, all the innocuous pastimes that one
expects to find at picnics.

Mary Hope wondered how in the world they
were all going to find room inside the schoolhouse
to dance. She had been frugal in the matter of
music, dreading to spend any money in hiring pro-
fessional musicians, lest she might not have enough
people to justify the expense. Now she wished
nervously that she had done as Lance Lorrigan had
done, and brought musicians from Lava. Of
course, there had been no piano when Lance gave
his party, which was different. She herself meant
to play, and Art Miller had brought his fiddle, and
Jennie had volunteered to "chord" with him.
But, Mary Hope felt much nervous apprehension
lest these Pocatello and Lava people should think
it was just Scotch stinginess on her part.

Late in the afternoon a few of the ranchers rode
hastily homeward to "do the chores", but the Lava
and Pocatello crowd remained, and began to drift
up to the schoolhouse and drum on the piano that
was actually going to pay for itself and free Mary
Hope's pride from its burden.

By sundown a dozen energetic couples were

waltzing while a Pocatello dentist with a stiff, sandy pompadour chewed gum and played loudly, with much arm movement and very little rhythm; so very little rhythm that the shuffling feet frequently ceased shuffling, and expostulations rose high above his thunderous chords.

By dusk the overworked ranch women had fed the last hungry mouth and put away the fragments of home-baked cakes and thick sandwiches, and were forming a solid line of light shirtwaists and dark skirts along the wall. The dance was really beginning.

As before, groups of men stood around outside and smoked and slapped at mosquitoes — except that at Lance's party there had been no mosquitoes to slap — and talked in undertones the gossip of the ranges. If now and then the name of Lorrigan was mentioned, there was no Lorrigan present to hear. At intervals the "floor manager" would come to the door and call out numbers: "Number one, and up to and including sixteen, git your pardners fer a two-step!" Whereupon certain men would pinch out the glow of their cigarettes and grind the stubs into the sod under their heels, and go in to find partners. With that crowd, not all could dance at once; Mary Hope remembered pridefully that there had been no dancing by numbers at the party Lance Lorrigan gave.

What a terrible dance that had been! A regular rowdy affair. And this crowd, big as it was, had as yet shown no disposition to rowdyism. It surely did make a difference, thought Mary Hope, what kind of people sponsored an entertainment. With the Devil's Tooth outfit as the leaders, who could expect anything but trouble?

Then she caught herself thinking, with a vague heaviness in her heart, how Lance had taken her away from that other dance; of that long, wonderful, silent ride through the starlight; how careful he had been of her — how tender! But it was only the way he had with him, she later reminded herself impatiently, and smiled over her shoulder at the whirling couples who danced to the music she made; and thought of the money that made her purse heavy as lead, the money that would wipe out her debt to the Lorrigans, — to Lance, if it really were Lance who had bought the piano.

A faint sound came to her through the open window, the rattle of a wagon coming down the hill in the dark. More people were coming to the dance, which meant more money to give to the Lorrigans. Mary Hope smiled again and played faster; so fast that more than one young man shook his head at her as he circled past, and puffed ostentatiously, laughing at the pace she set. She had a wild vision of other dances which she would give — Labor Day, Thanksgiving, Christmas, New Year's — and pay the Lorrigans for everything they had done; for the books, for the schoolhouse, everything. She felt that then, and then only, could she face Lance Lorrigan level-eyed, cool, calm, feeling herself a match for him.

The rattle of the wagon sounded nearer, circled the yard, came in at the gate. Mary Hope was giving the dancers the fastest two-step she could play, and she laughed aloud. More people were coming to the dance, and there might not be coffee and sandwiches enough at midnight, — she had over three hundred dollars already.

The dancers whirled past, parted to right and left, stopped all at once. Mary Hope, still playing, looked over her shoulder — into the dark, impenetrable gaze of Tom Lorrigan, standing there in his working clothes, with his big, black Stetson on his head and his six-shooter in its holster on his hip. Behind him Mary Hope saw Al and Duke and Belle, and behind them other Devil's Tooth men, cowboys whom she only knew slightly from meeting them sometimes in the trail as she rode to and from school. The cowboys seemed to be facing the other way, holding back the crowd near the door.

Mary Hope looked again into Tom's face, looked at Belle. Her fingers strayed uncertainly over the keys, making discords. She half rose, then sat down again. The room, all at once, seemed very still.

"I'm sorry to disturb yuh," Tom said, touching his hat brim and lifting his eyebrows at her, half smiling with his lips pulled to one side, like Lance

—oh, maddeningly like Lance!—"but I've come after the piano."

Mary Hope gasped. Her arms went out instinctively across the keyboard, as if she would protect the instrument from his defaming touch.

"I'll have to ask yuh to move," said Tom. "Sorry to disturb yuh."

"I — I'm going to pay for it," said Mary Hope, finding her voice faint and husky. She had an odd sensation that this was a nightmare. She had dreamed so often of the dance and of the Lorrigans.

"I paid for it long ago. I bought the piano — I've come after it."

Mary Hope slid off the stool, stood facing him, her eyes very blue. After all, he was not Lance. "You can't have it!" she said. "I won't let you take it. I'm raising money to pay you for it, and I intend to keep it." She reached for her purse, but Tom restrained her with a gesture.

"It ain't for sale," he said, with that hateful smile that always made her wonder just what lay behind it. "I own it, and I ain't thinking of selling. Here's the shipping bill and the guarantee and all; I brought 'em along to show you, in case you got curious about whose piano it is. You see the number on the bill — 86945. You'll find it tallies with the number in the case, if you want to look. Pete, Ed, John, take it and load it in the wagon."

"Well, now, see here! This is an outrage!

How much is the darn thing worth, anyway? This crowd is not going to stand by and see a raw deal like this pulled off." It was the Pocatello dentist, and he was very much excited.

"You saw a raw deal, and stood for it, when you saw the Lorrigans cold-shouldered out of the dance," Belle flashed at him. "We've stood for a lot, but this went a little beyond our limit."

"We're not going to stand for anything like this, you know!" Another man — also from Lava — shouldered his way up to them.

"Git outa the way, or you'll git tromped on!" cried Pete over his shoulder as he backed, embracing the piano and groping for handholds.

The Lava man gripped Pete, trying to pull him away. Pete kicked back viciously with a spurred heel. The Lava man yelled and retreated, limping.

Just how it happened, no two men or women afterward agreed in the telling. But somehow the merrymakers, who were merry no longer, went back and back until they were packed solidly at the sides and near the door, a few squeezing through it when they were lucky enough to find room. Behind them came four of the Devil's Tooth men with six-shooters, looking the crowd coldly in the eyes. Behind these came the piano, propelled by those whom Tom had named with the tone of authority.

The crowd squeezed closer against the wall as the piano went past them. There was not so much noise and confusion as one would expect. Then, at the last, slim, overworked, round-shouldered Mother Douglas, who had done little save pray and weep and work and scold all her life, walked up and slapped Belle full on the cheek.

"Ye painted Jezebel!" she cried, her eyes burning. "Long have I wanted to smack ye for your wickedness and the brazen ways of ye — ye painted Jezebel!"

Blind, dazed with anger, Belle struck back.

"Don't you touch my mother! Shame on you! Shame on you all! I didna ask you for your favors, for any gifts — and you gave them and then you come and take them —" This was the voice of Mary Hope, shrill with rage.

"You gave a dance in a house built for you by the Lorrigans, on Lorrigan land, and you danced to the music of a Lorrigan piano — and the Lorrigans were not good enough to be asked to come! Get outa my way, Hope Douglas — and take your mother with you. Call *me* a painted Jezebel, will she?"

The piano was outside, being loaded into the wagon, where Riley sat on the seat, chewing tobacco grimly and expectorating copiously, without regard for those who came close. Outside there was also much clamor of voices. A lantern held high by a Devil's Tooth man who had a gun in the other, lighted the platform and the wagon beside it.

At the last, Tom Lorrigan himself went back after the stool, and the room silenced so that his footsteps sounded loud on the empty floor. He looked at Mary Hope, looked at her mother, looked at the huddled, whispering women, the gaping children. He swung out of his course and slipped one arm around Belle and so led her outside, the stool swinging by one leg in the other hand.

"A painted Jezebel!" Belle said under her breath when they were outside the ring of light. "My God, Tom, think of that!"

Mary Hope had never in her life suffered such humiliation. It seemed to her that she stood disgraced before the whole world, that there was no spot wherein she might hide her shame. Her mother was weeping hysterically because she had been "slappit by the painted Jezebel" and because Aleck was not there to avenge her. The Pocatello and Lava crowd seemed on the point of leaving, and were talking very fast in undertones that made Mary Hope feel that they were talking about her. The rattle of the Lorrigan wagon hauling the piano away, the click of the horses' feet as the Devil's Tooth riders convoyed the instrument, made her wince, and want to put her palms over her ears to shut out the sound of it.

But she was Scotch, and a Douglas. There was no weak fiber that would let her slump before this emergency. She went back to the little platform, stood beside the desk that held the globe and the dictionary and a can of flowers, and rapped loudly with the ruler from the Pocatello hardware store. By degrees the room ceased buzzing with excited talk, the shuffling feet stood still.

"I am very sorry," said Mary Hope clearly, "that your pleasure has — has been interrupted. It seems there has been a misunderstanding about the piano. I thought that I could buy it for the school, and for that reason I gave this dance. But it seems — that — I'm terribly sorry the dance has been spoiled for you, and if the gentlemen who bought tickets will please step this way, I will return your money."

She had to clench her teeth to keep her lips from trembling. Her hands shook so that she could scarcely open her handbag. But her purpose never faltered, her eyes were blue and sparkling when she looked out over the crowd. She waited. Feet scuffled the bare floor, voices whispered, but no man came toward her.

"I want to return your money," she said sharply, "because without the piano I suppose you will not want to dance, and — "

"Aw, the dickens!" cried a big, good-natured cowpuncher with a sun-peeled nose and twinkly gray eyes. "I guess we all have danced plenty without no piano music. There's mouth harps in this crowd, and there's a fiddle. Git yore pardners for a square dance!" And under his breath, to his immediate masculine neighbors he added:

"To hell with the Lorrigans and their piano!"

Mary Hope could have hugged that cowpuncher who hastily seized her hand and swung her into place as the first couple in the first set.

When the three sets were formed he called the dance figures in a sonorous tone that swept out through the open windows and reached the ears of the Lorrigans as they rode away.

" *Honor* yore pardner — and the lady on your *left!*
  Join eight hands, an' a-circle to the *left!*
  Break an *Indian* trail home in the Indian *style,* with the
      lady in the *lead!*
  Swing the lady *behind* you once in a while! —
  The lady *behind* you once in a while! —
  Now your pardner, and go hog *wild!*"

The fiddle and two mouth harps were scarcely heard above the rhythmic stamping of feet, the loud chant of the caller, who swung Mary Hope clear of the floor whenever he put his arm around her.

" A — *second* couple out, and a-cir-cle *four!*
      Lay-dees do ce *do!*
  You swing me, an' I'll swing *you* —
  And *we'll* all dance in the same ole *shoe!*

" *Same* four on to the *next!* — dance the ocean *wave!*
  The *same* ole boys, the *same* ole trail,
  Watch that possum walk the *rail!*
  Cir-cle six, and a-do ce *do!*
  Swing, *every* one swing, and a — promenade *home!*"

"*Who* wants a piano? Couldn't hear it if yuh had it!" he cried, while the twelve couples paused

breathless. Then he wiped his face frankly and
thoroughly with his handkerchief, caught Mary
Hope's hand in his, lifted his voice again in his
contagious sing-song:

> " *Cir*-cle eight, till you get straight!
> *Swing* them ladies, like swingin' on a *gate!*
> *Left* foot up, and-a-right foot *down* —
> *Make* that big foot jar the *ground!*
>   Prom-e-*nade!*
> *Swing* yore corner, if you ain't too *slow!*
> *Now* yore pardner, and around you *go!*
> For the — *last* time — and a-*long* time —
> *You* know where, and a-I don't *care!*"

The dance was saved by the big cowpuncher with
the peeling nose and the twinkly gray eyes. Mary
Hope had never seen him before that day, but
whenever she looked at him a lump came in her
throat, a warm rush of sheer gratitude thrilled
her. She did not learn his name — two or three
men called him Burt, but he seemed to be a
stranger in the country. Burt saved her dance
and kept things moving until the sky was streaked
with red and birds were twittering outside in the
cottonwoods.

She wanted to thank him, to tell him a little of
her gratitude. But when she went to look for
him afterwards he was gone, and no one seemed
to know just where he belonged. Which was
strange, when you consider that in the Black Rim
country every one knows everybody.

CHAPTER EIGHTEEN

Peddled Rumors

IN the smoking compartment of a Pullman car
that rocked westward from Pocatello two days
after the Fourth, Lance sprawled his big body on a
long seat, his head joggling against the dusty
window, his mind sleepily recalling, round by
round, a certain prize fight that had held him in
Reno over the Fourth and had cost him some
money and much disgust. The clicking of the car
trucks directly underneath, the whirring of the
electric fan over his head, the reek of tobacco
smoke seemed to him to last for hours, seemed
likely to go on forever. Above it all, rising stri-
dently now and then in a disagreeable monotone,
the harsh, faintly snarling voice of a man on the
opposite seat blended unpleasantly with his dozing discomfort. For a long time the man had been
talking, and Lance had been aware of a grating
quality of the voice, that yet seemed humorous in
its utterances, since his two listeners laughed frequently and made brief, profane comment that en-
couraged the talker to go on. Finally, as he slowly
returned from the hazy borderland of slumber,

Lance became indifferently aware of the man's words.

From under the peak of his plaid traveling cap Lance lifted his eyelids the length of his black lashes, measured the men with a half-minute survey and closed his eyes again. The face matched the voice. A harsh face, with bold blue eyes, black eyebrows that met over his nose, a mouth slightly prominent, hard and tilted downward at the corners. Over the harshness like a veil was spread a sardonic kind of humor that gave attraction to the man's personality. In the monotone of his voice was threaded a certain dry wit that gave point to his observations. He was an automobile salesman, it appeared, and his headquarters were in Ogden, and he was going through to Shoshone on business connected with a delayed shipment of cars. But he was talking, when Lance first awoke to his monologue, of the sagebrush country through which the fast mail was reeling drunkenly, making up time that had been lost because of a washout that had held the train for an hour while two section crews sweated over a broken culvert.

"— And by gosh! the funniest thing I ever saw happened right up here in a stretch of country they call the Black Rim. If I was a story writer, I sure would write it up. Talk about the West being tame! — why, I can take you right now, within a few hours' ride, to where men ride with guns on 'em just as much as they wear their pants. Only reason they ain't all killed off, I reckon, is because they *all* pack guns.

"Hard boiled? Say, there's a bunch up there that's never been curried below the knees — and never will be. They pulled off a stunt the Fourth that I'll bet ain't ever been duplicated anywhere on earth, and never will be. I was in Pocatello, and I went on up with the crowd from there, and got in on the show. And sa-ay, it was some show!

"They've got a feud up there that's rock-bottomed as any feud you ever heard of in Kentucky. It's been going on for years, and it'll keep going on till the old folks all die off or move away — or land in the pen. Hasn't been a killing in there for years, but that's because they're all so damn tough they know if one starts shooting it'll spread like a prairie fire through dry grass.

"There's an outfit in there — the Devil's Tooth outfit. Far back as the country was settled — well, they say the first Lorrigan went up in there to get away from the draft in the Civil War, and headed a gang of outlaws that shot and hung more white men and Injuns than any outfit in the State — and that's going some.

"They were killers from the first draw. Other settlers went in, and had to knuckle under. The Devil's Tooth gang had the Black Rim in its fist. Father to son — they handed down the disposition — I could tell yuh from here to Boise yarns about that outfit.

"Now, of course, things have tamed down. As I say, there hasn't been a Devil's Tooth killing for years. But it's there, you know — it's in the blood. It's all under the surface. They're a good-hearted bunch, but it'll take about four generations to live down the reputation they've got, if they all turned Methodist preachers. And,'' the grating voice paused for a minute, so that one caught the full significance of his hint, "if all yuh hear is true, religion ain't struck the Devil's Tooth yet. It ain't my business to peddle rumors, and the time's past when you can hang a man on suspicion — but if you read about the Devil's Tooth outfit some time in the paper, remember I said it's brewing. The present Tom Lorrigan ain't spending *all* his time driving his cows to water. He was hauled up a few years ago, on a charge of rustling. An old Scotchman had him arrested. Tom was cleared — he had the best lawyer in the West — brought him from Boise, where they need good lawyers! — and got off clear. And since then he's been laying low. That's the one mistake he's made, in my opinion. He never did a damn thing, never tried to kill the Scotchman, never acted up at all. And when you think of the breed of cats he is you'll see yourself that the Black Rim is setting on a volcano.

"Tom Lorrigan has got more men working for him than any outfit in that country. He runs his own round-up and won't have a rep — that's a representative — from any other outfit in his camp. His own men haze outside stock off his range. He's getting rich. He ships more cattle, more horses than anybody in the country. He don't have any truck with any of his neighbors, and his men don't. They're outside men, mostly. There ain't a thing anybody can swear to — there ain't a thing said out loud about the Devil's Tooth. But it's hinted and it's whispered.

"So all this preamble prepares you for the funniest thing I ever saw pulled. But I guess I'm about the only one who saw how funny it was. I know the Black Rim don't seem to see the joke, and I know the Devil's Tooth don't.

"You see, it's so big and neighbors are so far apart that there ain't any school district, and a few kids were getting school age, and no place to send 'em. So a couple of families got together and hired the daughter of this old Scotchman to teach school. I ain't calling her by name — she's a nice kid, and a nervy kid, and I can see where she thought she was doing the right thing.

"Well, she taught in a tumble-down little shack for a while, and one day this Tom Lorrigan come along, and saw how the girl and the kids were sitting there half froze, and he hazed 'em all home. Broke up the school. Being a Lorrigan, all he'd have to do would be to tell 'em to git — but it made a little stir, all right. The schoolma'am, she went right back the next morning and started in again. Like shooing a setting hen off her nest, it was.

"Well, next thing they knew, the Devil's Tooth had built a schoolhouse and said nothing about it. Tom's a big-hearted cuss — I know Tom — tried to sell him a car, last fall. Darn near made it stick, too. I figured that Tom Lorrigan was maybe ashamed of busting up the school and making talk, so he put up a regular schoolhouse. Then one of his boys had been away to college — only one of the outfit that ever went beyond the Rim, as far as I know — and he gave a dance; a regular house-warming.

"Well, I wasn't at that dance. I wish I had been. They packed in whisky by the barrel. Everybody got drunk, and everybody got to fighting. This young rooster from college licked a dozen or so, and then took the schoolma'am and drove clear to Jumpoff with her, and licked everybody in town before he left. Sa-ay, it musta been some dance, all right!

"Then — here comes the funny part. Everybody was all stirred up over the Lorrigans' dance, and right in the middle of the powwow, blest if the Lorrigans didn't buy a brand new piano and haul it to the schoolhouse. They say it was the college youth, that was stuck on the schoolma'am. Well, everybody out that way got to talking and gossiping — you know how it goes — until the schoolma'am, just to settle the talk, goes and gives a dance to raise money to pay for the piano. She's all right — I don't think for a minute she's anything but *right* — and it might have been old Tom himself that bought the piano. Anyway, she went and sent invitations all around, two dollars per invite, and got a big crowd. Had a picnic in the grove, and everything was lovely.

"But sa-ay! She forgot to invite the Lorrigans! Everybody in the country there, except the Devil's Tooth outfit. I figure that she was afraid they might rough things up a little — and maybe she didn't like to ask them to pay for something they'd already paid for — but anyway, just when the dance was going good, here came the whole Devil's Tooth outfit with a four-horse team, and I'm darned if they didn't walk right in there, in the middle of a dance, take the piano stool right out from under the schoolma'am, and haul the piano home! They —"

A loud guffaw from his friends halted the narrative there. Before the teller of the tale went on, Lance pulled his cap down over his eyes, got up and walked out and stood on the platform.

"They hauled the piano *home!*" He scowled out at the reeling line of telegraph posts. "They — hauled — that piano — home!"

He lighted a cigar, took two puffs and threw the thing out over the rail. "She didn't ask the Lorrigans — to her party. And dad —"

He whirled and went back into the smoking compartment. He wanted to hear more. The seat he had occupied was still empty and he settled into it, his cap pulled over his eyes, a magazine before his face. The others paid no attention. The harsh-voiced man was still talking.

"Well, they can't go on forever. They're bound to slip up, soon or late. And now, of course, there's a line-up against them. It's in the blood, and I don't reckon they can change — but the country's changing. I know of one man that's in there now, working in the dark, trying to get the goods — but of course, it's not my business to peddle that kind of stuff. I was tickled about the piano, though. The schoolma'am was game. She offered to give us back our two dollars per, but of course nobody was piker enough to take her up on it. We went ahead and had the dance with harmonicas and a fiddle, and made out all right. Looks to me like the schoolma'am's all to the good. She's got the dance money —"

It was of no use. Lance found he could not listen to that man talking about Mary Hope. To strike the man on his fish-like, hard-lipped mouth would only make matters worse, so he once more left the compartment and stood in the open doorway of the vestibule just beyond. The train, slowing to a stop at a tank station, jarred to a standstill. In the compartment behind him the man's voice sounded loud and raucous now that the mechanical noises had ceased.

"Well, I never knew it to fail — what's in the blood will come out. They've lived there for three generations now. They're killers, thieves at heart — human birds of prey, and it don't matter if it is all under the surface. I say it's *there.*"

At that moment, Lance had the hunger to kill, to stop forever the harsh voice that talked on and on of the Lorrigans and their ingrained badness. He stepped outside, slamming the door shut behind him. The voice, fainter now, could still be heard. He swung down to the cinders, stood there staring ahead at the long train, counting the cars, watching the fireman run with his oil can and climb into the engine cab. He could no longer hear the voice, but he felt that he must forget it or go back and kill the man who owned it.

In the car ahead a little girl leaned out of the window, her curls whipping across her face. Jubilantly she waved her hand at him, shrilled a sweet, "Hello-oh. Where *you* goin'? I'm goin' to my grandma's house!"

The rigor left Lance's jaw. He smiled, showing his teeth, saw that a brakeman was down inspecting a hot box on the forward truck of that car, and walked along to the window where the little girl leaned and waited, waving two sticky hands at him to hurry.

"Hello, baby. I know a grandma that's going to be mighty happy, before long," he said, standing just under the window and looking up at her.

"D'you know my gran'ma? S'e lives in a green house an' s'e's got five — hundred baby kittens for me to see! An' I'm goin' to bring one home wis me — but I *do'no* which one. D'you like yellow kittens, or litty gray kittens, or black ones?"

Gravely Lance studied the matter, his eyebrows pulled together, his mouth wearing the expression which had disturbed Mary Hope when he came to mend the lock on her door.

"I'd take — now, if your grandma has one that's all spotted, you might take that, couldn't you? Then some days you'd love the yellow spots, and some days you'd love the black spots, and some days —"

"Ooh! And I could call it *all* the nice names I want to call it!" The little girl pressed her hands together rapturously. " When my kitty's got its yellow-spotty day, I'll call him Goldy, and when —"

The engine bell clanged warning, the wheels began slowly to turn.

"Ooh! You'll get left and have to walk!" cried the little girl, in big-eyed alarm.

"All right, baby — you take the spotted one!" Lance called over his shoulder as he ran. He was smiling when he swung up the steps. No longer did he feel that he must kill the harsh-voiced man.

He went forward to his own section, sat down and stared out of the window. As the memory of the little girl faded he drifted into gloomily reviewing the things he had heard said of his family. Were they really pariahs among their kind? Outlawed because of the blood that flowed in their veins?

Away in the back of his mind, pushed there because the thought was not pleasant, and because thinking could not make it pleasant, had been the knowledge that he was returning to a life with which he no longer seemed to be quite in tune. Two weeks had served to show him that he had somehow drifted away from his father and Duke and Al, that he had somehow come to look at life differently. He did not believe in the harsh man's theory of their outlawry; yet he felt a reluctance toward meeting again their silent measurement of himself, their intangible aloofness.

The harsh-voiced man had dragged it all to the surface, roughly sketching for the delectation of his friends the very things which Lance had been deliberately covering from his own eyes. He had done more. He had told things that made Lance wince. To humiliate Mary Hope before the whole Black Rim, as they had done, to take away the piano which he had wanted her to have — for that Lance could have throttled his dad. It was like Tom to do it. Lance could not doubt that he had done it. He could picture the whole wretchedly cheap retaliation for the slight which Mary Hope had given them, and the picture tormented him, made him writhe mentally. But he could picture also Mary Hope's prim disapproval of them all, her deliberate omission of the Lorrigans from her list of invited guests, and toward that picture he felt a keen resentment.

The whole thing maddened him. The more, because he was in a sense responsible for it all. Just because he had not wanted that lonely look to cloud the blue eyes of her, just because he had not wanted her to be unhappy in her isolation, he had somehow brought to the surface all those boorish qualities which he had begun to hate in his family.

"Cheap — cheap as dirt!" he gritted once, and he included them all in the denunciation.

Furiously he wished that he had gone straight home, had not stopped in Reno for the fight. But on the heels of that he knew that he would have made the trouble worse, had he been at the Devil's Tooth on the day of the Fourth. He would have quarreled with Tom, but there was scant hope that he could have prevented the piano-moving. Tom Lorrigan, as Lance had plenty of memories to testify, was not the man whom one could prevent from doing what he set out to do.

At a little junction Lance changed to the branch line, still dwelling fiercely upon his heritage, upon the lawless environment in which that heritage of violence had flourished. He was in the mood to live up to the Lorrigan reputation when he swung off the train at Jumpoff, but no man crossed his trail.

So Lance carried with him the full measure of his rage against Mary Hope and the Devil's Tooth, when he rode out of Jumpoff on a lean-flanked black horse that rolled a wicked eye back at the rider and carried his head high, looking for trouble along the trail.

CHAPTER NINETEEN

Mary Hope Has Much Trouble

MARY HOPE, still taking her own point of view, had troubles in plenty to bear. In her own way she was quite as furious as was Lance felt quite as injured as did the Devil's Tooth outfit, had all the humiliation of knowing that the Black Rim talked of nothing but her quarrel with the Lorrigans, and in addition had certain domestic worries of her own.

Her mother harped continually on the piano quarrel and the indignity of having been "slappit" by the painted Jezebel. But that was not what worried Mary Hope most, for she was long accustomed to her mother's habit of dwelling tearfully on some particular wrong that had been done her. Mary Hope was worried over her father.

On the day of the Fourth he had stayed at home, tinkering up his machinery, making ready for haying that was soon to occupy all his waking hours, — and they would be as many as daylight would give him. He had been doing something to an old mower that should have gone to the junk heap long ago, and with the rusty sickle he had managed to cut his hand very deeply, just under the ball of the thumb. He had not taken the trouble to cleanse the cut thoroughly, but had wrapped his handkerchief around the hand and gone glumly on with his work. Now, on the third day, Mary Hope had become frightened at the discoloration of the wound and the way in which his arm was swelling, and had begged him to let her drive him to Jumpoff where he could take the train to Lava and a doctor. As might be expected, he had refused to do anything of the kind. He would not spend the time, and he would not spend the money, and he thought that a poultice would draw out the swelling well enough. Mary Hope had no faith in poultices, and she was on the point of riding to Jumpoff and telegraphing for a doctor when her father cannily read her mind and forbade her so sternly that she quailed before him.

There was another thing, which she must do. She must take the money she had gotten from the dance and with it pay Tom Lorrigan for the schoolhouse, or stop the school altogether. Jim Boyle, when she had ridden over to the AJ to tell him, had said that she could do as she pleased about paying for the schoolhouse; but if she refused to teach his kids, he would get some one else who would. Jim Boyle seemed to feel no compunctions whatever about accepting favors from the

Devil's Tooth. As to Sederson, the Swede, he was working for Boyle, and did what his boss said. So the matter was flung back upon Mary Hope for adjustment according to the dictates of her pride or conscience, call it which you will.

Her mother advised her to keep the money and buy another piano. But Mary Hope declared that she would not use the schoolhouse while it was a Lorrigan gift; whereupon Mother Douglas yielded the point grudgingly and told her to send Hugh, the gawky youth, to the Devil's Tooth with the three hundred dollars and a note saying what the money was for. But her father would not permit Hugh to go, reiterating feverishly that he needed Hugh on the ranch. And with the pain racking him and making his temper something fearful to face, Mary Hope dared not argue with him.

So she herself set out with her money and her hurt pride and all her troubles, to pay the Devil's Tooth outfit for the schoolhouse — approximately, since she had only a vague idea of the cost of the building — and then be quit of the Lorrigan patronage forever.

It happened that she found Tom at home and evidently in a temper not much milder than her father's. Two of the Devil's Tooth men were at the stable door when she rode up, and to them Tom was talking in a voice that sent shivers over Mary Hope when she heard it. Not loud and declamatory, like her father's, but with a certain implacable calm that was harder to face than stormy vituperation.

But she faced it, now that she was there and Tom had been warned of her coming by Coaley, who pointed his ears forward inquiringly when she neared the stable. The two cowpunchers gave Tom slanting glances and left, muttering under their breaths to each other as they led their sweaty horses into a farther corral.

Tom lifted his hand to his hat brim in mute recognition of her presence, gave her a swift inquiring look and turned Coaley into the stable with the saddle on. Mary Hope took one deep breath and, fumbling at a heavy little bag tied beside the fork of her saddle, plunged straight into her subject.

"I've brought the money I raised at the dance, Mr. Lorrigan," she said. " Since you refused to take it for the piano, I have brought it to pay you for the schoolhouse — with Mr. Boyle's approval. I have three hundred and twelve dollars. If that is not enough, I will pay you the balance later." She felt secretly rather well satisfied with the speech, which went even better than her rehearsals of it on the way over.

Then, having untied the bag, she looked up, and her satisfaction slumped abruptly into perturbation. Tom was leaning back against the corral rails, with his arms folded — and just *why* must he lift his eyebrows and smile like Lance? She was going to hand him the bag, but her fingers bungled and she dropped it in the six-inch dust of the trail.

Tom unfolded his arms, moved forward a pace, picked up the bag and offered it to her. "You've got the buying fever, looks like to me," he observed coldly. "I haven't got any schoolhouse to sell."

"But you have! You built it, and —"

"I did build a shack up on the hill, awhile back," Tom admitted in the same deliberate tone, "but I turned it over to Jim Boyle and the Swede and whoever else wanted to send their kids there to school." Since Mary Hope refused to put out her hand for the bag, Tom began very calmly to retie it on her saddle. But she struck his hand away.

"I shall not take the money. I shall pay for the schoolhouse, Mr. Lorrigan. Unless I can pay for it I shall never teach school there another day!" Her voice shook with nervous tension. One did not lightly and unthinkingly measure wills with Tom Lorrigan.

"That's your business, whether you teach school or not," said Tom, holding the bag as though he still meant to tie it on the saddle.

"But if I don't they will hire another teacher, and that will drive me away from home to earn money —" Mary Hope had not in the least intended to say that, which might be interpreted as a bid for sympathy.

"Well, Belle, she says no strange woman can use

that schoolhouse. They might not find anything
to teach school in, if they tried that."

"You've got to keep that money." Mary Hope
turned the Roman-nosed horse half away, meaning to leave Tom there with the money in his hand.

Tom reached calmly out and caught the horse
by the bridle.

"I want to tell you something," he drawled, in
the voice which she had heard when she came up.
"I haven't *got* to do anything. But I tell you
what I *will* do. If you don't take this money back
and go ahead with your school-teaching as if nothing had happened, I'll burn that schoolhouse to
the last chip in the yard. And this money I'll take
and throw down that crevice under the Tooth,
up there. The money won't do nobody any good,
and the schoolhouse won't be nothing at all but a
black spot. You can suit yourself — it's up to
you."

Mary Hope looked at him, opened her lips to
defy him, and instead gave a small sob. Her
Scotch blood chilled at the threat of such wanton
destruction of property and money, but it was not
that which made her afraid at that moment of
Tom Lorrigan, — held her silent, glaring impo-
tently.

She trembled while he tied the money to the
saddle fork again, using a knot she had never seen
tied before. She wanted to tell him how much she
hated him, how much she hated the whole Lorri-

gan family, how she would die before she ever
entered the door of that schoolhouse again unless
it was paid for and she could be free of obligation
to him.

But when his head was bent, hiding all of his face
but the chin, she had a wild fleeting notion that he
was Lance, and that he would lift his head and
smile at her.　Yet when he lifted his head he was
just Tom Lorrigan, with a hardness in his face
which Lance did not have, and a glint in his eye
that told her his will was inexorable, that he would
do exactly what he said he would do, and perhaps
more, if she opposed him.

Without a word she turned back, crushed under
the sense of defeat.　Useless destruction of property and money did not seem to mean anything at
all to a Lorrigan, but to her the thought was horrible.　She could not endure the thought of what
he would do if she refused to use the schoolhouse.
Much less could she endure the thought of entering the place again while it remained a Lorrigan
gift.

Blindly fighting an hysterical impulse to cry
aloud like a child over her hurt, she reined Jamie
into the short-cut trail of the Slide.　Coming down
she had followed the wagon road, partly because
the longer trail postponed a dreaded meeting, and
partly because Jamie, being uncertain in his temper and inclined to panicky spells when things did
not go just right with him, could not safely be

trusted on the Slide trail, which was strange to him.

Until she reached the narrow place along the shale side hill she did not realize what trail she was taking. Then, because she could not leave the trail and take the road without retracing her steps almost to the stable, she went on, giving Jamie an impatient kick with her heel and sending him snorting over the treacherous stuff in a high canter.

"Go on and break your neck and mine too, if ye like," she sobbed. " Ye needn't think I'll give an inch to *you; it's bad enough.*" When Jamie, still snorting, still reckless with his feet, somehow managed to pass over the boulder-strewn stretch without breaking a leg, Mary Hope choked back the obstreperous lump in her throat and spoke again in a quiet fury of resentment. "Burn it he may if he likes; I shall *not* put my foot again inside a house of the Lorrigans!"

Whereat Jamie threw up his head, shied at a white rock on the steep slope beneath, loped through the sagebrush where the trail was almost level, scrambled up a steep, deep-worn bit of trail, turned the sharp corner of the switch-back and entered that rift in the cap-rock known as the Slide.

Mary Hope had traveled that trail many times on Rab, a few years ago. She had always entered the Slide with a little thrill along her spine, knowing it for a place where Adventure might meet her face to face — where Danger lurked and might one day spring out at her. To-day she thought nothing about it until Jamie squatted and tried to whirl back. Then she looked up and saw Adventure, Danger and Lance Lorrigan just ahead, where the Slide was steepest.

Lance pulled up his hired horse, his thoughts coming back with a jerk from the same disagreeable subject that had engrossed Mary Hope. The hired horse jumped, tried his best not to sit down, lunged forward to save himself, found himself held back with a strength that did not yield an inch, and paused wild-eyed, his hind feet slipping and scraping the rock.

Jamie in that moment was behaving much worse. Jamie, finding that he could not turn around, was backing down the Slide, every step threatening to land him in a heap. Mary Hope turned white, her eyes staring up at Lance a little above her. In that instant they both remembered the short turn of the switch-back, and the twelve-foot bank with the scrambling trail down which no horse could walk backwards and keep his legs under him.

"Loosen the reins and spur him!" Lance's voice sounded hollow, pent within that rock-walled slit. In the narrow space he was crowding his own horse against the right wall so that he might dismount.

Mary Hope leaned obediently forward, the reins hanging loose. "He *always* backs up when he's scared,'' she panted, when Jamie paid no attention.

Instinctively Lance's hand felt for his rope.   On the livery saddle there did happen to be a poor sort of grass-rope riata, cheap and stiff and clumsily coiled, but fortunately with a loop in the end.

"Don't lasso Jamie!   He always fights a rope. He'll throw himself!''   Mary Hope's voice was strained and unnatural.

Lance flipped a kink out of the rope.   In that narrow space the loop must be a small one; he had one swift, sickening vision of what might happen if the little loop tightened around her neck. "Put up your hands — close to your head,'' he commanded her.   "It's all right.   Don't be afraid — it's all right, girl —''

He shot the loop straight out and down at her, saw it settle over her head, slip over her elbows, her shoulders.   "It's all right — can you get off!''

She tried, but the space was too narrow to risk it, with Jamie still going backward in a brainless panic.   He would have trampled her beneath him had she done so.

"Stay on — but be all ready to jump when he leaves the Slide.   Don't be afraid — it's all right. He won't hurt you; he won't hurt you at all.''   He was edging closer to the horse, holding the rope taut in his right hand, his left ready to catch Jamie by the bridle once he came near enough. His one fear was that the horse might fall before he was out of the gash, and in falling might crush Mary Hope against the rocks.

As Lance came on, Jamie backed faster, his haunches dropped, his feet slipping under him. Lance dared not crowd him, dared not reach for the bridle, still more than an arm's length away. So Jamie came out of the Slide backwards, saw with a sudden panic-stricken toss of his head that he had open daylight all around him, whirled short and gave one headlong leap away from the place that had terrified him so.

Lance jumped, reaching for Mary Hope as the horse went over the bank. By the length of his hand he missed her, but the rope pulled her free from Jamie, and she fell prone on the trail and lay still.

"Are you hurt? Good God! are you hurt?" Lance gathered her in his arms and carried her to where the rock wall made a shady band across the steep slope.

Mary Hope was very white, very limp, and her eyes were closed. On her cheeks he saw where tears had lately been. Her mouth had a pitiful little droop. He sat down, still holding her like a child, and felt tentatively of her arms, her shoulders, vaguely prepared to feel the crunch of a broken bone. There was no water nearer than the ranch. Jamie, having rolled over twice, was lying on his side near a scraggly buck-brush, looking back up the hill, apparently wondering whether

it would be worth while to get up. The hired
horse, having found a niche wherein to set his hind
feet, stood staring down through the Slide, afraid
to come farther, unable to retreat.

One side of Mary Hope's face was dusty, the
skin roughened with small scratches where she had
fallen. With his handkerchief Lance very gently
wiped away the dust, took off her hat and fanned
her face, watching absently two locks of hair that
blew back and forth across her forehead with the
breeze made by the swaying hat brim.

She was not dead! She could not be dead, with
that short fall. Then he saw that she was breathing faintly, unevenly, and in another minute he
saw her lashes quiver against her tanned cheek.
But her eyes did not open, the color did not flow
back into her face.

"Oh, girl — girl, wake up!" With a little shake
he pulled her close to him. "Open your eyes. I
want to see your eyes. I want to see if they are
just as blue as ever. Girl — oh, you poor little
girl!"

He had been hating her, furious at the insult
she had given his family. Angry as he was with
the Lorrigans, resenting fiercely what they had
done, he had hated Mary Hope Douglas more, because the hurt was more personal, struck deep into
a part of his soul that had grown tender. But he
could not hate her now — not when she lay there in
his arms with her tear-stained cheek against his

heart, her eyes shut, and with that pathetic droop to her lips. Gently he tucked back the locks of hair that kept blowing across her forehead. Very tenderly, with a whimsical pretense at self-pity, he upbraided her for the trouble she was giving him.

"Must I go clear down to the ranch and pack up water in my hat, and slosh it on your face? I'll do that, girl, if you don't open your eyes and look at me. *You're* not hurt; *are* you hurt? You'd better wake up and tell me, or I'll have to take you right up in my arms and carry you all the way down to the house, and ride like heck for a doctor, and —"

"Ye will not!" she retorted faintly, and unexpectedly he was looking into her eyes, bluer than he had remembered them; troubled, questioning — but stubborn against his suggestion. She moved uneasily, and he lifted her to the bank beside him and put one arm behind her, so that she leaned against him.

"Oh, very well — then I will not. You'll walk with me to the house, and we'll let Belle —"

"I will not! Never in my life will I enter the house of a Lorrigan!" Mary Hope brushed a palm against her forehead, straightened herself as if she resented her weakness, wished to hold herself aloof from him. She did not look at Lance, but stared across the narrow valley to the sage-clothed bluff beyond.

"Why not? You've just come from the Lorrigans, haven't you?" Lance studied her face.
"You must have, or you wouldn't be on this trail."

"I went down to pay for the schoolhouse, since
your father took the piano away. — And he would
not take the money, and he said he would burn the
house if I don't teach in it — and I'll *die* before
ever I'll open the door again, unless he takes the
money. And he said if I left the money he would
throw it down the crevice yonder — and he would
do it! And do you think I'll be under any obligation to Tom Lorrigan? You called my father
hard, but your father is the hardest man that ever
lived. The Lorrigans shall *not* —"

Lance laughed, set her hat wrong side before on
her head, tucked the elastic band under her chin,
laughed again when she pettishly removed it and
set the hat straight. "I wouldn't worry over the
schoolhouse right now — nor Tom Lorrigan
either," he said. "Look at your horse down there.
If you're all right, I'll go down and see how many
bones he's broken. You had a chance for a nasty
pile-up. Do you know that?"

"I'm grateful," said Mary Hope soberly.
"But it was Lorrigan meanness brought me here;
it was a Lorrigan got me into the trouble now, and
a Lorrigan got me out of it. It's *always* the Lorrigans."

"Yes, and a Lorrigan's got to see you a little
farther before you're through with them, so cheer

up." Lance laughed again, an amused little chuckle that was calculated to take the droop out of Mary Hope's lips, and failed completely.

He saw her cheeks were reddening, saw too that her face gave evidence of no particular bodily pain. She had probably fainted from fright, more than anything else, he decided, and her fright was now forgotten in her animosity. He slid off the bank, went down to where Jamie lay, took him by the bridle and urged him to stand. Which Jamie, after one or two scrambling attempts, managed to do. But the horse was hurt. He could scarcely hobble to the trail.

Without paying any visible attention to Mary Hope, Lance removed her saddle from Jamie, and brought it up to where she sat dispiritedly watching him. His manner was brisk, kind enough, but had an aloofness which made her keenly aware that he accepted her adherence to the feud and tacitly took his own place with the Lorrigans. Over this emergency she felt that he had unspokenly set a flag of truce. His attitude depressed her.

"There are just two things to do," he said, laying the saddle at her feet. "You may ride that livery horse back home, and I'll come along to-morrow and pick him up and take him in with me to Jumpoff; or you can let me go down to the ranch and bring up a gentle horse, and you can ride that home. I can get him when I come out to-morrow with my traps. I advise you to take the gentle horse from the ranch, after the shake-up you've had. This town horse is not easy gaited, by any means. Your horse I'll manage to get down to the ranch and do what I can for him. It's his shoulder, I think, from the way he acts. He may be all right after a while.''

Mary Hope looked distressfully at Jamie, standing dejected where Lance had left him, his head sagging, every line of him showing how sick of life he was. She glanced swiftly up at Lance, bent her head suddenly and pressed the tips of her fingers along her cheek bones, wiping away tears that came brimming over her eyelids.

''You'd better let me bring up a horse and take you home,'' Lance urged, the caressing note creeping into his voice.

''Oh, no! I can't! I — what do I care how I get home? But if your father won't take the money — You don't *know!* The whole Rim talks and gossips until I wish I were dead! And I can't go on using the schoolhouse — and Tom Lorrigan says if I don't —'' She was crying at last, silently, miserably, her face hidden behind her hands.

''He'll take the money.'' Lance, after an indeterminate minute while he watched her, laid his hand lightly on her shoulder. ''I'll see that dad takes it. And I'll give you a bill of sale that ought to shut the Black Rim mouths. I'm a Lorrigan and I'm not going to apologize for the blood that's in me, but I want you to know that if I had been home on the night of the Fourth the Lorrigans wouldn't have done the rotten cheap thing they did."

Mary Hope heard him tearing a leaf out of his memorandum book, looked up at him while he wrote rapidly. Without any comment whatever he gave her the paper, went up to where the hired horse stood, and coaxed it down through the Slide. Quickly, with the deftness that told of lifelong intimacy with horses and saddles, he set her own saddle on the hired horse, while Mary Hope read the terse bill of sale that set forth the legal "Ten dollars and other valuable considerations," and was signed "Thomas Lorrigan, per L. M. Lorrigan." It all seemed very businesslike, and heartened her so much that she was willing to be nice to Lance Lorrigan. But Lance remained strictly neutral.

"I'll lead him up the Slide for you," he said unemotionally when the horse was ready. "After he's over that, I think you'll be all right; you're a good rider. And you need not feel under any obligations then to the Lorrigans. I was practically through with the horse, anyway, and it will be no trouble at all to drive by your place and get him to-morrow."

"I can lead him up —" Mary Hope began, but Lance had already turned the horse and started him up the Slide, so there was nothing for her to do but follow.

At the top she gave him the money bag, which he took without any words whatever on the subject. He held the horse until she had mounted, made sure that she was all right, chilled by his perfect politeness her nervous overture toward a more friendly parting, lifted his hat and turned immediately to go back down the Slide.

Mary Hope glanced back over her shoulder and saw his bobbing hat crown. "Ah, he's just a Lorrigan, and I hate them all. But he let me pay — I'm quits with them now — and I'll never in my life speak to one of them again!"

CHAPTER TWENTY

As He Lived, So He Died

BELLE LORRIGAN, with Lance beside her on the one seat of the swaying buckboard, swung through the open gate of the Douglas yard and drove to the sun-baked, empty corral. In the doorway of the house, as they dashed past, the bent body of Mother Douglas appeared. She stood staring after them, her eyes blurred with tears. "It's that huzzy, the Lorrigan woman," she said flatly, wiping her face on her checked apron, stiffly starched and very clean. "Do you go, Mary Hope, and get them the horse they've come for. If Hugh were here —"

From somewhere within the house the voice of Aleck Douglas rose suddenly in a high-keyed vindictive chanting. Mother Douglas turned, but the old man came with a rush across the floor, brushed past her and went swaying drunkenly to the corral, shouting meaningless threats. After him went Mary Hope, her eyes wide, her skirt flapping about her ankles as she ran.

"Oh, please do not pay any attention to father!"

she cried, hurrying to overtake him before he reached the buckboard. "He's out of his head with pain, and he will not have a doctor — Father! listen! They only came for the horse I borrowed yesterday — they're going directly — come back and get into your bed, father!"

Aleck Douglas was picking up a broken neck yoke for a weapon when Lance sprang out over a wheel and grappled with him. The old man's right arm was swollen to twice its natural size and bandaged to his shoulder. His eyes were bloodshot, his breath fetid with the fever that burned him when he turned his face close to Lance.

"It's his arm makes him crazy," said Mary Hope breathlessly. "Last night it began, and mother and I cannot keep him in his bed, and we don't know *what* to do! He will not have a doctor, he says —"

"He'd better have," said Belle shortly, hanging to the pintos that danced and snorted at the excitement. "I'll send one out. Lance, you better stay here and look after him — he'll kill somebody yet. Aren't there any men on the place, for heaven's sake?"

Mary Hope said there wasn't, that Hugh was not expected back before night. They had bought a horse from the Millers, and it had jumped the fence and gone home, and Hugh had gone after it. Then she ran to do what she could to calm her father. Scotty, it would seem, wanted to drive the

Lorrigans off his land because they were thieves and cutthroats and had come there to rob him boldly in the broad light of day.

"Bat him on the head if you have to, Lance," Belle called, cold-eyed but capable. "He'll get sunstroke out here in this heat. And if you can get him into the house you had better tie him down till a doctor comes." Then she left, with the pintos circling in a lope to get out through the gate and into the trail.

The last she saw of them, Lance and Mary Hope were both struggling with the old man, forcing him foot by foot to the house, where Mother Douglas stood on the doorstep crying, with her apron to her face.

She had the tough little team in a white lather, with their stubborn heads hanging level with their knees, when she stopped at the little railroad station and sent a peremptory wire to the Lava doctor who was most popular in the Black Rim. She waited until he arrived on the train which he luckily had time to catch, and then, the pintos having somewhat recovered under the solicitous rubbing-down of a hollow-chested stableman, she hustled the doctor and his black case into the buckboard and made the return drive in one hour and fifty minutes, which was breaking even her own record, who was called the hardest driver in the whole Rim country.

They found Lance with his coat off and the perspiration streaming down his face, battling with Aleck Douglas who was raving still of the Lorrigans and threatening to kill this one who would not leave him alone to die in peace. Mary Hope and her mother were in the hot little kitchen where the last of the sunlight streamed through the faded green mosquito netting that sagged in and out as the breeze of sundown pushed through lazily.

The Lava doctor did not say much. He quieted the raving with his hypodermic needle, removed the amateurish bandage from the hand and the arm, looked at the wound, applied a cooling lotion, and dexterously wound on a fresh bandage. It seemed very little, Mary Hope thought dully, for a doctor to come all the way from Lava to do.

He would stay all night, he said. And the Lorrigans went home silent, depressed, even Belle finding nothing to say.

"I'll ride over in the morning and see how he is," Lance observed, as the tired little team climbed the Devil's Tooth Ridge. "I'll have to get the horse, anyway."

The next morning, when he arrived rather early, he learned from Mary Hope that her father had died just before daylight, and that Hugh had not come back, and the doctor wanted to be taken to Jumpoff, and she could not leave her mother there alone, and a coffin must be ordered, and she did not know *what* to do. She was past tears, it seemed to Lance. She was white and worn and worried, and there was something in her eyes that made them too tragic to look at. He stood just outside the kitchen door and talked with her in a low voice so that Mother Douglas, weeping audibly in the kitchen, need not know he was there.

"The doctor can ride that livery horse in," he said soothingly. "And I'll wire to Lava for anything that you want, and notify any friends you would like to have come and see you through this." He was very careful not to accent the word friends, but Mary Hope gave him a quick, pathetic glance when he said it.

"You've been kind — I — I can't say just what I would like to say — but you've been kinder than some friends would be."

She left the doorstep and walked with him to the stable, Lance leading his horse and slowing his pace to match her weary steps. "It — seems unreal, like something I'm dreaming. And — and I hope you won't pay any attention to what father — said. He was out of his mind, and while he had the belief, he —"

"I'd rather not talk about that," Lance interrupted quietly. "Your father believed that we're all of us thieves, that we stole his stock. Perhaps you believe it — I don't know. We've a hard name, got when the country was hard and it took hard men to survive. I don't think the Lorrigans, when you come right down to it, were any worse than their neighbors. They're no worse now.

They got the name of being worse, just because they were — well, stronger; harder to bully, harder to defeat. The Lorrigans could hold their own and then some. They're still holding their own. There never was a Lorrigan ever yet backed down from anything, so I'm not going to back down from the name the Rim has given us. I'm *glad* I'm a Lorrigan. But I'm not glad to have you hate me for it.''

They were at the stable door, which Mary Hope pulled open. The hired horse stood in the second stall. Lance dropped the reins of his own horse, turned to Mary Hope and laid his hands on her shoulders, looking down enigmatically into her upturned, troubled face.

''Girl, don't let us worry you at all. You've got trouble enough, and I'm going to do all I can to help you through it. I'll send out friends; and then the Lorrigans won't bother you. We won't come to the funeral, because your father wouldn't like to see us around, and your mother wouldn't like to see us around, and you —''

''Oh, don't!'' Mary Hope drooped her face until her forehead rested on Lance's arm.

Lance quivered a little. ''Girl — girl, what is it about you that drives a man mad with tenderness for you, sometimes?'' He slipped his free arm around her shoulders, pressed her close. ''Oh, girl — girl! Don't hate Lance — just because he's a Lorrigan. Be fairer than that.'' He bent his head to kiss her, drew himself suddenly straight, his brows frowning.

"There — run back and ask your mother what all she would like to have done for her in town, and tell the doctor that I'll have the horse ready for him in about two minutes. And be game — just go on being game. Your friends will be here just as soon as I can get them here." He turned into the stable and began saddling the horse.

Mary Hope, after a moment of indecision, went back to the house, walking slowly, as though she dreaded entering again to take up the heavy burden of sorrow that must be borne with all its sordid details, all the meaningless little conventions that attend the passing of a human soul. She had not loved her father very much. He was not a man to be loved. But his going was a bereavement, would leave a desolate emptiness in her life. Her mother would fill with weeping reminiscence the hours she would have spent in complaining of his harshness. She herself must somehow take charge of the ranch, must somehow fill her father's place that seemed all at once so big, so important in her world.

She looked back, wistfully, saw Lance leading out the horse. He had told her to be game — to go on being game. She wondered if he knew just how hard it was going to be for her. He had said that the Lorrigans were strong, were harder to defeat, had always held their own. He was proud because of their strength! She lifted her head, carefully wiped the tears from her cheeks — Mary Hope seemed always to be wiping tears from her cheeks lately! — and opened the door. The Lorrigans? Very well, there was also the Douglas blood, and that was not weaker than the Lorrigan.

She was quite calm, quite impersonal when she gave Lance a list of the pitifully small errands she and her mother would be grateful if he would perform for them. Her lips did not quiver, her hands did not tremble when she took her father's old red morocco wallet from the bureau drawer and gave Lance money to pay for the things they would need. Or if he would just hand the list to the Kennedys, she told him, they would be glad to attend to everything and save him the bother. They would come out at once, and perhaps Mrs. Smith would come. She thanked him civilly for the trouble he had already taken and added a message of thanks for Belle. She thanked him for the use of the horse and for attending to the schoolhouse matter for her. She was so extremely thankful that Lance exploded in one two-word oath when he rode away. Whereupon the doctor, who knew nothing of Lance's thoughts, looked at him in astonishment.

CHAPTER TWENTY-ONE

LANCE TRAILS A MYSTERY

LANCE, rising at what he considered an early hour — five in the morning may well be considered early, — went whistling down to the corral to see what plans were on for the day. It was the day of Aleck Douglas's funeral, but the Devil's Tooth outfit would be represented only by a wreath of white carnations which Belle had ordered sent up from Pocatello. White carnations and Aleck Douglas did not seem to harmonize, but neither did the Devil's Tooth and Aleck Douglas, and the white wreath would be much less conspicuous and far more acceptable than the Lorrigans, Lance was thinking.

He paused at the bunk-house and looked in. The place was deserted. He walked through it to the kitchen where the boys ate — the chuckhouse, they called it — and found nothing to indicate that a meal had been eaten there lately. He went out and down to the stable, where Sam Pretty Cow was just finishing his stall cleaning. Shorty, who now had a permanently lame leg from falling under his horse up in the Lava Beds a year ago,

was limping across the first corral with two full
milk buckets in his hands.

"Say, what time does this ranch get up, for heck
sake?" Lance inquired of Sam Pretty Cow, stepping aside so that Sam might carry in a forkful of
fresh hay.

"I dunno — long time ago." Sam Pretty Cow
turned the hay sidewise and went in to stuff his
fragrant burden into the manger.

"I was going out with the boys, if they went anywhere. Where have they all headed for, Sam?
I could overtake them, maybe."

Sam Pretty Cow, returning to the doorway,
shifted a quid of tobacco from one cheek to the
other and grinned.

"I dunno, me," he responded amiably.

"You don't *know?* Didn't dad say anything?
Didn't the boys?" And then, with faint exasper-
ation, "Doesn't any one ever talk any more on this
ranch?"

Sam Pretty Cow gave him a swift, oblique glance
and spat accurately at a great horsefly that had
lighted on a board end.

"Not much, you bet. Nh-hn."

Lance called to Shorty, who had set his milk
buckets down that he might open the little gate
that swung inward, — the gate which horses were
not supposed to know anything about.

"Oh-h, Shorty! Where did dad and the boys
go this morning?"

Shorty turned slowly, pulling the gate open and propping it with a stick until he had set the buckets through. Deliberation was in his manner, deliberation was in his speech.

"Las' night, you mean. They hit out right after midnight."

"Well, where did they *go?*" Lance ground his cigarette under his heel.

"You might ask 'em when they git back," Shorty suggested cryptically, and closed the gate just as carefully as if forty freedom-hungry horses were milling inside the corral.

Lance watched him go and turned to Sam Pretty Cow who, having thrust his hay fork behind a brace in the stable wall, was preparing to vary his tobacco-chewing with a smoke.

"What's the mystery, Sam? Where did they go? I'm here to stay, and I'm one of the family — I *think* — and you may as well tell me."

Sam Pretty Cow lipped the edge of his cigarette paper, folded it down smoothly on the tiny roll of tobacco leaned his body backward and painstakingly drew a match from the small pocket of his grimy blue overalls.

"I'm don' *know* nothing," he vouchsafed equably. "I'm don' ask nothing. I'm don' hear nothing. You bet. Nh-hn — yore damn right."

From under his lashes Lance watched Sam Pretty Cow. "I was over helping hold old Scotty in his bed, the other day," he said irrelevantly.

"He was crazy — out of his head. He kept yelling that the Lorrigans were stealing his stock.
He kept saying that a few more marks with a
straight branding iron would turn his Eleven into
an NL, ANL, DNL, LNL — any one of the Devil's
Tooth brands. Crazy with fever, he was."

Sam Pretty Cow studied the match, decided
which was the head of it, and drew it sharply along
his boot sole.

"Yeah — yo're damn right. Crazy, you bet
yore life. Uh-huh."

"He said the Miller's Block brand could easily
be turned into the N Block — Belle's brand. He
said horses had been run off the range —"

"He's dead," Sam observed unemotionally.
"You bet. He's gettin' fun'ral to-day."

"How long will the boys be out?" Lance pulled
a splinter off the rail beside him and began sep-
arating the fibers with his finger nails that were
too well cared for to belong to the Black Rim folk.

"I dunno, me."

"Scotty sure was crazy, Sam. He tried twice to
kill me. Once he jumped up and ran into the
kitchen and grabbed a butcher knife off the table
and came at me. He thought I was there to rob
him. He called me Tom."

"Yeah," said Sam Pretty Cow, blowing smoke.
"He's damn lucky you ain't Tom. Uh-huh — **you**
bet."

Lance lifted his eyebrows, was silent while he

watched Shorty limping down from the house, this time with table scraps for the chickens.

"Scotty was certainly crazy," Lance turned again to Sam. "Over and over he kept saying, while he looked up at the ceiling, 'The Lorrigan days are numbered. Though the wicked flourish like a green bay tree, they shall perish as dry grass. The days are numbered — their evil days are numbered.' "

Sam Pretty Cow smoked, flicked the ash from his cigarette with a coppery forefinger, looked suddenly full at Lance and grinned widely.

"Uh-huh. So's them stars numbered, all right. I dunno, me. Tom Lorrigan's damn smart man." He reached down for an old bridle and grinned again. "Scotty, I guess he don' say how many numbers them days is, you bet." He started off, trailing his bridle reins carelessly in the dust.

"If you're going to catch up a horse, Sam, I wish you'd haze in the best one on the ranch for me."

Sam Pretty Cow paused, half turned, spat meditatively into the dust and jerked a thumb toward the stable.

"Me, I dunno. Bes' horse on the ranch is in them box stall. Them's Coaley. I guess you don' want Coaley, huh?"

Lance bit his lip, looking at Sam Pretty Cow intently.

"You needn't catch up a horse for me, Sam.

I'll ride Coaley," he said smoothly. Which brought a surprised grunt from Sam Pretty Cow, Indian though he was, accustomed though he was to the ways of the Lorrigans.

But it was not his affair if Lance and his father quarreled when Tom returned. Indeed, Tom might not return very soon, in which case he would not hear anything about Lance's audacity unless Lance himself told it. Sam Pretty Cow would never mention it, and Shorty would not say a word. Shorty never did say anything if he could by any means keep silence.

Lance returned to the house, taking long strides that, without seeming hurried, yet suggested haste. He presently came down the path again, this time with a blanket roll and a sack with lumpy things tied in the bottom. He wore chaps, his spurs, carried a yellow slicker over his arm. On his head was a black Stetson, one of Tom's discarded old hats.

He led Coaley from the box stall where he had never before seen him stand, saddled him, tied his bundles compactly behind the cantle, mounted and rode down the trail, following the hoof prints that showed freshest in the loose, gravelly sand. Coaley, plainly glad to be out of his prison, stepped daintily along in a rocking half trot that would carry him more miles in a day than any other horse in the country could cover, and bring him to the journey's end with springy gait and head held proudly, ears twitching, ready for more miles if his rider wanted more.

The tracks led up the road to the Ridge, turned sharply off where the brush grew scanty among the flat rocks that just showed their faces above the surface of the arid soil. Lance frowned and followed. For a long way he skirted the rim rock that edged the sheer bluff. A scant furlong away, on his right, a trail ran west to the broken land of Indian Creek. But since the horsemen had chosen to keep to the rocky ground along the rim, Lance followed.

He had gone perhaps a mile along the bluff when Coaley began to toss up his head and perk his ears backward, turning now and then to look. Lance was sunk too deep in bitter introspection to observe these first warning movements which every horseman knows. He was thinking of Mary Hope, who would be waking now to a day of sorrowful excitement. Thinking, too, of old Aleck Douglas and the things that he had said in his raving.

What Douglas had shouted hoarsely was not true, of course. He did not believe, — and yet, there was Shorty's enigmatical answer to a simple question; there was Sam Pretty Cow, implying much while he actually said very little; there was this unheralded departure of all the Devil's Tooth riders in the night, in the season between round-ups. There was Coaley feeling fit for anything,

shut up in the box stall while Tom rode another
horse; and here was Lance himself taking the trail
of the Devil's Tooth outfit at a little after sunrise
on a horse tacitly forbidden to all riders save Tom.

Coaley, in a place where he must pick his way
between boulders, paused and lifted his head, staring back the way they had come. Lance roused
himself from gloomy speculations and looked back
also, but he could not see anything behind them
save a circling hawk and the gray monotone of the
barren plateau, so he urged Coaley in among the
boulders.

There must be something back there, of course.
Coaley was too intelligent a horse to make a mistake. But it might be some drifting range stock,
or perhaps a stray horse. Certainly it was no one
from the Devil's Tooth, for Sam Pretty Cow had
set off to mend a fence in the lower pasture, and
Shorty never rode a horse nowadays for more than
a half mile or so; and six o'clock in the morning
would be rather early for chance riders from any
other ranch. With a shrug, Lance dismissed the
matter from his mind.

Where a faint, little-used trail went obliquely
down the bluff to the creek bottom, Lance saw
again the hoofprints which the rocky ground had
failed to reveal. He could see no reason for taking this roundabout course to go up the creek, but
he sent Coaley down the trail, reached the bottom
and discovered that the tracks once more struck

off into rocky ground. His face hardened until his resemblance to Tom became more marked than usual, but where the tracks led he followed. Too often had he trailed stray horses in the past to be puzzled now, whether he could see the hoofprints or not.

They must have made for the other side of the creek, gone up Wild Horse gulch or the Little Squaw. There was just one place where they could cross the creek without bogging in the tricky mud that was almost as bad as quicksand. He therefore pulled out of the rocky patch and made straight for the crossing. He would soon know if they had crossed there. If they had not, then they would have turned again up Squaw Creek, and it would be short work cutting straight across to the only possible trail to the higher country.

He had covered half of the distance to the creek when Coaley again called his attention to something behind him. This time Lance glimpsed what looked very much like the crown of a hat moving in a dry wash that he had crossed not more than five minutes before. He pulled up, studied the contour of the ground behind him, looked ahead, saw the mark of a shod hoof between two rocks. The hoof mark pointed toward the crossing. Lance, however, turned down another small depression where the soil lay bare and Coaley left clean imprints, trotted along it until a welter of rocks made bad footing for the horse, climbed out

and went on level. Farther up the valley an
abrupt curve in Squaw Creek barred his way with
scraggly, thin willow growth that had winding cow
trails running through it.   Into one of these Lance
turned, rode deep into the sparse growth, stopped
where the trail swung round a huge, detached
boulder, dismounted and dropped Coaley's reins to
the ground and retraced his steps some distance
from the trail, stepping on rocks here and there
and keeping off damp spots.

He reached the thin edge of the grove, stood
behind a stocky bush and waited.   In two or three
minutes — they seemed ten to Lance — he saw the
head and shoulders of a rider just emerging from
the gully he himself had so lately followed.

Back on Coaley, following the winding trail,
Lance pondered the matter.   The way he had come
was no highway — no trail that any rider would
follow on any business save one.   But just why
should he be followed?   He had thought at first
that some one was trailing the Devil's Tooth outfit, as he had been doing, but now it seemed plain
that he himself was the quarry.

He flicked the reins on Coaley's satiny neck, and
the horse broke at once into a springy, swift trot,
following the purposeless winding of the cow path.
When they emerged upon the other side where the
creek gurgled over a patch of rocks like cobble-
stones, Lance stopped and let him take a sip or two
of water, then struck off toward the bluff, letting

Coaley choose his own pace, taking care that he kept to low ground where he could not be seen.

For an hour he rode and came to the junction of Mill Creek and the Squaw. Then, climbing through chokecherry thickets up a draw that led by winding ways to higher ground, Lance stopped and scrutinized the bottomland over which he had passed. Coaley stood alert, watching also that back trail, his ears turned forward, listening. After a moment, he began to take little mincing steps sidewise, pulling impatiently at the reins. As plainly as a horse could tell it, Coaley implored Lance to go on. But Lance waited until, crossing an open space, he saw a rider coming along at a shambling trot on the trail he had himself lately followed.

He frowned thoughtfully, turned Coaley toward home and rode swiftly in a long, distance-devouring lope.

He reached the ranch somewhere near ten o'clock, surprising Belle in the act of harnessing her pintos to a new buckboard at which they shied hypocritically. Belle stared at him round-eyed over the backs of her team.

"My good Lord, Lance! You — you could be Tom's twin, in that hat and on that horse! What you been doing — doubling for him in a lead?"

Lance swung down and came toward her. "Belle, where did dad and the boys go?"

"Oh — fussing with the stock," said Belle

vaguely, her eyes clouding a little. "We're getting so many cattle it keeps Tom on the go day and night, seems to me. And he *will* keep buying more all the while. Did — did you want to go with them, honey? I guess Tom never thought you might. You've been away so long. You'd better not ride Coaley, Lance. Tom would just about murder you if he caught you at it. And where did you get hold of that hat?"

Lance laughed queerly. "I just picked it off the table as I came out. Mine is too new and stiff yet. This seemed to fit. And Coaley's better off under the saddle than he is in the stable, Belle. He's a peach — I always did want to ride Coaley, but I never had the nerve till I got big enough to lick dad."

He caught Belle in a quick, breath-taking hug, kissed her swiftly on the cheek and turned Coaley into the corral with the saddle still on.

"Are you going over — to the funeral?" he asked as he closed the gate.

"I'm going to town, and I've got the letters you left on the table to be mailed. No, I'm not going to the funeral. I don't enjoy having my face slapped — and being called a painted Jezebel," she added dryly.

Under his breath Lance muttered something and went into the house, not looking at Belle or making her any reply.

"Lance," said Belle to the pintos, "thinks we're

rough and tough and just about half civilized. Lord, when you take a Lorrigan and educate him and *polish* him, you sure have got a combination that's hard to go up against. Two years — and my heavens, I don't *know* Lance any more! I never thought any Lorrigan could feaze *me* — but there's something about Lance —''

In the house Lance was not showing any of the polish which Belle had mentioned rather regretfully. He was kneeling before a trunk, throwing books and pipes and socks and soft-toned silk shirts over his shoulder, looking for something which he seemed in a great haste to find. When his fingers, prying deep among his belongings, closed upon the thing he sought, he brought it up, frowning abstractedly.

A black leather case, small and curved, opened when he unbuckled the confining strap. A binocular, small but extremely efficient in its magnifying power he withdrew, dusting the lenses with the sleeve of his shirt. He had bought the glasses because some one had advised him to take a pair along when he went with a party of friends to the top of Mount Tamalpais one Sunday. And because he had an instinctive dislike for anything but the best obtainable, he had bought the highest-priced glasses he could find in San Francisco,— and perhaps the smallest. He buckled them back into their case, slapped them into his pocket and closed the trunk lid with a bang. From the mantel

in the living room he gleaned a box of cartridges
for an extra six-shooter, which he cleaned and
loaded carefully and tucked inside the waistband
of his trousers, on the left side, following an instinct that brought him close to his grandfather,
that old killer whom all men feared to anger.

"The horse and the hat; he thought it was dad
he was trailing!" he said to himself, with his teeth
clamped tight together.   "Oh, well, when it comes
to that kind of a game —"

He went out and down to the corral, watered
Coaley and mounted again, taking the trail across
pastures to Squaw Creek.

CHAPTER TWENTY–TWO

Lance Rides Another Trail

WITH a two-days' growth of beard on his chin and jaws, a new, hard look in his eyes and the general appearance of a man who has been riding long and has slept in all his clothes, Lance rode quietly up to the corral gate and dismounted. A certain stiffness was in his walk when he led Coaley inside and turned a stirrup up over the saddle horn, his gloved fingers dropping to the latigo. Lance was tired — any one could see that at a glance. That he was preoccupied, and that his preoccupation was not pleasant, was also evident to the least observing eye.

Tom, coming out of the bunk house, studied him with narrowed lids as he came walking leisurely down to the corral. Tom's movements also betrayed a slight stiffness of the muscles, as though he had ridden hard and long. He did not hurry. Lance had pulled off the saddle and the sweaty blanket and the bridle, and had turned Coaley into the corral before he knew that some one was coming. Even then he did not turn to look. He was staring hard at a half-dozen horses grouped in the farther corner of the corral, — horses with gaunt flanks and the wet imprint of saddles. They were hungrily nosing fresh piles of hay, and scarcely looked up when Coaley trotted eagerly up to join them. Six of them — a little more than half of the outfit that had ridden away the other night.

"Well! I see you helped yourself to a new saddle horse," Tom observed significantly, coming up behind Lance.

"Yes. Coaley acted lonesome, shut up in the box stall. Thought a little riding would do him good." Lance's eyes met Tom's calmly, almost as if the two were mere acquaintances.

"You give him a plenty, looks like. Where yuh been?"

"I? Oh — just riding around." Lance stooped indifferently to untie his slicker and blanket from the saddle.

"Thought I'd like to use him myself. Thinking some of riding into town this afternoon," Tom said, still studying Lance.

"Well, if you want to ride Coaley, he's good for it. I'd say he has more miles in him yet than any of that bunch over there." With slicker and blanket roll Lance started for the house.

Tom did not say anything. He was scowling thoughtfully after Lance when Belle, coming from the chicken house with a late hatching of fluffy little chicks in her hat, looked at him inquiringly. To her Tom turned with more harshness than he had shown for many a long day.

"Schoolin' don't seem to set good on a Lorrigan," he said. "How long's he goin' to stay this time?"

"Why, honey, don't you *want* Lance home? He rode Coaley — but that's no crime. Lance wouldn't hurt him, he's too good a rider and he never was hard on horses. And Coaley just goes *wild* when he has to stand shut up all day —"

"Oh, it ain't riding Coaley, altogether. He can ride Coaley and be darned. It's the new airs he's putting on that don't set good with me, Belle. You wanted to make something of Lance, and now, by Henry, you'll have to name the job you've made of him — I'd hate to!"

Belle put a hand into the cheeping huddle in her hat, lifted out a chick and held it to her cheek. "Why, you're just imagining that Lance is different," she contended, stifling her own recognition of the change. "He'll settle right down amongst the boys —"

"The boys ain't cryin' to have him, Belle. Black Rimmers had ought to stay Black Rimmers, or get out and stay out. Lance ain't either one thing or the other."

"Why, Tom Lorrigan!" Belle dropped the chick into her hat and tucked the hat under her arm. Her eyes began to sparkle a little. "I don't think Lance liked it about the piano, but he's the same Lance he always was. I've watched him, and he hasn't said a thing or done a thing outa the way — he's just the *dearest* great big fellow! And I can't for the life of me see why you and the whole outfit hang back from him like he was a stranger. Education ain't catching, Tom. And Lance don't put on any airs at all, so why in the name of heaven you all —''

''Well, well, don't get all excited, Belle. But if education was ketching, a lot of the boys would be rollin' their beds. I'm going to town. Anything yuh want brought out?''

Belle did not answer. She went away to the house with her hatful of chicks, and put them into a box close to the stove until the mother hen made sure whether the four other eggs were anything more than just stale eggs. It would have been hard for Belle to explain just what the heaviness in her heart portended. Certainly it was not in her nature to worry over trifles, — yet these were apparent trifles that worried her. On the surface of the Devil's Tooth life only faint ripples stirred, but Belle felt somehow as though she were floating in a frail boat over a quiet pool from whose depths some unspeakable monster might presently thrust an ominous head and drag her under.

In the crude yet wholly adequate bathroom she heard a great splashing, and guessed that it was Lance, refreshing himself after his trip. That, she supposed, was another point that set him apart from the other boys. From June to September, whenever any of the male inhabitants of the Devil's Tooth felt the need of ablutions beyond the scope of a blue enamel wash basin, he took a limp towel and rode down across the pasture to the creek, and swam for half an hour or so in a certain deep pool. Sometimes all of the boys went, at sundown, and filled the pool with their splashings. Only Lance availed himself of tub and soap and clean towels, and shaved every morning before breakfast.

She heard him moving about in his room, heard him go into the kitchen and ask Riley what the chances were for something to eat. She did not follow him, but she waited, expecting that he would come into the living room afterwards. She went to the piano and drummed a few bars of a new dance hit Lance had brought home for her, and with her head turned sidewise listened to the sound of his footsteps in the next room, his occasional, pleasantly throaty tones answering Riley's high-pitched, nasal twang.

Her eyes blurred with unreasoning tears. He was her youngest. He was so big, so handsome, so like Tom,— yet so different! She did not believe that Tom could really see anything to cavil at in Lance's presence, in his changed personality. Tom, she thought, was secretly as proud of Lance as she was, and only pretended to sneer at him to hide that pride. The constraint would soon wear off, and Lance would be one of the boys again.

The screen door slammed. With a lump in her throat, Belle went to a window and looked out. Lance, in his new Stetson and a fresh shirt and gray trousers tucked into his riding boots, was on his way to the stable again. She watched him pick up a rope and go into the far corral where a few extra saddle horses dozed through the hot afternoon. She saw him return, leading a chunky little roan. Saw him throw his saddle on the horse. Saw him ride off — the handsomest young fellow in all the Black Rim — but with apparently never a thought that his mother might like a word with him, since he had been gone for two days without any explanation or any excuse. Which was not like Lance, who had always before remembered to be nice to Belle.

Up the Slide trail Lance rode, perhaps two hours behind Tom. The marks of Coaley's hoofs were still fresh in the trail, but Lance did not appear to see them at all. He let the roan scramble over the shale as he would, let him take his own pace among the boulders and up through the Slide. At the top he put him into an easy lope which did not slacken until he reached the descent on the other side of the Ridge.

Presently, because the roan was an ambitious young horse and eager to reach the end of the trail, and Lance was too preoccupied to care what

pace he traveled, they arrived at Cottonwood
Spring, circled the wire fence and whipped in
through the open gate at a gallop.

The little schoolhouse was deserted. Lance dismounted and looked in, saw it still dismal with the
disorder of the last unfortunate dance. It was
evident that there had been no school since the
Fourth of July.

Then he remembered that Mary Hope's father
had been sick all of the week, and it was now only
two days since the funeral. She would not be
teaching school so soon after his death.

He closed the door and remounted, his face
somber. He had wanted to see Mary Hope.
Since the morning after Scotty died he had fought
a vague, disquieting sense of her need of him.
There had been times when it seemed almost as
though she had called to him across the distance;
that she wished to see him. To-day he had obeyed
the wordless call. He still felt her need of him,
but since she was not at the school he hesitated.
The schoolhouse was in a measure neutral ground.
Riding over to the Douglas ranch was another
matter entirely. Too keenly had he felt the cold
animosity of Mother Douglas, the wild, impotent
hate of old Scotty mouthing threats and accusa-
tions and vague prophecies of future disaster to
the Lorrigans. He rode slowly out through the
gate and took the trail made by the Devil's Tooth
team when they hauled down the materials for the

schoolhouse. The chunky roan climbed briskly, contentedly rolling the cricket in his bit. The little burring sound of it fitted itself somehow to the thought reiterating through Lance's tired brain. "She wouldn't want me — to come. She wouldn't — want me — to come."

The roan squatted and ducked sidewise, and Lance raised his head. Down the rough trail rode a big cowpuncher with sun-reddened face and an air of great weariness. His horse plodded wearily, thin-flanked, his black hair sweat-roughened and dingy. The rider looked at Lance with red-veined eyes, the inflamed lids showing sleepless nights.

"How'r yuh?" he greeted perfunctorily, as they passed each other.

"Howdy," said Lance imperturbably, and rode on.

Lance's eyebrows pulled together. He had no need of looking back; he had seen a great deal in the one glance he had given the stranger. He scrutinized the trail, measured with his eyes the size and the shape of the horse's footprints.

After a little he left the wagon road and put the roan to the steep climb up the trail to the great Tooth of the ridge. He still frowned, still rode with bent head, his eyes on the trail. But now he was alert, conscious of his surroundings, thinking of every yard of ground they covered.

At a little distance from the base of the Tooth he

dismounted, tying the restive roan to a bush to prevent him from wandering around, nibbling investigatingly at weeds, bushes, all the things that interest a young horse.

Slowly, walking carefully on rocks, Lance approached the Tooth. A new look was in his face now, — a look half tender, half angry because of the tenderness. Several times he had met Mary Hope here at the Tooth, when he was just a long-legged youth with a fondness for teasing, and she was a slim, wide-eyed little thing in short skirts and sunbonnet. Always the meetings had pretended to be accidental, and always Mary Hope had seemed very much interested in the magnificent outlook and very slightly interested in him.

From the signs, some one else was much interested in the view. Lance came upon a place where a man had slipped with one foot and left the deep mark of his boot in the loose, gravelly soil. Sitting on a boulder, he made a leisurely survey of the place and counted three cigarette stubs that had fallen short of the crevice toward which they had evidently been flung. How many had gone into the crevice he could not tell. He slid off the boulder and, walking on a rock shelf that jutted out from the huge upthrust rock, examined the place very thoroughly.

At a certain spot where Mary Hope had been fond of sitting on the rock shelf with her straight little back against the Tooth's smooth side, a splendid view of the Devil's Tooth ranch was to be had. The house itself was hidden in a cottonwood grove that Belle had planted when she was a bride, but the corrals, the pastures, the road up the Ridge was plainly visible. And in the shallow crack in the rock was another cigarette end, economically smoked down to a three-quarter-inch stub.

Lance returned by way of the shelf to the outcropping of rocks that would leave no trace of his passing. He untied and mounted the roan and circled the vicinity cautiously. Two hundred yards away, down the slope and on a small level place where the brush grew thick, he found where a horse had stood for hours. He looked at the hoofprints, turned back and rode down the schoolhouse trail again, following the tracks of the fagged black horse.

When another fifty yards would bring the basin in sight, Lance turned off the trail and dismounted, tied the roan again and went forward slowly, his eyes intent on the tops of the trees around Cottonwood Spring. A rattler buzzed suddenly, and he stopped, looked to see where the snake was coiled, saw it withdraw its mottled gray body from under a rabbit weed and drag sinuously away, its ugly head lifted a little, eyes watching him venomously. An unwritten law of the West he broke by letting the snake go. Again he moved forward, from bush to bush, from boulder to boulder. When all of the basin and the grove were revealed to him, he stopped, removed his gray range hat and hung it on a near-by bush. He took his small field glasses from his pocket, dusted the lenses deliberately and, leaning forward across a rock with his elbows steadied on the stone and the glasses to his eyes, he swept foot by foot the grove.

He was some minutes in discovering a black horse well within the outer fringe of the cottonwoods, switching mechanically at the flies and mosquitoes that infested the place, and throwing his head impatiently to his side now and then when the sting was too sharp to ignore. With the glasses he could see the sweat-roughened hide ripple convulsively to dislodge the pestering insects, could see the flaring nostrils as the horse blew out the dust gathered from his hungry nosing amongst the coarse grass and weeds. The man Lance did not at once discover, but after a little he saw him rolled in canvas to protect himself from the mosquitoes. He seemed already fast asleep.

"He needs it," said Lance grimly, with his twisted smile, and went back to the roan.

CHAPTER TWENTY-THREE

LANCE PLAYS THE GAME

THAT night Lance sauntered into the bunk house, placidly ignoring the fact that Tom was there, and that some sort of intermittent conference was taking place. Cool and clean and silk-shirted and freshly shaved, the contrast was sharp between him and the men sprawled on their beds or sitting listlessly around the table playing keno. Tom lifted an eyebrow at him; Lance sent him a look to match and went over to the card players.

They did not want him in the bunk house. He who had spent nearly all of his life on the Devil's Tooth ranch knew that he was not wanted. They did not want him to know that he was not wanted, and by their very effort to hide it did they betray themselves.

"Didn't go to Jumpoff after all, dad," Lance remarked idly, a rising inflection turning the phrase into a question.

Tom grunted and got up to go. His men cast furtive glances at one another, looked at Lance from under their brows, noted the silk shirt and the low, tan Oxfords, and the texture and cut of his gray trousers with the tan leather belt that had a small silver buckle. Plain as it was they knew that buckle was silver. They saw how clean-cut was the hairline at the back of his head and over his ears — sure sign that he was "citified." And toward the man who is citified your purely range-bred product cherishes a distinct if secret grudge. His immaculate presence made them all feel frowsy and unwashed and ill-clad. And to hide how conscious he was of his own deficiencies, the man who sat nearest Lance lifted his hat and rumpled his hair still more.

"Duke and Al didn't get in yet, eh?" Lance picked up an extra deck of cards and began to shuffle them absent-mindedly but nevertheless dexterously.

"Nope — they stayed out," replied a blond man named Winters. They called him "Chilly."

"Hot weather for working cattle," Lance observed indifferently.

"Yeah — sure is," responded Ed Moran, who was low-browed and dark and had an ugly jaw.

"Yeah — *damn* hot," testified Jim Bloom. "How's Californy for weather?"

"Oh-h — it has all kinds, same as here." Lance did not want to talk about California just then, but he followed the lead easily enough. "You can get anything you want in California. In two hours you can go from twenty-five feet of snow to orange groves. You can have it all green, fruit trees and roses blooming in midwinter, or you can hit into desert worse than anything Idaho can show.''

''Yep — that's right, all right. Great place, Californy,'' Chilly tried to make his voice sound enthusiastic, and failed. ''Great place.''

''Speaking about climate —'' Lance sat down on a corner of the table, eased his trousers over his knees, crossed his tan Oxfords and began a story. It was a long story, and for some time it was not at all apparent that he was getting anywhere with it. He shuffled the deck of cards while he talked, and the keno game, interrupted when he began, trailed off into ''Who's play is it?'' and finally ceased altogether. That was when Lance's Jewish dialect began to be funny enough to make even Chilly Winters laugh. At the end there was a general cachinnation.

''But that's only a sample of the stuff they pull out there, on tourists,'' said Lance, when the laughter had subsided to a few belated chuckles. ''There's another one. It isn't funny — but I'm going to *make* it funny. You'll think it's funny — but it isn't, really.''

He told that one and made them think it was funny. At least they laughed, and laughed again when he had finished.

''Now here's another. This one really *is* funny — but you won't feel like laughing at it. I'll tell it so you won't.''

He told that story and saw it fall flat. "You see?" He flipped the cards, tossed them on the table with a whimsical gesture. "It isn't what you do in this world — it's how you do it that counts. I'm sitting on your keno game, am I? All right, I'll get off."

He went out as abruptly as he had entered, and he paused long enough outside to know that a silence marked his going. Then he heard Ed Moran's voice depreciating him. Frankly he listened, lighting a cigarette.

"Aw — his mother was an actress, wasn't she? *That* guy ain't going to cut no ice around here whatever."

"Looks an awful darn lot like Tom," ventured Chilly. "I dunno — you take a Lorrigan —"

"Him? Lorrigan? Why, say! He may *look* like a Lorrigan, but he ain't one. Tom's damn right. He don't set in. Why, like as not he'd —"

"Aw, cut out the gabbling!" Ed's voice growled again. "It's yore play, Bob."

Stepping softly, Lance went on to the house. "I just — *look* like one!" he repeated under his breath. "Fine! At any rate," he added dryly, "I've proved that I *can* go into the bunk house now and then."

He went up and sang songs with Belle then, until after ten o'clock. He would have sung longer, but it happened that in the middle of a particularly pleasing "Ah-*ee,* oh-*ee,* hush-a-bye-

ba-by" yodel, Tom put his head out of the bedroom and implored Lance to for-the-Lord-sake go
up on the Ridge to howl. So Lance forbore to
finish the "ah-*ee,* oh-*ee*", much to Belle's disappointment.

"But you know Tom's been out riding hard and
not getting much sleep, so I guess maybe we better
cut out the concert, honey," she told Lance, getting
up and laying her plump, brown arms across his
shoulders. "My heavens, Lance, you kinda make
me think the clock's set back thirty years, when I
look at you. You're Tom, all over — and I did
think you were going to be like me."

Lance scowled just a little. "No, I'm not Tom
all over — I'm Lance all over."

"You're Lorrigan all over," Belle persisted.
"And you're just like Tom when he was your age.
Good Lord, how time does slip away! Tom used
to be so full of fun and say such funny things —
and now it's just ride and ride and work, and eat
and sleep. Honey, I want you to know that I'm
glad you learned something a little different.
What's the use of having a million, if you work
yourself to death getting it? Look at the boys —
look at Al and Duke. They're like old men, the
last year or two. We used to have such good times
on the ranch, but we don't any more — nobody
ever thinks of anything but work."

She lowered her voice to a whisper, her arms
still lying on Lance's shoulders, her clouded blue

eyes looking up into his. "That trouble with Scotty Douglas kind of — changed Tom and the boys. You went away. You've changed too, but in a different way. It *soured* them, just a little. Tom wants to make his million quick and get outa here. I was glad when you stirred things up a little, last spring, and gave that dance. Or I was glad, till it ended up the way it did. It was the first dance we'd been to since you left, Lance! And I thought it would kind of patch up a little more friendliness with the folks around here. But it didn't. It just made a lot of talk and trouble — and, Lance, honey, I'm awfully darn sorry about that piano. It's down in the chicken house this minute. Tom wouldn't even have it in the house. And now, I don't suppose there ever will be any chance to make friends with any one. Tom — well, all of us were so *darn* mad to think she never even asked us —"

"Don't care any more about that, Belle. Please don't. And by the way, I took the money Mary Hope wanted to give dad for the schoolhouse. Perhaps he didn't tell you, but he threatened to burn the house down if she left the money, so I took it and gave her a bill of sale in his name. I wish you'd keep the money. And some day, maybe dad will take it."

"Tom never told me a word about it," Belle whispered pitifully, dropping her forehead on Lance's broad chest. "Honey, it never used to be this way. He used to tell me things. But now, he doesn't — much. Last spring, when he built the schoolhouse and all, I was so *glad!* It was more like old times, and I thought — but the fight turned him and the boys again, and now they're just as far off as ever. Lance, I don't whine. You never heard Belle whine in your life, did you, honey? But I'll tell you this: The only things that haven't changed, on the Devil's Tooth, are Riley and the pintos. And even they let you drive 'em to Jumpoff and back last spring without busting things up. They're getting old, I guess. Maybe we're all getting old. Still, Rosa and Subrosa are only ten past, and I haven't had a birthday for years —

"It's — Lance, do you mind if Belle lets go and tells you things, just this once? You've changed, some, but not like the rest. Please, Lance, I want to lean against you and — and feel how strong you are —"

A great tenderness, a great, overwhelming desire to comfort his mother, who had never let him call her mother, seized Lance. His arms closed around her and he backed to an armchair and sat down on it, holding her close.

"Don't care, Belle — it's all right. It's *going* to be all right. I'm just Lance, but I'm a man — and men were made to take care of their women. Talk to me — tell me what's been eating your heart out, lately. It's in your eyes. I saw it when I came home last spring, and I see it now every time I look at you.''

"You've seen it, honey?" Belle's whisper was against his ear. She did not look at his face. "There's nothing to see, but — one feels it. Tom's good to me — but he isn't *close* to me, any more. The boys are good to me — but they're like strangers. They don't talk about things, the way they used to do. They come and go.''

Lance's big, well-kept hand went up to smooth her hair with a comforting, caressing movement infinitely sweet to Belle. "I know," he said quietly.

"And it isn't anything, of course. But the old boys have gone, and these new ones — Lance, what *is* the matter with the Devil's Tooth ranch? Tell me, for heaven's sake, if I'm getting to be an old woman with notions!''

"You'll never be an old woman," said Lance in the tone Mary Hope built her day-dreams around. "Age has nothing to do with you — you just *are*. But as to notions — well, you may have. Women do have them, I believe." He kissed her hair and added, "What do you think is the matter with the ranch?''

"I don't *know*. When I try to pin it to one thing, there's nothing to put a pin in. Not a thing. You remember Cheyenne? I was afraid Tom would kill him, after the trial. You know it was practically proven that he was a spy, and was

working to get something on the outfit. I was on
the warpath myself, over that trial. I would a shot
up a few in that courtroom if Tom had been con-
victed. You know and I know that Tom didn't
have a thing to do with that darned spotted yearling of Scotty's.

"But Cheyenne just — just faded out of exist-
ence. Tom's never mentioned him from the day of
the trial to this. And I know he hates the whole Rim,
and won't have anything much to do with anybody
— but he acts just as if nothing had happened, as
if nobody had ever tried to make him out a cow-
thief. He won't talk about it. He won't talk
about anything much. When we're alone he just
sits and *thinks*. And honey, the Lorrigans have
always been men that *did* things.

"He and the boys woke up, and the ranch acted
human about the schoolhouse, but it's other times,
when there's no excitement around, that I feel as
if — I don't know what. It's something underneath. Something that never comes to the top.
Something that's liable to reach up and grab."
She put a hand up and patted Lance's lean, hard
jaw. "I'd shoot any one that said Belle Lorrigan's *afraid* — but that's about what it amounts
to," she finished with a little mirthless laugh.

"Belle Lorrigan's not afraid. There's nothing
to be afraid of. You've lived in the Rim too long,
Belle, and you've been watching dad and the boys
chasing that million. I've seen other men work-

ing at it, and it always gets hold of them until they
don't seem to care for anything else. Now, I
know an ageless lady who's going to bed and forget all about her nerves and her notions. Or if
she doesn't forget, she'll remember too that she
has somebody around who knows — and who cares
a heap for his mother." Lance pulled her close
and kissed her comfortingly.

"That helps," whispered Belle. "You've
changed, too — but not like the rest, thank God.
And I thought maybe you had noticed things —"

"I have noticed that the Devil's Tooth is mighty
busy chasing dollars on the hoof," soothed Lance.
"It has left our Belle alone too much, and it has
gotten on her nerves. Go to bed, woman — and
dream of pleasant things."

He took her by the shoulders and pushed her
playfully to the very door of her bedroom, gave
her another kiss and turned the knob for her, and
watched her go in with a smile on her face. His
own smile lasted only until the door was closed.
He went to the lamp, blew it out and entered
his own room, removed his shoes and dropped
them on the floor with more noise than was
considerate of his father's slumber, lighted his
lamp and moved aimlessly about the room for a
time.

He sat down on the edge of the bed while he
smoked a cigarette, his elbows on his knees, his
thoughts traveling far trails. Abruptly he rose,

put on a pair of well-worn tennis shoes, opened a
door leading outside and went quietly down to the
corrals.

The first corral he crossed and found it empty of
any horses save the pintos and Coaley. The second corral held three horses, one of them the
chunky roan he had ridden that afternoon. The
third and largest corral was empty, the gate
swinging open.

"All right — no horses caught up for night-
riding — *yet*," he said to himself, and returned
to the house, leaving the straighter path to pass
close to the bunk house. He listened there for a
full two minutes, decided that it would take at least
five men to do all of that snoring, and went to bed
thankful for the comfort of a felt mattress under
his tired body.

The next day passed without any incidents save
trivial ones that did not count. Lance rode to
the creek with his trout-rod and reel — more citified innovations which the ranch eyed askance —
and spent four hours loitering along the bank, his
fly floating uselessly over shallow pools where was
never a fish. It was not the right time of day for
fishing, but Lance seemed to have forgotten the
lore he had learned along that same creek and
others farther away.

Sometimes he could be seen from the ranch
buildings, more often he could not. When he
could not be seen was when he was crouched

among the rocks, studying the Devil's Tooth Ridge with his powerful glasses.

"Hope he's comfortable," he said once, when, satisfied that his guess was correct, he put the glasses away and settled down seriously to fishing.

He rode home with four trout, and Riley fried them for supper. During supper Lance criticized Squaw Creek, and hinted that Mill Creek and Lava Creek were better fishing waters, and that he meant to try them.

That night at eleven o'clock he made another silent tour of the corrals and went to bed feeling pretty sure that the ranch would show its present complement of men in the morning.

On the second day, four of the hired cowboys rode in at sundown, and with them came Al. Their horses were fagged. They themselves were dirty, hungry, tired. Their faces were glum — and the glumness remained even after they had washed and eaten ravenously. Al did not come to the house at all, but stayed down in the bunk house, whither Tom presently went. Lance did not follow.

Belle looked worried and asked Lance constrainedly if he knew why Duke had not come with the others. Lance laughed.

"Duke? Oh — he's on the trail of another dollar. By heck, Belle, I'm afraid you've raised one son to be a shirk. I don't seem to need all of that dollar chasing to make me happy."

Tom came in then, glanced swiftly from one to the other, said something unimportant, rolled a cigarette with elaborate care, and observed that Duke would find it hot, riding all the way to Shoshone, and that he'd be darned if he'd go that far for any girl. He sat down and disposed himself comfortably, got up, muttered something about forgetting to turn Coaley out, and left the house.

Belle turned and looked at Lance. "Honey, it's that kind of thing —"

"I used to think, Belle, that you had the bluest eyes in the whole world," Lance drawled quizzically. "They're blue enough, in all conscience — by heck, Belle! Does a Lorrigan always love blue eyes?"

"I was going to say that —"

"You were going to say that you were not going to say a darned thing, madam. You need a vacation, a trip somewhere. Why don't you beat it, and get your nerves smoothed down a little?"

"Lance, you don't believe Duke —"

"Belle, your boys are old enough to think of girls a little bit, now and then. Even your baby thinks of girls — a little bit. Now and then. I'm going fishing, Belle. I'm going to fish where there are fish. And if I'm not back by the clock, for heck's sake don't get yourself excited and call *me* a mystery."

She called after him. "Lance, come back here and tell me the truth! You don't believe —"

"Belle, I'll tell you the truth.   Sure, I'll tell you the truth.   I tell you to cut out this worrying over nothing.   Why, don't you know the world is plumb full of real things to worry about?"   He came close, patting her on the shoulder as one pats a child who feels abused for slight cause.   "This notion of yours — it's all damned nonsense.   Cut it out."

He went off whistling, and Belle gazed after him dubiously, yet reassured in spite of herself.   After all, there was nothing.

CHAPTER TWENTY-FOUR

When a Lorrigan Loves

FOLLOWED a day of sweltering heat, when the horses in the corral switched flies and sweated doing nothing; when all of the chickens crawled under the coolest shelter they could find, and panted with their wings spread away from their bodies; when the wind was like a blast from an open furnace, and no man of his own choice remained in the sun.

In the shade of the biggest haystack, Tom and Al squatted on their boot heels with their faces toward the corral and the houses beyond, and talked for two hours in low monotones while they broke spears of fragrant hay into tiny bits and snapped the bits from them with thumb and finger. From the house porch Lance saw them there and wondered what they were talking about so long. He even meditated committing the crime of eavesdropping, but he decided against it. Even if there had been any point from which he could approach the two unseen, his soul rebelled against such tactics employed in cold blood.

Devil's Tooth Ranch dragged somehow through its third day of inaction, and that night prepared itself to sleep if possible, though the hot wind still blew half a gale and the sky was too murky to show any stars.

Daylight found Lance awake and brooding as he had done ever since his return. He heard no sound in the house, and after a while he dressed and went down to the bunk house. It was empty. No extra horses had been corralled the night before, of that he was sure. Yet the boys were gone again, and with them had gone Tom and Al. He looked and saw Coaley in the box stall.

On this morning Lance asked no questions of Sam Pretty Cow or Shorty, who presently appeared and went listlessly about their tasks. He returned to the house, heard Riley grinding coffee, and dressed for riding while he waited for breakfast. He was drinking his first cup of coffee when Belle appeared in a thin blue kimono and a lacey breakfast cap which Lance knew had been ordered from the big, dog-eared catalogue on the living-room table. He roused himself from scowling meditation and gave her a smile.

"Sleep any?"

"Not much," sighed Belle. "Tom —" she stopped and looked at Lance hesitatingly. "Tom had to push the cattle back from Lava Bed way — he says this weather's drying up Lava Creek and the stock'll suffer if they're left drifting up and

down the mud-holes where they've watered all
summer. He took the boys and started about
two in the morning — to get out of the heat. I —
I didn't think you'd want to go, honey —"

"You thought right. I didn't want to go; it's
too hot," Lance assured her, and refrained from
looking at her face and the pathetic cheerfulness
she was trying so hard to make real.

"It's sultry. I thought yesterday I couldn't
stand another hour of that wind — but now I wish
it would blow. It's going to storm —"

"Yes. It's going to storm." Lance set down
his empty cup. "I may go fishing, Belle. Don't
look for me back — I may ride over and see how
the AJ is making out. The little Boyle girl is not
married yet, I hope?"

"Oh — no. No, she isn't. Lance, honey —"

Lance waited beside her chair, but Belle seemed
to forget that she had anything to say. She sat
leaning her head on one hand, the other stirring
her coffee absent-mindedly. "Don't get caught
out," she said apathetically.

"I won't." Lance lifted the lace frill of the cap
and kissed her temple lightly. "Go back to bed.
It's too early for you to be up."

At the stable Sam Pretty Cow looked a question,
grunted and went on with his stall-cleaning.
Lance saddled Coaley, tied on an emergency ra-
tion of grub.

"Fishin's good t'day. Storm's coming. Uh-huh — you bet," Sam Pretty Cow observed as Lance mounted.

"Maybe," Lance assented non-committally and rode away.

There were no horse tracks in the trail, yet Lance followed it doggedly, the new-risen sun burning his back through two thin shirts. He seemed in no doubt this morning as to the course he should take. He scarcely gave a glance at the trail. His eyes were staring straight before him at a sullen row of blue-black "thunder heads" that showed above the gray skyline. Yet he did not see them, did not give a thought to their meaning.

He was thinking poignantly of Mary Hope, fighting the vivid impression which a dream last night had left with him. In his dream Mary Hope had stood at her door, with her hands held out to him beseechingly, and called and called: "Lance! Oh, Lance! I dinna hate you because you're a Lorrigan — Oh, *Lance!*"

It had been a curious dream from start to finish. Curious because, in various forms, this was the third time he had seen her stand with hands outstretched, calling to him. He did not believe in dreams. He had neither patience for presentiments nor faith in anything that bordered on the occult.

It had been against much inner protest that he had ridden to the schoolhouse in obedience to the persistent idea that she needed him. That he had not found her there seemed to him conclusive proof that there was nothing in telepathy. The dreams, he felt sure, were merely a continuation of that persistent idea — and the persistent idea, he was beginning to believe, was but a perverse twist given to his own longing for her.

"— And I can't go to her — not yet. Not while the Lorrigan name —" What came before, what came after those incomplete phrases he would not permit his mind to formulate in words. But he could not shake off the effect of the dream, could not stifle altogether the impulse that plucked at his resolve.

For more than an hour he rode and tried to fix his mind upon the thing he had set out to do. He knew perfectly well where he was going — and it was *not* to see Mary Hope. Neither was his destination Lava Creek nor the drying range on either side. His first two days of hard riding had been not altogether fruitless, and he had enough to think of without thinking of Mary Hope. Certain cold facts stared at him, and gibbered their sinister meaning, and dared him to ride on and discover other facts, blood-brothers of these that haunted him o' nights.

Coaley, feeling his rider's mood, sensing also the portent of the heavy, heat-saturated atmosphere and the rolling thunder heads, slowed his springy trot to a walk and tossed his head uneasily from side to side. Then, quite without warning, Lance wheeled the horse short around and touched the reeking flanks with his heels.

"I'm seventeen kinds of a damn fool — but I can't stand any more of this!" he muttered savagely, and rode at a sharp trot with his back to the slow-gathering storm.

He found Mary Hope half a mile from the Douglas house, at the edge of the meadow round which Hugh was driving a mower, the steady, metallic clicking of the shuttle-like sickle sounding distinct from the farther side of the motionless green expanse. Mary Hope was standing leaning against one lone little poplar tree, her hat in her hand, and her eyes staring dully into the world of sorrowful thoughts. Relief and a great, hungry tenderness flooded the soul of Lance when he saw her. He pulled up and swung off beside her.

"Girl — thank the good God you're all right," he said, and took her in his arms, the veins on his temples beating full with his hot blood. "I had to come. I had to see you. You've haunted me. Your voice has called me — I was afraid — I had to come — and now I'm not going to let you go. Oh, girl, you're mine! By all the powers of heaven and earth, you're mine! The Lorrigan name — what does it matter? You're mine — I love you. You'll love me. I'll *make* you love me. You'll love me till you won't care who I am or who you are, or whether there are any other people in the world — you'll love me so! And I'll love you always, always, — to death and beyond, and beyond what lies after that. Girl, girl — you do need me! You need my love. You need it because it's the biggest thing in the world — and your love is going to match it. We'll get married — we'll make a world of our own, just you and I. We won't care where we make it — it will be our world, the world of our love. Are you game? Are you game to love Lance the way Lance loves you? Oh, girl, tell me!"

A chill breath swept them like the memory of her father's hate. A deep, basso rumble drowned whatever reply she stammered. He sheltered her in his arms, kissed her lips, her eyes, her hair, went back to her lips again.

"Oh, girl — when a Lorrigan loves —!" He cried softly, exultantly. "I tried not to — but I had to love you. It's Fate. Are you afraid to love me back? Are you afraid?"

"No Lorrigan can cry coward to a Douglas," Mary Hope panted. "But — but my mother will be that —"

"My mother will be that — all of that, and more," Lance stopped her, still exulting in her love. "All the Lorrigans — what does it matter? Life's for you and me to live, you girl with the bluest eyes in the world. When will you marry me? To-day? Tell me to-day!"

"Oh!" gasped Mary Hope, breathless still from

the suddenness of it all. "Oh, not to-day — oh, but the headlong way you have! I — I canna think. I —''

"I don't want you to think. I didn't ask you to think. Just love me — that's all. And marry me soon, Girl-with-the-blue-eyes. Soon. It must be soon — sooner than to-morrow —''

Splittingly the thunder crashed close behind them, a vivid white line cleaving sharply the snarling clouds. Like a sleeper Lance opened the eyes he had closed against her hair and lifted his head. "I must take you home," he said more calmly. "It's going to storm — hard. But let me tell you, sweetheart, — it can't storm as hard as I can love. I'll take you home, and then you'll marry me.''

Mary Hope's face was pale and radiant. She did not say that she would marry him — nor did she say that she would not. Her eyes were misty with tears until she winked hard, when they shone softly. Lance had never seen them so blue. She stood still, her hands clasped together tightly while he gathered up the reins and mounted. He pulled his foot from the left stirrup, reached down to her and smiled. Never had she seen him smile like that. Never had she seen that look in his eyes. She breathed deep, reached up and caught the saddle horn, put her foot in the stirrup and let him lift her beside him.

Against Coaley's nervous pull at the bit Lance

held a steadying hand and laughed. "It's Fate, girl. Let the storm come. We'll beat it — it can't hurt us. Nothing can hurt us now." He had to shout above the crashing thunder. "Do you love me, sweetheart?" His eyes, close to her own, flamed softly, making Mary Hope think dizzily of altar fires.

"I do — I do!" She gasped. "Oh, I cannot think how I love you — it scares me to think!" Her arm was around his neck, her face was turned to his.

He saw her lips form the words, guessed what it was she was saying. The crash on crash of thunder beat the sound of her voice to nothingness. The white glare of the lightning flashes blinded them. Coaley, quivering, his nostrils belling until they showed all red within, his big eyes staring, forged ahead, fighting the bit.

"He's rinning away wi' us!" shouted Lance, his lips close to her ear, and laughed boyishly.

"Mother —" he heard her say, and pulled her higher in his arms, so that he could be sure that she heard him.

"I'll just pick your little old mother up in my arms and make her love me, too!" he cried. "Nothing can spoil our love — *nothing!*"

As though the gods themselves chided his temerity, the very heavens split and shattered all sound with rending uproar. Coaley squatted, stopped and stood shaking, his heart pounding so that Lance felt its tremulous tattoo against his thigh. The rumbling after-note of the thunder seemed like silence.

"It struck close. That shed — look!" Lance's voice was no longer the voice of the young male whose love would override Fate itself. It was the voice of the man who will meet emergencies quietly, unflinchingly, and soothe the woman's fear. "Don't be afraid — it's all right, sweetheart."

He forced Coaley to go on. He smiled at Mary Hope's pallor, he reassured her as they neared her home. A shed, sufficiently detached to keep its fire to itself, was blazing. The wind puffed suddenly from nowhere and waved the high, yellow flames like torn ribbons. Great globules of water splashed upon them from the pent torrent above. Coaley galloped through the gate, passed the house, shied at something lying on the ground, stopped abruptly when Lance pulled sharply on the bit.

" Girl — sweetheart — *be game!* " Lance said sternly when Mary Hope screamed.

He let her to the ground, swung off and passed her, running to the pitifully still little figure of Mother Douglas lying in the pathway, her checked apron flapping, its starchy stiffness showing limp dark spots where the raindrops splashed.

"She's only shocked. She's all right — *stop that screaming!* Good God, girl, where's your nerve?"

His severity steadied her. Mary Hope stopped screaming, both hands held tightly over her mouth. Lance was already on his way to the house, carrying Mother Douglas like a sleeping child in his arms. And the rain came, a white curtain of water that drenched them to the skin in the first ten seconds.

On the bed where Aleck Douglas had stared at the ceiling, and raved, and died, Lance laid her carefully as though he feared to waken her. He tore open the faded calico dress at the throat, laid his ear upon her heart.

" She's alive, sweetheart," he said hearteningly. "It's only a shock. Bring a basin of water. We'll have her all right in no time."

He worked over the old woman, using all the means he could remember or invent, while the house shook with the fury of the wind, and the lightning dazzled them and the rain drummed incessantly on the roof. Mary Hope watched him, her eyes wide, her lips refusing to form any words. For her own sake he sent her on many little errands, kept her busy at useless little tasks. After what seemed an interminable time he stood looking down at the gently heaving breast.

"How game is my girl?" he asked, taking Mary Hope in his arms. "Is she game enough to stay here while Lance goes for a doctor? It won't be long —" He paused while he made a rapid mental calculation of the distance, and of what a

horse may endure. "Three hours. Will my girl
be brave enough to stay here three hours? I'll
call the man who was mowing — if I can find him.
But that will take minutes. Three hours — and
you won't weaken, will you, dear?"

Mary Hope leaned against him, clutched him,
shivered at the crashing thunder. "It's awful,"
she moaned. "I'm afraid you might be hit —"

"Afraid? A Douglas not as game as a Lorrigan?" He shook her, lifted his eyebrows at her,
pursed his lips at her, shook her again and kissed
her. "I can't love a girl who's afraid of thunder.
Your mother's all right, you know. We saw where
that bolt struck — fifty yards, almost, from where
she was. She got a shock, that's all. But we'll
have a doctor here and make him take the responsi-
bility. And I'll be back in three hours, and you're
going to be game — just as game as you've always
been."

He pulled his hat down over his eyes, buttoned
his wet coat to the chin, laid his hand for a minute
over the faintly pulsating heart of Mother Douglas, swept Mary Hope up in his arms and kissed
her again, pulled open the door and was gone.

Through a rain-blurred window Mary Hope saw
him run to the stable, lead out Coaley who had
taken refuge there, vault into the saddle without
troubling about the stirrup, and come thundering
back past the house and out of the gate, his head
bent to the storm.

She looked at the clock. Three hours? He could never do it in three hours! She went back and knelt beside the bed, and prayed as her mother had taught her to pray. And not all of her petition was for her mother. Every lightning flash, every crack, every distant boom of the thunder made her cringe. Lance — Lance was out in the storm, at the mercy of its terrible sword-thrusts that seemed to smite even the innocent. Her mother — even her own mother, who had held unswervingly to her faith — even she had been struck down!

A mile down the road Lance was leaning forward, encouraging Coaley to more speed, because there the trail ran level and fairly free from rocks. Later, he pulled the horse down to a walk, breathing him up a hill; let him trot down the slope beyond, picked him into a swift gallop when they again struck the level. He gauged, with cold-blooded attention to certain rough miles in the journey, just how swiftly Coaley could cover ground and live. He knew horses. He knew Coaley, and he knew that never yet had Coaley been pushed to the actual limit of his endurance. But the girl Lance loved — ah, it was a Lorrigan who loved! — was back there alone, and she would be counting the minutes. It might be that he might return to find her weeping over her dead. So Lance counted miles and a horse's strength, and bent to the storm and rode.

Ten minutes past the hour, and he was snapping orders to the telegraph operator. The storm, happily, had swept on down the canyon and had given Jumpoff little more than a wetting and a few lightning flashes.

"And order out a special engine and coach, — what do I care what it will cost? I'll pay. Wire your Lava chief that the money is here. Send the doctor on ahead of the regular train — can't wait for that."

He had the Lorrigan habit of carrying a good deal of money on his person, and he counted out banknotes until the operator lifted his hand and said it was enough. He slammed out, then, mounted and rode to a livery stable and gave orders there.

"— And I'll *buy* the damn team, so kill 'em if you have to. Only get the doctor out there." He was in the saddle and gone again before the stableman had recovered from his sag-jawed astonishment.

"Guess there's something in that talk of him and the Douglas girl," the stableman gossiped to a friend while he harnessed his swiftest team.

In ten minutes under the three hours Lance stopped at the house, went in and saw that Mary Hope was still being game, and was very glad to be in his arms, and that Mother Douglas was alive and staring up at the ceiling, her face set in a deadly kind of calm.

"She moves her eyes to me, sometimes — she's been awake for almost an hour. But she hasn't moved —" Her voice broke.

"It's all right — the doctor is on his way. And I'm here, sweetheart — you won't be alone again. Where's that man of yours? I'll send him over with a note to Belle. She'll come — she's a wonder with sick folks."

"Mother — I'm afraid mother wouldn't let her — she's that *set!*"

Lance looked at the corpse-like figure with the wide-open eyes and a flicker of the lids now and then to show that she was alive, and swallowed a lump in his throat. Mother Douglas would probably not know who was with her, he thought.

Coaley, the proud-spirited, shambled slowly to the stable, his head drooping, his eyes dulled with exhaustion. He had done his part. Lance rubbed him down, blanketed him, working swiftly, his thoughts with Mary Hope and her love and her fresh grief. He found Hugh, scribbled a note to Belle and got him started on Jamie.

Mother Douglas moved her eyes, stared at him sharply when he went to her. But she did not speak, did not move a muscle of her face. The heart of Lance went heavy, but he could smile still at Mary Hope and tell her that it was all right, and that the doctor ought to be there in an hour or so, and that Belle would come, and that he loved her, loved her, loved her.

CHAPTER TWENTY-FIVE

Belle Lorrigan Wins

IN the second-best suit of Aleck Douglas, with his wrists showing strong and shapely below the coat sleeves, and wrinkles across his back, Lance turned his own steaming apparel before the kitchen fire and waited to hear what the doctor had to say.

In his mind was a great wonder at the inscrutable operations of Fate, that had twice brought tragedy into the Douglas house while he himself was permitted to bring all his love, which without the tragedies might have been rejected; which had sent him hurrying to Mary Hope on this day of all the days when he had longed to come. He could not believe that blind Chance had irresponsibly twisted the threads of Mary Hope's life so that these things had come upon her. He was abashed, humbled, filled with awe of the tremendous forces that rule our destinies. For perhaps the first time in his life he stood face to face with something beyond his understanding, something against which his arrogant young strength was powerless.

The doctor presently came to him, beckoned him to the doorway and preceded him into the rain-washed yard, where the late afternoon sun shone with dazzling brightness after the storm.

"I think she'll live through this," the doctor began abruptly. "It was not the lightning, altogether, though she undoubtedly did receive a severe shock. There has been a predisposition to paralysis, which is the true nature of this attack. Her right side is completely paralyzed, and so far as I can determine after a more-or-less superficial examination, her vocal chords are also affected, making speech impossible. Her left arm is not affected, and her mind seems fairly normal. Too much work, too much worry, too much monotony — and she has reached the time of life when these things are most apt to occur. Her husband's death was undoubtedly a contributary cause. With proper medical attention she may recover from this attack — partially, at least. She should be removed to a good hospital, or a trained nurse placed in charge of the case here. That will be expensive. Do you know whether the family can afford —"

"The family can afford anything she needs, anything that will give her a chance," Lance told him brusquely.

"She will probably be an invalid as long as she lives," the doctor went on. "She will be a great care. Are there any relatives, other than the girl?

It's a tremendous burden to fall on her shoulders, Mr. Lorrigan.''

"The burden," said Lance, "will not fall on her shoulders. I don't mind telling you that Miss Douglas and I will be married very soon. As soon as possible."

The doctor brightened visibly. "Congratulations, Mr. Lorrigan! I should strongly advise you, then, to have the old lady removed to a nice, quiet hospital. You will not want the care of her — young people should not be handicapped in that way. I can make the necessary arrangements. She should not be subjected to the discomforts of the journey just at present — it's a long way by team, and a long way by train. I should like to have her as quiet as possible for a few days, at least."

"We'll look after that," said Lance, and hurried in to tell Mary Hope that her mother was not going to die, and that Belle was coming — he could hear the rattle of the buckboard.

"I don't know what mother will say," Mary Hope began, and stopped and hid her eyes behind her hands. Her mother, poor soul, could not say anything. It seemed terrible to Mary Hope that her mother must lie there and endure the presence of the painted Jezebel in her home, and be unable to utter one word of denunciation, one bitter reproach. It was like a judgment; and she could not bear the thought that her mother must suffer it. A judgment, or treachery on her part, — the terrible treason of a child betraying her mother.

"It's all right, girl; you don't *know* our Belle. We'll just leave it to her. She'll find a way. And I'll go out now and tell her all about it, and leave her to manage."

"I'll go," Mary Hope decided unexpectedly. "I have things to say — you shall not go, Lance Lorrigan. You will please let me see her alone — first. I'm that afraid of Belle Lorrigan I could creep under the table and hide! And so I shall go alone to her."

Lance surrendered, and rolled a cigarette and smoked it in the kitchen, and wondered if a cigarette had ever been smoked in that house before, and whether the ghost of Aleck Douglas was somewhere near, struggling vainly against the inevitable. It certainly was unbelievable that a Lorrigan should be there, master — in effect, at least — of the Douglas household, wearing the shoddy garments of Aleck Douglas, and finding them at least three sizes too small.

They were an unconscionably long time out there, — those two women who meant so much to him. He glanced in at Mother Douglas, in bed now and looking terribly shrunken and old. The doctor was with her, sitting close to the bed and leaning forward a little, watching her eyes while he talked soothingly. Lance was not wanted there, either. He returned to the kitchen and put more wood in the stove, and felt tentatively his drying clothes.

Belle came in, holding Mary Hope by the hand. The eyes of both were moist, shining, blue as the sky outside.

"Lance, honey, I'm glad," she whispered, kissing him on the cheek. "Hope told me. And don't you two kids worry about me. I'll win my way somehow. I always have — and I guess maybe you've got it in you, too, Lance. It sure took something more than Lorrigan nerve to win Mary Hope — though I'll admit Lorrigan nerve won *me*. No, I won't go in there now. Don't tell her I'm here, we'll wait awhile."

It was dusk, and the lamp had not yet been lighted. Through the unshaded window Mother Douglas could look out at the first pale stars. The doctor had gone. The house was very quiet, the snapping of the kitchen fire, the steady *tick*-tock, *tick*-tock of the old-fashioned clock blending with, rather than breaking, the silence.

Mother Douglas closed her eyes. Her groping left hand ceased its aimless plucking at a yarn knot in the patchwork comforter. Her breath came evenly — Mary Hope wondered if she slept. A hand fell on Mary Hope's shoulder, though she had not heard a footfall. She seemed prepared, seemed to know what she must do. She slipped out of the chair, and Belle slipped into it. Mother Douglas opened her eyes, turned them that way; infinite weariness marked the glance. Her left hand resumed again its vague groping, the work-worn fingers plucking at the coverlet.

Sitting there in the dusk, her fingers faintly outlined in the old wooden armchair in which Aleck Douglas had been wont to sit and brood somberly over his work and his wrongs, Belle began softly to sing:

> *"Ye banks and braes o' bonnie Doon,*
> *How can ye bloom sae fresh and fair?"*

The withered hand lay still, the fingers clutching tightly a fold of cotton cloth. Mother Douglas looked and closed her eyes. Leaning close, when the song was finished, Belle saw that the grim lips were trembling, that tears were slipping down the too calm face. With her handkerchief she wiped away the tears, and sang again. The "Girl with a Thousand Songs" had many Scottish melodies in her repertoire, and the years had not made her forget.

At the last, the groping left hand reached painfully across, found Belle's hand waiting, and closed on it tightly. Whenever Belle stopped singing the hand would clutch hers. When she began again the fingers would relax a little. It was not much, but it was enough.

In the kitchen Mary Hope moved quietly about, cooking supper, straining and putting away the milk Hugh brought in. In the kitchen Lance sat

and watched her, and made love to her with his eyes, with his voice that made of the most commonplace remark a caress.

But that night, when Mary Hope was asleep and Belle was dozing beside the stricken woman, Lance saddled Jamie and led Coaley home. And while he rode, black Trouble rode with him and Love could not smile and beat back the spectre with his fists, but hid his face and whimpered, and was afraid.

For Lance was face to face again with that sinister, unnamed Something that hung over the Devil's Tooth ranch. He might forget it for a few hours, engrossed with his love and in easing this new trouble that had come to Mary Hope; he might forget, but that did not make his own trouble any the less menacing, any the less real.

He could not tell her so, now while she had this fresh worry over her mother, but Lance knew — and while he rode slowly he faced the knowledge — that he could not marry Mary Hope while the cloud hung over the Devil's Tooth. And that there was a cloud, a black, ominous cloud from which the lightning might be expected to strike and blast the Lorrigans, he could not deny. It was there. He knew it, knew just how loud were its mutterings, knew that it was gathering swiftly, pushing up over the horizon faster than did the storm of the morning.

He would not put Coaley down the Slide trail,

but took him around by the wagon road. They plodded along at a walk, Coaley's stiffened muscles giving him the gait of an old horse. There had been no urgent need to take Coaley home at once, but it was an excuse, and Lance used it. He could not think, — he could not face his own trouble when he was near Mary Hope. She drove everything else from his mind, and Lance knew that some things must not be driven from his mind. He had set himself to do certain things. Now, with Mary Hope loving him, there was all the more reason why he should do them.

The ranch seemed deserted, though of course it was late and he knew that every one would be in bed. He found a lantern, put Coaley into the box stall again, and spent a long time rubbing him down and carrying him fresh hay and water. He went up then and roused Sam Pretty Cow, who was sleeping in the small cabin he had elected to make his own private habitation on the ranch. Sam Pretty Cow told him that no one had come home as yet.

"Two, three days, I dunno. Mebby Tom comes then," he hazarded, blinking at Lance. "This too quick. Nobody comes back same day, you bet."

Lance stood looking down at him, scowling thoughtfully. "Sam, you've been a long time with the outfit. You've been a good man. You aren't crippled up — and you're the best rider of the bunch of us. Why don't *you* go out any more?"

Sam lighted a cigarette, blew out the blazing match and laid the burnt stub carefully on a box. He smoked stolidly, gazing at the dingy wall before him.

"Bust them bronks in the corral," he said at last, grinning briefly. "You stay long, you see me ride. Uh-huh — yo' bet."

"Well, yes. That's all right. But why don't you go with the outfit?" Lance leaned against the wall, arms folded, studying him. It was almost hopeless, trying to get anything out of Sam Pretty Cow; still, Lance tried it.

Sam Pretty Cow looked up at him, looked down at his bare feet that he had swung out of bed when Lance wakened him.

"Uh-huh. That's why. That all right, I'm go. That ain't all right, I'm don' go. You bet."

Lance tap-tapped his right arm with the fingers of his left hand, chewed his lip and looked at Sam Pretty Cow.

"Still, dad lets you stick around the outfit," he drawled meaningly.

Sam Pretty Cow shot a quick glance toward him, looked at the door, relaxed again and studied his toes which he wriggled on the dirty floor.

"I'm good man, you bet. I'm mind my business." He drew a long breath, glanced again from the door to Lance's face. "Tom's damn smart man — me, I'm mebby smarter. I dunno."

Lance looked down at him, smiling strangely.

"Sam, I'm minding my business, too.   I'm doing it by — not minding my own business.   Tom Lorrigan's a smart man — but I'm Tom Lorrigan's son."

Sam turned his foot over, looked critically at the calloused sole of it, turned it back again and blew a mouthful of smoke.   "Yeah — uh-huh.   You damn smart — you don't like them damn jail. I'm don't. We both smart, you bet."

Lance lifted an eyebrow.   "What's the Piegan word for *accomplice,* Sam?" he asked softly.

Sam Pretty Cow considered.   "Me, I'm don' know them damn word," he decided.

"It's a word that sends smart men to jail, Sam. It means the man that stays at home and — *knows.*"

Sam Pretty Cow tucked his feet under the thin blanket, laid his half-smoked cigarette on the box, with the burning end out over the edge.

"Uh-huh.   Yeah.   You bet."   He looked up at Lance, for the first time meeting his eyes squarely. "I'm know them damn word you call. Nh-hn. Long time I'm got that what it mean on my heart. You're damn right."   He waited a minute, saw the Lorrigan look on Lance's face, on his lips that smiled enigmatically.   "Them Californy got bronks to bust?"

"Surest thing you know, Sam. But that's all right. You stay."

Sam Pretty Cow looked doubtful as an Indian may ever be expected to look.

"You stay, Sam. There'll be bronks to bust on the Devil's Tooth for a long while yet." He moved to the door, pulled it open and stood looking out. Only a few miles away Mary Hope lay asleep, loving him in her dreams, please God. Here, the Shadow hung black over the Devil's Tooth. He turned to Sam Pretty Cow whose hand was stretched toward the smoky lamp.

"You forget that word, Sam. It doesn't mean anything at all — to a Piegan. And Sam, if I'm not around to-morrow morning, you ride over to the Douglas ranch, and take back the horse I borrowed. Belle may want to send you to town. She's there."

Sam Pretty Cow's eyes widened appreciably. "Uh-huh — all right. I'm go," he promised, and blew out the light.

Lance went slowly up to the house and lay face downward on his bed.

CHAPTER TWENTY-SIX

The Dope

TRAVELING lightly, Lance had covered a hundred and fifty miles in four days, through country where trails were few and rough. He had made wide detours, had slept on the ground in his slicker, had eaten bacon and bannocks cooked in the small frying pan which he carried in the sack with his meager rations. He had missed altogether the Devil's Tooth outfit, and was swinging back now by way of the Lava Beds, where Tom had said that they were going. It was because Tom had named that as his destination that Lance had ridden elsewhere to find him; good reasoning, but so far unproductive of results.

Four days, and he had not heard from Mary Hope, had learned nothing conclusive, either for or against the Devil's Tooth. Some clues he had gleaned, some evidence that strengthened his suspicions, but nothing to make him feel that the trip had been worth the hardship.

Without knowing just why, he had ridden out expecting to learn the best or the worst and have done with nagging suspicion. It had seemed to him that Fate meant to be kind, that his destiny and Mary Hope's pointed the way to happiness. Now he was beginning to doubt. How was happiness possible, if the outlaw blood of the Lorrigans ran at high pressure through the veins of his family? He did not know to a certainty that it did, but until he knew that it did not he could never marry Mary Hope. He had to know. It had been pure madness, going to her as he had gone. While his horse plodded up the hill to where the lava outcroppings began, Lance meditated gloomily on the madness that had driven him to her. He had felt so sure of himself and his future, so much the master of his destiny and hers! Yet, even while he wooed her tempestuously he had known that it was madness, that Trouble was reaching even then to pluck him by the sleeve. Mary Hope and her stern, Scotch integrity linked to the blackened Lorrigan name that might soon stand on the roster of the State's prison? It was impossible, inconceivable. He had been a hound to say to her what he had said.

True, when her mother was stricken he had been there to help her, to comfort her. But it would be small comfort to Mary Hope when the storm broke over the Devil's Tooth.

"And I said Fate was with us — I said nothing could hurt her! And it will hurt her all her life."

His sweaty horse paused to breathe, heaving a great sigh, looking discouragedly at the climb yet before him. Lance came to himself and swung off, giving the horse an apologetic slap on the shoulder. "You ought to kick me cold, Sorry, for making you pack my hulking carcase up this hill. Why didn't you stop at the bottom?"

Sorry looked at him, waited for Lance to take the lead, and climbed after him more briskly. He was a big-boned, well-muscled animal, but two hundred pounds had been a heavy load to carry up hill, and he was glad to be rid of it.

At the top Lance did not remount. The thickly strewn flat rocks made treacherous footing, and more than one man had taken a nasty fall because he had chosen to ride that mile of lava when he should have walked. It was somewhere along this stretch of rock outcropping that Shorty had broken his knee so that he would never ride again to the round-up.

Lance was walking along with his head down, brooding over his trouble, when he fancied he heard a faint halloo. Sorry stopped and craned his head. But Lance could see nothing save the barren stretch of lava and the monotonous wilderness beyond, with mountains in the far background and the Black Rim stretching grim on the left of him. He started on, thinking that perhaps some animal or bird was responsible for the sound. But he had gone but a short distance when it came again, more distinctly because he was half listening for it.

He waited, made a guess at the location of the person who shouted, and turned that way, changing the reins from his right hand to his left and pulling his holstered six-shooter within easy reach of his hand. This was not the country, his was not the errand, for carelessness, and Lance was taking no risk.

As he walked his eyes roved continually over the brown expanse of rocks and stunted juniper that formed the Lava Beds. Behind him came Sorry, his worn shoes slipping now and then on a smooth rock, his head bobbing patiently, close to Lance's shoulder. As so often happens, it was the horse that first discovered the object of their search. He pulled away from the direct line, looking and looking at what Lance, keen-eyed though he was, mistook for a black rock with a juniper bush growing beside it.

Lance turned that way, focussed his glasses upon the object and saw what had happened. A horse had fallen with its rider, the two lying together, the man pinned under the horse. A black horse which he recognized, and a big, red-faced cowpuncher with gray eyes that did not twinkle. While Lance looked, the man lifted his head, seemed to be staring straight into Lance's face, opened his mouth and contorted his pain-racked face in a shout. It was strange to have the sound reach Lance's ears thinned and weakened by distance, while the glasses brought the injured man

so close that he could see the wild look of entreaty
in his eyes. Lance put up the glasses and began
running, with Sorry stumbling and slipping behind him.

"I been here since morning," the big cowpuncher chattered feverishly when Lance came up
to him. "I'm fixed, all right! I was dozing and
I didn't jump and he caught me when he fell. I
guess his leg is broke, but so is mine, fur's that
goes. I come down hard on a rock and I guess I
broke some ribs or something. Hurt like hell for
a few hours — it ain't so bad now. Look out when
you go to make him git up — if he rolls on me it's
all off. I guess it's all off, anyway, but I don't
want to be squashed to death."

Lance bit his lip. It was hard to hear the man
talking, talking, in that rapid, headlong fashion,
while his leg lay under the full weight of the black
horse and the sun blazed on his uncovered head.
It was hard to see his shirt all blood-soaked on
the left side where he had fallen across an uptilted,
thin-edged rock.

The horse, too, was in sorry state. A weed-
grown crevice had cheated him with its semblance
to sound footing, and he lay with front leg broken,
groaning a little now and then while the man talked
and talked. And while he examined the two it
seemed to Lance that Fate was pointing, and saying that here, too, was one of the inscrutable instruments by which he worked out the destinies

of men. A slippery rock, a man riding that way half asleep —

"I'll have to shoot this horse, I'm afraid," Lance said pityingly. "His leg is broken — it's the most merciful thing I can do. And if I try to lift him off you while he's alive he may struggle —"

"Sure thing! Go on and shoot him! I woulda done it myself if you hadn't come along purty soon. I knowed it would be all off with us both if we had to lay out all night, so I was going to finish us both off, when I seen you. Thought I'd take a gambling chance till dark — but the sun has been baking me to a crisp —"

"It's all right — I'll get you to a ranch. We'll fix you up, so don't think about the finish." A little of the color had left Lance's face. Shooting a horse was to him next thing to shooting a human. He had to do it, though. There was no other way.

He took the horse by the cheek-piece of the bridle, spoke to him gently, turned the head a little away from him so that the horse could not look him in the eyes. "Poor old fellow, it's all I can do for you," he muttered when he pulled his gun from the holster.

"Maybe you better do the same for me," said the man, still speaking in the rapid tone which told of fever. "You ain't able to heave him off me, are you?"

"Sure, I'm able to. Lie still, now, and grit your teeth, old man. It may hurt, when I lift him off your leg. I'll raise him up and put a rock under, and pull you out. Can you stand that?"

"Me? Hell, yes. Ain't I been standing pain since before daylight? Me, I can stand anything if I have to!"

Yet he fainted when Lance took him by the shoulders and pulled him free, and Lance used half the water in the canteen on the saddle in bringing him back to consciousness. When the fellow opened his eyes, Lance remembered that he had half a pint of whisky in his coat pocket, and offered it to the injured one.

"Golly, that's a life-saver!" he ejaculated when he had taken two swallows. He reached down and felt his crushed leg, grimacing at the pain of returning circulation.

"She's busted all right. Busted *right*, if I'm any judge. And my side — things are all busted up in there. I know it. Say, oldtimer, how do you figure you're going to get me outa here? Do you know it's all of ten miles to the nearest ranch? I've got a map of the whole country in my coat pocket. I'll show yuh if you don't know. You're a stranger, I guess. I don't recollect seeing yore horse before. I always know horses. What's his brand?"

Lance did not say. He himself was wondering how he was going to get the man out of there. If

the fellow thought he was a stranger, all the better. Still, it did not matter much. Already the
whisky was whipping the man's brain to quicker
action, loosening his tongue that had already been
set wagging by fever.

"Think you can stand it to ride?" he asked solic-
itously. "I can heave you into the saddle, if you
can stand being moved. I'd ride to the next ranch
and bring a wagon — but the country's too rough.
A rig couldn't get within five miles of here."

"You're right. Not even Belle Lorrigan's buckboard could make it across that canyon on beyond.
Say, speaking of the Lorrigans —" he hesitated,
then plunged recklessly on. "I'm going to pass
you some dope I've got on that outfit. The
chances are I'm done for. The way my insides
feel — and you do something for me, will you? If
I cash in, you turn in this dope. We may as well
'tend to this business right now, before I tackle
the job of riding."

Lance stood looking down at him while he fum-
bled in his pocket, pulled out a small leather note-
book and some papers.

"I'm a stock detective, see. My name's Burt
Brownlee. I was just about ready to turn in the
dope and have the whole outfit pulled. Well, it's
all here. They been rustling right and left, see.
But they're cute — they're *damn* cute. We been
trying to work up the case on the outside, and it
seemed like somebody in the Black Rim was send-

ing stock out, and so I've been working on this end.
Now here's the data. I followed 'em, and I've got
the dope. I know now how they work it, and my
evidence and this dope here, that can be verified
later on when the time comes, will put the whole
bunch over the road, see. They're outlaws — always have been — but they won't be by the time
they get outa the pen."

"You better keep that," Lance cut in gruffly.
"Man, that's nothing you want to be gabbling to a
stranger. Shut up, and let me put you on my
horse."

"No, I want to tell yuh," Burt insisted with all
the obstinacy of a man half crazy with pain and
whisky. "I want to tell yuh, and I'm going to
tell yuh! Get down here and listen. Here's a
map, and here's the brands they worked, and
here's how they worked 'em. And here's the
dates."

On one knee Lance kneeled and listened, his jaws
set hard together. Fast as the man talked the
thoughts of Lance flew ahead, snatched at the
significance of every detail, every bit of evidence.
Some things puzzled Burt Brownlee, but Lance
knew the answer to the puzzle while Burt talked
and talked. Finally he laid his hand over the
finely traced maps that showed secret trails, un-
guessed, hidden little draws where stolen stock
had been concealed, all the fine threads that would
weave the net close around the Lorrigans.

"Here, put that stuff up. This is not getting you to a doctor, and this can wait. Put it up."

"No, you take it. And if I don't pull through, you turn it in. You keep it. I don't want to be found dead with that dope on *me* — you can't tell who might get hold of it." He thrust the papers and the book eagerly into Lance's unwilling hand.

"No-o, you can't tell who might get hold of it," Lance admitted, biting his lip. "Well, let me take your riding outfit off this horse and then we'll go."

While he pulled saddle and bridle off the dead horse, Burt Brownlee talked and talked and talked. He wanted more whisky, which Lance promised him he should have when he was ready to get on the horse. He told further evidence against the Devil's Tooth, told how he had followed Tom for two days only to see him later at the ranch where he had returned while Burt had for a time lost the trail. On that trip, he said, he would have gotten the full details of one "job" had he not turned off to follow Tom Lorrigan.

While he worked Lance listened stoically. When he was ready to start he led Sorry close, lifted the fellow as tenderly as he could, saw him faint again with the pain, and somehow got him on the horse while he was still unconscious. Burt Brownlee was a big man, but he was not of great weight. Lance bound him to the saddle with his own riata, revived him with a little more whisky, and started for Conley's, who lived nearest.

It was ten miles to Conleys, as riders guessed the distance. Lance walked and led Sorry, and tried to hold Burt Brownlee in the saddle, and listened to his rambling talk, and gave him more whisky when he seemed ready to die. During certain intervals when Burt seemed lucid enough to realize his desperate condition, Lance heartened him with assurance that they were almost there.

On the way into the canyon Burt Brownlee suffered greatly on the steep trail, down which the horse must go with forward joltings that racked terribly the man's crushed side. The whisky was gone; he had finished the scanty supply at the canyon's crest, because he begged for it so hard that Lance could not steel himself to refuse. At the bottom Lance stopped Sorry, and put an arm around Burt. Lance's face was set masklike in its forced calm, but his voice was very tender, with the deep, vibrant note Mary Hope loved so ardently.

"Lean against me, old man, and rest a minute. It's pretty tough going, but you're game. You're dead game. You'll make it. Wait. I'll stand on this rock — now lean hard, and rest. Ho, there's no whisky — water will have to do you, now. I've a little in my canteen, and when you've rested —"

"I'm going," said Burt, lurching against Lance's steady strength. "You're a white man. That Lorrigan dope — don't forget what I told you — turn it in —"

Lance's mouth twisted with sudden bitterness. "I won't — forget," he said. "I'll turn it — in."

"I'm — a goner. Just — stand and let me — lean —"

Lance stood, and let him lean, and with his handkerchief he very gently dried Burt's cold, perspiring face. It seemed an endless time that he stood there. Now and then Burt clutched him with fingers that gripped his shoulders painfully, but Lance never moved. Once, when Sorry turned his head and looked back inquiringly, wondering why they did not go on, Lance spoke to the horse and his voice was calm and soothing. But when it was all over, Lance's underlip was bleeding at the corner where he had bitten into it.

He walked into Conley's yard an hour after that, his face drearily impassive, a dead man lashed to the saddle. He asked for paper and a pen, and in a firm, even handwriting he described tersely the manner of Burt Brownlee's death, told where the dead horse and the saddle would be found, and as an afterthought, lest there be trouble in locating the spot, he drew a sketch of that particular part of the Lava Beds. He signed the statement, and had the excited Conleys, shaking man and half hysterical wife, sign also as witnesses. His matter-of-fact treatment of the affair impressed them to the point of receiving his instructions as though they were commands which must on no account be disobeyed in any particular.

"I'll be back and tell the coroner. He'll want to see the horse and saddle, perhaps. Mr. Conley, you can find them without any trouble. If he wants an inquest, tell him I'll be on hand. Thank you, Mrs. Conley,—no, I'll not wait for anything to eat. I'm not hungry. I must get home. Good-by—sorry I can't do any more for you."

He mounted Sorry, pricked him into a gallop, and presently disappeared around a bend of the trail that led in the direction of the Devil's Tooth ranch.

CHAPTER TWENTY–SEVEN

DARKNESS falls late on the Black Rim country in midsummer. It was just deepening from dusk when Lance rode up to the corral gate, pulled the saddle and bridle off Sorry with swift jerks that bespoke a haste born of high nervous tension, and strode up to the house. From the bunk house, when he passed, came the murmur of low-keyed voices. The outfit, then, was at home once more. From the shaded window of Belle's bedroom a thin silver of light shone, where the blind was curled back at the edge, but the rest of the house was dark. He went in, moving softly, but Belle must have heard his step on the porch, for she came out with her bedroom lamp in her hand, the other raised to impress quiet upon him.

"Lance, honey! Where on earth have you been?" She set the lamp down on the table and came close, putting her arms around him, her eyes searching the impenetrable calm of his face, the veiled purpose behind his eyes. It was the Lorrigan fighting look; she had seen it once or twice in Tom's face and it had frightened her. She was

frightened now, but her own intrepid soul pushed
back her fear.

"*Sh-sh,* honey," she whispered, though Lance
had neither moved nor spoken since she touched
him. "*Sh-sh* — Mary Hope and her mother are
here, and they're both asleep.   I — honey, we were
so worried, when you didn't come back.   That note
you sent didn't say a *thing,* and I was afraid —
And I was between the devil and the deep sea,
honey.   I couldn't stay away from here, when I
didn't know — and I couldn't leave Hope there,
and the women that came flocking when they heard
the news were just *cows* for brains.   And the old
lady won't have a nurse and she *wouldn't* let me
out of her sight — she keeps me singing about all
the time she's awake, or reciting poetry — Bobbie
Burns, mostly, and Scott.   Would you ever *think*
she'd stand for Bobbie Burns?   But I can do it
as Scotch as she can, and she likes it.

"So she wouldn't let me leave, and I couldn't
stay — and I had Hugh make up a bed in the
spring wagon, and brought her over here.   If you
and Hope are going to be married right away, the
old lady will need to be here, anyway.   The doctor
tried to talk hospital — he just *tried.*   The old
lady can write now with her left hand so we can
make it out, and when he said hospital to her she
— she almost *swore.*

"So it's all right, Lance, honey — my God,
Lance, *what is it?*   Have you heard from Duke?"

She broke down suddenly, and clutched him in a
way that reminded him poignantly of that dying
man in the canyon. Her whisper became sibilant,
terrified. *"What is it?* What has happened?
Lance, *tell* me! Tom is here, and Al; they were
here when we came, to-day —"

Lance took a deep breath. Very gently he
leaned and kissed her on the forehead, reached
back and pulled her hands away from his shoulders.

"It's nothing, Belle. I'm — tired. And you —
you surprised me. Will it waken them if I —
clean up a little before I go to bed? I'll — be careful." He forced his eyes, his lips, to smile at
her. "Good girl, Belle. I'm — you're a trump.
Now go back to bed. Lance is on the job — Lance
won't leave again like that — he'll — settle down."

He sat down on the nearest chair and pulled off
his boots. He made an imperative gesture toward
her bedroom, and Belle, giving him a strange,
searching look, went in and closed the door after
her. He gave a sigh of relief when she was gone,
never dreaming how little he had imposed upon
her.

In his stocking feet he went to the kitchen, found
hot water in the teakettle, carried it to his room and
shaved, cleansing his body as well as he could from
the dust of the trip without making any sound that
might disturb the sleeping invalid and Mary Hope.
He dressed himself carefully as though he **were**

going to meet guests. The set look was still in
his face when he stood before the dresser mirror,
knotting the blue tie that harmonized best with the
shirt he wore. He pulled the tan leather belt
straight, so that the plain silver buckle was in the
middle, took something off the bed and pushed
it carefully inside the waistband of his trousers,
on the left side, taking great care that its position
was right to the fraction of an inch. He took his
tan Oxford shoes in his hand, pulled open his door
as quietly as any burglar could have done, stepped
down upon the ground and put on the shoes, lacing
them carefully, tucking in the bow ends fastidi-
ously.

Then, moving very softly, he went down the path
to the bunkhouse, opened the door and walked in,
never dreaming that Belle was no more than a
dozen steps behind him, or that, when he closed
the door, she was standing just outside, listening.

The blood of his actress mother carried him
insouciantly over the pregnant silence that received him. He leaned negligently against the
wall beside the closed door, his arms folded, his
eyebrows tilted upward at the inner ends, his lips
smiling quizzically.

"I've another funny story to tell you fellows,"
he drawled, just before the silence became awk-
ward. "Glad you're all here — it's too good to
keep, too good to waste on part of the outfit. I
want you all to get the kick. You'll enjoy it —

being cattlemen. It's a joke that was pulled on an outfit down in Arizona.''

Like a trained monologist, he had them listening, deceived by his smiling ease, waiting to hear the joke on the Arizona outfit. Tom and Al, at the table with some papers before them, papers that held figures and scribbled names, he quite overlooked. But they, too, listened to the story, were imposed upon by that quizzical smile, by his mimicry, by the bold, swift strokes with which he painted word pictures which their imaginations seized upon as fast as they were made.

It was Tom who first felt a suspicion of Lance's purpose, and shifted his position a little, so that his right hand would be free. As he did so, without looking toward him Lance's left fingers began tapping, tapping the muscles of his right arm; his right hand had sagged a little. Tom's eyebrows pulled together. Quite well he knew that pose. He waited, listened with closer attention to the story.

Lance paused, as your skillful *raconteur* usually does pause before the climax. His glance went impersonally over the faces of his audience. Most of them were leaning forward, a few were breathing hard. They were listening, straining unconsciously to get the meaning he withheld from them. Lance's right hand sagged another half inch, his lips pulled sidewise in the enigmatical smile of the Lorrigans.

"I lied, of course — about the outfit this joke is on. It's really the Devil's Tooth I'm talking about. But the kick remains, so listen, folks, just listen.

"I'm a Lorrigan. Two of you are Lorrigans, and you know what I mean when I say that. The rest of you had better *guess* what I mean, if you don't know — and guess right!

"I'm talking to you with my back against the wall — in more ways than one. Don't think I'm fool enough not to know it. But you're listening with your backs against another wall; I believe it is of stone, usually, and the windows have bars. I don't think you're such fools you fail to grasp my meaning. I'm talking — and you're going to listen.

"What I said — well, I have the dope, you know. I know where you took that last bunch of stolen horses, and I know the date when you turned them over. I have a map or two — I know those secret trails you made, that lead into that hidden little basin that the Rim has not discovered yet. I've dope enough to indict the whole outfit on five separate counts — and any one of them will put every man of you in the pen for a term of years — well, from five to ten up to fifteen or twenty — a mere detail.

"I know why Duke didn't come back. There's a yellow streak in Duke, and he lost his nerve and drifted to parts unknown. Where, I'm not curious to discover. It doesn't matter, so long as his destination *remains* unknown.

"That's the story. And now, here's the point: Others, detectives working at the other end of the business, have an inkling of some of this dope. They haven't got what I've got, but they may possibly get it. They may — possibly. And if they do — wel-ll —" He smiled at them, his eyebrows pointing his meaning, his fingers tapping, tapping on his arm.

"You've got to quit. Now, without turning the deal you're working on, you've got to quit. Get that. Get it right into your souls. You men that have been hired to steal, you've got to drift. Where, does not concern me at all. Where Duke went is good — Parts Unknown. Or if it's to hell — why, the going is good. Never better. You'll go quicker, but there won't be any coming back, so I advise — Parts Unknown.

"You two Lorrigans — I'm not thinking of you now as my brother and my father — the same advice applies to you. You're Lorrigans. You'd rather fight it out than pull out, but you won't. You'd rather kill me than go. That's all right; I understand perfectly. But — I'm Lorrigan, too. You'll go, or I'll kill you. Tom Lorrigan, your hand is pret-ty close to your gun! But so is mine. You'd kill me, because I stand in the trail you've been traveling. But you wouldn't kill me a damn bit quicker than I'd kill *you!* I do stand in the trail — and you're going to take another, both you Lorrigans.

"You had a debt — a bill of damages against the Black Rim. We-ll," he smiled, "you've collected. Now, to-night, you write 'paid' across that bill. You tried to be honest, and the Black Rim wouldn't give you credit for it; they tried to frame something on you, tried to send you 'over the road' on a damned, measly charge you weren't small enough to be guilty of. I understand. The trail ends right here. You quit. You sit there ready to kill. But I'm just as ready as you are. You'll quit, or *I'll kill you!*"

He waited, watching Tom. Tom, watching Lance, got up and faced him cold-eyed, unafraid, weighing not chances, but values rather.

"You'd kill me, would you?" he asked, his voice matching the drawl of Lance.

"Sure, I'd kill you!" Lance smiled back.

Eyes on a level, the two stared at each other, smiling that deadly, Lorrigan smile, the smile of old Tom Lorrigan the killer.

"You would, all right," Tom said. Then his stiffened muscles relaxed. A twinkle came into his eyes. "If you're game enough to do that, kid, by God, I'm game enough to quit!"

Lance unfolded his arms, reached out with his open right hand and met Tom's hand in a close grip. "That's the stuff, dad! I knew you had it in you — I knew it!"

Outside the door, Belle hugged her six-shooter to her breast and leaned against the wall, her knees shaking under her. "Thank God! Oh, thank God a Lorrigan can be bigger than all the Lorrigan blood that's in him!" she whispered. "Oh, Lance, honey — oh, thank God!"

CHAPTER TWENTY-EIGHT

THE MAKING OF NEW TRAILS

A T the corral, that time-honored conference
ground of all true range men, the three Lorrigans leaned their backs against the rails and
talked things over in true range style: laconic
phrases that stated their meaning without frills or
mental reservations, and silences that carried their
thoughts forward to the next utterance.

"Al can take the outfit and drift," said Tom,
as though he were discussing some detail of the
round-up. "He knows where — and they can scat-
ter. I'll give 'em a horse apiece as a — a kinda
bonus. I'll have to stay, looks like. Fall round-
up's coming on."

"Wel-l," said Lance, throwing an arm over a
rail and drumming with his fingers, "I was raised
on round-ups. I don't suppose I've forgotten all
about it. You might turn the management over
to me for a year or so, and take a trip. Belle
needs it, dad. I think I could keep things riding
along, all right."

"Sounds kinda like you had that idea for a

joker up your sleeve," Al observed meaningly. "Are you plumb sure of that dope, Lance?"

Lance removed his arm from the corral rail, and reached into his pocket. "I didn't think you had it in you, Al, to be that big a fool. But since you've said it, here's the dope. Take it, dad. I said I'd turn it in, but I didn't say who'd receive it. The stock detective that's been camping on your trail for the last few weeks was killed on the Lava Beds to-day. I found him. He's at Conley's, now, waiting for the coroner. You might ride over, Al, and see for yourself. And on the way, you might ride up the Slide trail and take a look around the Tooth. You'll see signs where he's watched the ranch from up there. And you can go on down and find where he camped several times at Cottonwood Spring.

"The coroner won't get on the job before to-morrow or next day, and it will take a little time, I suppose, for Brownlee's employers to wake up and wonder what became of the evidence he was sent to collect. You'll have, perhaps, a week in which to make your getaway. They're waiting outside the Rim for the evidence this Burt Brownlee was collecting, so that they could make one big clean-up.

"I'm not setting myself up as a judge, or anything like that — but — well, the going's good, right now. It may not be so good if you wait."

He lighted a match and held it up so that Tom

could glance at the maps and skim the contents of the memorandum book.   By the blaze of the match Lance's face still looked rather hard, determined to see the thing through.

"You'd better burn that stuff, dad.   And in the morning — how would it be if we went to town and got the legal end of my new job straightened out!   I'll want a Power of Attorney.   You may be gone for some time.   I suppose you know," he added, "that Mary Hope and I are going to be married.   So you and Belle can take a trip somewhere.   They say it's worth while going down to the big cattle country in the Argentine — South America, you know."

Tom did not reply.   He had lighted a second match and was studying attentively the data in Burt Brownlee's book.   The third match told him enough to convince him.   He gave a snort when darkness enveloped them again.

"I sharpened my pencil pretty darn fine when I made out my bill against the Black Rim a few years ago — and by the humpin' hyenas, these figures here kinda go to show I overcharged 'em. Some.   Not so damn much, either, if you look at my side.   Better get up the horses, Al, and you'n the boys take the trail.   The kid's right.   The go-in's dern good, right now.   Better'n what it will be."

In the scuffed sand before the corral gate Tom made a small fire, with a few crumpled papers and one small book, which he tore apart and fed, leaf by leaf, to the flames. The light showed him grimly smiling, when he tilted his head and looked up at Lance who watched him.

"So you'n the Douglas kid is figuring on getting hitched! Well, don't ever try to eye her down like you done to yore dad. She'll brain yuh, likely — if you wait long enough for her to make up her mind."

Lance laughed. Up at the house Belle heard him and caught her breath. She stared hard at the three forms silhouetted like Rembrandt figures around the little fire, started toward them and stopped. She was a wise woman, was Belle. Some things a woman may know — and hide the knowledge deep in her heart, and in the hiding help her mate.

Black Rim folk, who always knew so much of their neighbors' affairs, once more talked and chortled and surmised, and never came within a mile of the truth. The young college rooster had come home to the Devil's Tooth, they gossiped, and had a row with Al; so Al left home, and Duke too. The Lorrigans always had been hard to get along with, but that Lance — he sure must be a caution to cats, the way he'd cleaned off the ranch.

Marrying the Douglas girl, and taking that paralyzed old lady right to the ranch, had probably had a lot to do with it. Lance might be willing to forget that old trouble with Scotty, but the rest of the

Lorrigans sure never would. And it was queer, too, how all that rustling talk petered out. Mebby there hadn't been much in it, after all.

Not even Mary Hope guessed why she and Lance were left so completely in charge of the ranch. Sometimes, when the invalid was captious and showed too plainly that she preferred Belle's playing and singing to the musical efforts of her own daughter, and scrawled impatient questions about Belle's return, Mary Hope would wonder if Tom Lorrigan really hated her, and if her coming had practically driven him out of his own home. She would cry a little, then, — unless Lance happened to be somewhere near. If he were, there was no crying for Mary Hope.

"He's a good son," Mother Douglas once wrote, "I wish Aleck was alive, to see how the Lord has changed the Lorrigans."

THE END